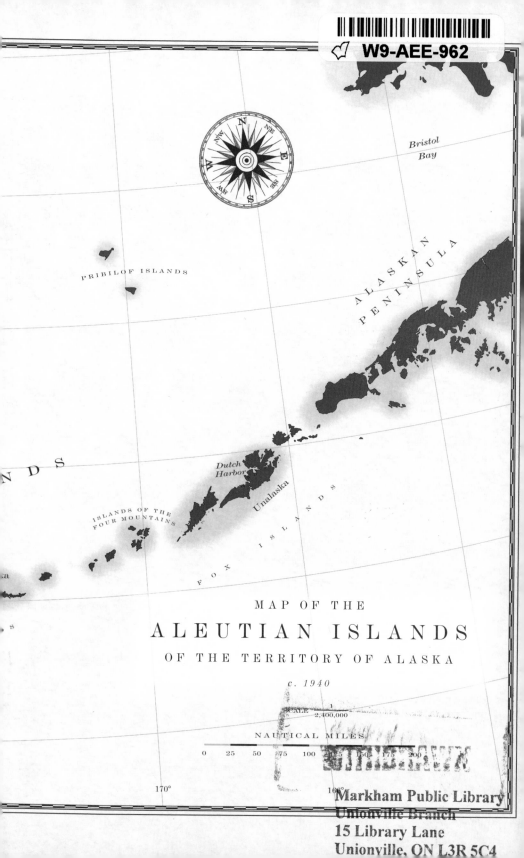

Bristol
Bay

ALASKAN

PENINSULA

PRIBILOF ISLANDS

Dutch
Harbor

Unalaska

ISLANDS OF THE
FOUR MOUNTAINS

FOX ISLANDS

N D S

ka

s

MAP OF THE

ALEUTIAN ISLANDS

OF THE TERRITORY OF ALASKA

c. 1940

SCALE $\frac{1}{2,400,000}$

NAUTICAL MILES

0   25   50   75   100   125   150   175   200

170°

168°

The Wind Is Not a River

"What a great-hearted, beautifully written, and utterly riveting novel. *The Wind Is Not a River* has a power that brings to mind the old Greek stories of war, love, and journey."

—Ron Rash, author of *Serena* and *Nothing Gold Can Stay*

"[A] top-notch WWII historical novel. . . . Payton has delivered a richly detailed, vividly resonant chronicle of war's effect on ordinary people's lives."

—*Publishers Weekly*

"*The Wind Is Not a River* is a gripping tale of one man's battle to survive the physical elements, the tides of war, and terrifying isolation. Brian Payton gives us a compelling look at how primal, how essential, the links between lovers become when everything else is stripped away."

—Natalee Caple, author of *In Calamity's Wake*

"Part adventure tale, part love story, this beautifully written novel offers a moving portrait of a couple whose lives are forever changed by the only battle of WWII to take place on American soil. . . . Payton, in the loveliest of prose, illuminates a little-known aspect of WWII while portraying a devoted couple who bravely face down the isolation, pain, and sacrifice of wartime."

—*Booklist*

"Brian Payton's *The Wind Is Not a River* is both ethereal and entrancing: once inside John Easley's head, escape is neither easy nor safe. This book shows all too well the way isolation chews through civilization and leaves only bones."

—Russell Wangersky, author of *Whirl Away*
and *The Glass Harmonica*

"Payton knows how the brutality and horror of war scar the human spirit and the power and tenderness of love sustain it. In this lyric and deeply moving novel, he connects the two with imagination and brio. *The Wind Is Not a River* is a heart-stopping, heart-rending read."

—Ellen Feldman, author of *Scottsboro*, *Next to Love*,
and *The Boy Who Loved Anne Frank*

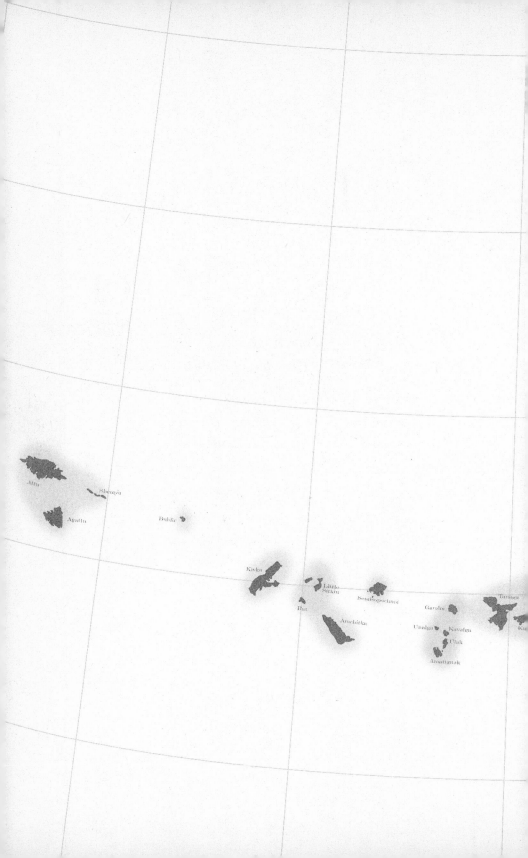

Attu

Shemya

Agattu

Buldir

Kiska

Little
Sitkin

Semisopochnoi

Gareloi

Tanaga

Rat

Amchitka

Unalga   Kavalga

Ulak

Kis

Amatignak

The Wind Is Not a River

A NOVEL

BRIAN PAYTON

Patrick Crean Editions
HarperCollins*PublishersLtd*

Published by Patrick Crean Editions, an imprint
of HarperCollins Publishers Ltd.

First Canadian edition

HarperCollins books may be purchased for educational, business, or
sales promotional use through our Special Markets Department.

HarperCollins Publishers Ltd
2 Bloor Street East, 20th Floor
Toronto, Ontario, Canada
M4W 1A8

www.harpercollins.ca

Designed by Suet Yee Chong
Maps by Suet Yee Chong

Library and Archives Canada Cataloguing in Publication
information is available upon request.

ISBN 978-1-44342-373-1

Printed and bound in the United States of America
14 15 16 17 18   OV/RRD   10 9 8 7 6 5 4 3 2 1

for Lily

PART ONE

ONE

WHEN JOHN EASLEY OPENS HIS EYES TO THE MID-day sky his life does not pass before him. He sees instead a seamless sheet of sky gone gray from far too many washings. He blinks twice, then focuses on the tiny black specks drifting across the clouds. They pass through his field of vision wherever he turns to look. Last winter, the doctor pronounced them *floaters*. Said that by Easley's age, thirty-eight, plenty of people had them. Little bits of the eyeball's interior lining had come free and were swimming inside the jelly. What Easley actually sees are not the specks themselves, but the shadows they cast as they pass over his retina. To avoid their distraction, the doctor advised him to refrain from staring at a blank page, the sky, or snow. These are his first conscious thoughts on the island of Attu.

He sits up straight. When he does, it feels as if his head has a momentum all its own, as if it wants to continue its upward trajec-tory. A dull pain jabs his ribs. He places bare hands in the snow to keep from keeling over. The parachute luffs out behind him—a jaundiced violation against the otherwise perfect white. Fog so thick he can't see the end of the silk. For a moment, he is anxious it might catch a breeze and drag him farther upslope.

Planes whine and circle overhead, unseen.

Easley flexes his hands. The gloves were ripped away by the velocity of the fall. He gazes down his long legs and moves his boots from side to side. He slides the flight cap from his head, runs fingers through his hair, checks for signs of blood. Finding none, he unclips the harness, rolls over on his stomach, pushes himself up. He is, unaccountably, alive and whole. And so it begins.

The fog is better than an ally; it is a close, personal friend. It covers his mistakes and spreads its protective wing over him, allowing him to escape detection. But it also separates him from the crew, if indeed anyone else has survived. Then a red flash of memory: an airman's lapel suddenly blooms like a boutonnière before the man's head slumps forward and lolls.

Not far downslope, the snow gives way to an empty field that spreads off into the mist. Yard-long blades of last year's ryegrass are brown, laid flat from the full weight of winter. Easley returns to the parachute, gathers it up, hastily shoves it back into its pack. It does not go willingly. He hoists the pack onto his shoulders, winces at the pain in his side, then stands defiantly erect, wondering what to do.

The occasional report of Japanese antiaircraft fire begins to define space. Between distant bursts—five, ten miles?—is the nearby cascade of breakers. But like staring into deep water, the fog misdirects, distorts. Within the hundred-yard range of visibility, there is no cover. He is fully, completely exposed. He unshoulders the pack and uses it as a seat.

He stares at the backs of his hands, which have gone pink with the cold. Lately they have been putting him in mind of his father. They are no longer the hands of a young man, clear and smooth. Suddenly it seems as if every pore and vein reveal themselves. A topography of thin lines and faded scars.

John Easley was all of seven years old when he let go of his brother's sticky hand in London's Victoria Station. They had arrived from Vancouver, by way of Montreal, only the day before, destined to spend the next eight months in a tiny flat as their father advanced his engineering credentials. John would have responsibilities. For the moment, however, while their mother was off searching for a job and their father stood in line for tickets to the Underground, John's only task was to remain on the bench and watch over three-year-old Warren. But those magnificent trains easing into and out of the station drew him like a spell. He is sure he had his brother's hand when he first wandered down the concourse, just as he knows that he was the one who let go.

The guilt came on like a fever. After all these years he can feel it still. He turned round, but the benches, the platforms all looked the same. There were numerous toddlers from which to choose, each firmly attached to other families. What started as a trot turned into a sprint, out of the station and into the conviction that it was already too late. Adrenaline gave way nausea, then dizziness overtook him.

He awoke to a ring of female faces and the vague idea that he had risen from the dead. But his father soon appeared, cradling his brother Warren, his face twisted and pale. He thanked the women and grabbed John by the upper arm. Once a discreet distance away from the scene, he set Warren down on the pavement, then turned to his eldest son. "How could you leave your brother? Where on earth did you think you were going?" Then, for the first and only time, Easley watched his father break down. Unwilling to let anyone see him cry, he reached up with both big hands and covered his face in shame.

Antiaircraft fire grows sporadic then stops altogether. The wind begins to stir. Easley rises and stares into the mist. He makes his way downhill two hundred yards, off the last patch of snow and onto flattened rye. The terrain, soft and spongy underfoot, slopes toward the beach. Not a single tree presents itself, no bush of any description.

A small stream bisects his path. Less than a yard across, it snakes through the weathered grass. Easley lies down on his stomach with his head above the water. He puts his lips to the cold little stream and drinks so deep his head begins to ache. When the pain subsides, he drinks again as if he hasn't seen water in days.

He pushes himself up and notices a glimmer in the current, a suggestion of reflected sun. A gust blows the fur-lined collar of the flight suit against his cheek, then lays it down again. The far-off scream of an arctic tern is followed, strangely, by what sounds like a cough. Easley spins around. He now has perhaps a hundred feet of visibility and that is improving rapidly. The farther he sees, the more he realizes how completely exposed he is. No stump or boulder to duck behind, no ditch to conceal him. His heart trips a beat. Easley strains to hear the cough again but detects only the breaking of waves. He stands with thumbs hooked in the straps of his harness, at a loss for what to do.

And then he turns to see a rift open up in the fog. Like endless curtains parting, the rift widens and moves his way, brightening the land, warming the air on approach. Finally, the sheet splits open and the sun spills down directly overhead. It is such a miraculous thing that he forgets, for a moment, that he is behind enemy lines.

The opening extends down the slope and onto the beach. He can make out the waves' pealing white under pale blue sky. As the opening expands and liberates more and more terrain, Easley hears the faint cough again and stares through the vapor for its source. Unarmed, he can only watch as a form takes shape near the edge of the beach. Japanese? A member of the crew? It is clear that the man has seen him. Easley doesn't know whether to raise his hands or run.

The fog slips like satin from the slopes of a dormant volcano, revealing a frigid beauty. All is laid bare in the bold relief of the rare Aleutian sun—patches of white, tan husk of last year's grass, blood blue North Pacific. When Easley recognizes the lone figure, he stifles the urge to shout for joy. He unhooks his thumb from the harness, raises his hand, and waves.

A fresh bust of antiaircraft fire and they both buckle at the knees.

Then, just as swiftly as it began, the fog stalls its retreat. Like a wave racing down a beach to the sea, it hesitates, reverses course, then comes flooding back again. They walk toward each other in the gathering mist, the preceding color and light now seeming like a dream. They approach each other with widening grins, like they're the only ones in on the joke. And when they meet, they hug long and hard, like men who had cheated death together—like men convinced the worst is behind them.

THE BOY, KARL BITBURG, is spent. Easley realizes he is soaked to the skin as soon as they embrace. The boy stands smiling, shivering. Easley guesses him to be no more than nineteen years of age and finds himself doubting he'll ever see twenty.

"Find anyone else?" The boy speaks in a lonesome drawl.

"No. You come down in the water?"

"About thirty yards from shore. Got out, as quick as I could, and hauled in the silk. Hid it under a rock over there." The boy nods down the beach. "Don't think any Japs ever saw. They're clear on the far side of the ridge."

It was only luck, Easley says, that he himself landed on shore. The fog was so thick he only saw what was coming seconds before his feet hit the ground. He saw no other parachutes and completely lost track of the plane. As Easley tells his tale, he observes the boy shake and considers—for the very first time—the true power of the cold and wet arrayed against them. The boy's face is bloodless and pale, his stature weighed down. He looks nothing like the cocky, pumped-up kid Easley met two days before.

"We should search for the others," the boy announces.

"We need to dry you off."

"We find my goddamn friends. That's what we do." The boy stands a little taller, sticks out his chin. "I know those guys. I live with those guys. You're just along for the ride."

"We don't get you dried off and stop your shivering, you'll be dead by morning."

Seeing the boy pulls Easley out of the daze he's been wandering in, presenting a point of focus. It also gives him his first real notion of a future since touching down on the patch of snow.

"Airman first class," the boy says, declaring his rank. "You're not even supposed to be here. I'm responsible 'til we find the lieutenant."

"Suit yourself," Easley says. "But now that the fog's back we might want to make a fire, dry you off. Have somewhere to bring your friends—if there's anyone left to find." He can see that the boy wants to listen to reason. "Could be Japs on the lookout. We should find some kind of cover."

"They might smell the smoke."

"You get hypothermia out here, you're finished."

The boy puts his hands on his hips and looks into the fog. "My lighter's soaked."

Easley reaches into his pocket and finds his own shiny Zippo. He pulls it out, flips it open, snaps a sharp orange flame.

Driftwood is in short supply, dry wood is but a dream. Easley well knows not a single tree grows in the entire Aleutian Chain, the only wood available being tattered logs and branches pushed in from distant shores. The best pieces are found where beach gives way to sedge and rye, where rogue waves have reached up and pulled the earth out from under the tangle of roots. Beneath the resulting ledges, a few sticks and logs collect. This wood and withered grass provide kindling enough for a fire.

They locate a ravine just up from the high tide line. Soon the light will fail. The boy stands across the fire from Easley, stripped to the waist, holding his heavy shearling jacket over the flames.

The boy's body is pale and wiry. He is of average height, somewhat shorter than Easley. Although he has the frame of an athlete, Easley reckons it won't do him much good out here. The complete absence of fat is not encouraging. A new tattoo is etched on his shoulder: the anchor and eagle of the U.S. Navy. The mark of a warrior. It strikes Easley as ridiculous on the pale, helpless skin. It makes the boy look even younger. The soaked flight suit, his only real protection, will probably never dry.

Easley watches him shudder near the flames, then walks over beside him. He takes off his own flight jacket and puts it around his shoulders. The boy wraps himself in the warmth and nods with gratitude. Then Easley steps out of his leather flight pants and hands them over. This leaves Easley with cotton trousers, shirt, and jacket.

The boy slips off the rest of his wet clothes and pulls on Easley's pants. Then, with trembling arms, he holds his wet drawers out over the fire. "I usually don't get to flash the family jewels on the first date," he says, "although I always give it a try."

The ravine is less than ten feet deep, but it is enough to conceal the campfire light except, perhaps, from the mountains a few miles away, or directly out at sea. Things could be worse. They remain uninjured, the enemy seems unaware of their presence, and the boy is livening up by the minute. They will make it through the night.

When darkness falls, the fog clears and the stars shine defiantly. The mountains loom purple-black and the phosphorus ribbon of surf provides the only demarcation between darkened land and sea.

Easley feels the descending realization that they are only marking time. Six planes left on the bombing run. The Navy knows only which did not return. Perhaps one of the other gunners saw his plane crash into the frigid sea. He is convinced they will no longer be looking for them—not looking for him in particular. They are presumed drowned or captured. Each man who makes this run knows there is no hope of rescue. Back on the island of Adak, the boy's comrades will count him and his crew as missing in action and lift a glass to their memory tonight. In a few weeks' time, his parents will be handed a vague letter buttered in platitudes. Their son went beyond the call, fought with distinction.

Easley's wife will receive no such correspondence. Helen will know by now that he has returned to Alaska, but even she won't have imagined he's made it all the way back to the Aleutians. Easley summons her elegant hands, her crooked smile, the soft hair at the back of her neck, but is left holding the guilt of having left her behind. He imagines her before the war, before everything changed, sitting by the roaring fire in her father's house, bathed in warmth and light.

* * *

EASLEY AWAKES to an aching rib. The boy is wedged against him, asleep in the parachute. The shelf of roots remains overhead, the sea did not invade. When the fire died down last night, they covered the coals, then sought shelter where they found wood at the high tide line. There was barely enough room for the two of them. Ignoring the protocol of keeping watch, they pulled out Easley's silk, wrapped themselves up, and quickly fell asleep.

Easley turns his head and peers out into the blinding white. A pair of boots can been seen about a dozen yards away in the new accumulation of snow. A moment later, a thin yellow stream. Easley holds his breath. When the soldier finishes, he tramps across the beach and stares out to sea. He is soon joined by four more shuffling soldiers, all shooting glances back over the hills and peaks. They overlook the narrow hiding place. A mere two inches of snow has covered all previous tracks and indiscretions. The Japanese appear weary and bored. They don't see a thing.

Easley reaches over, clamps his hand over the boy's mouth and cheeks. The boy comes to with a start, meets Easley's eyes, then slowly turns to look as the men light cigarettes, shift rifle slings from one shoulder to the other. When they disappear from view, Easley sighs and lies back down again.

"Damn." The boy rubs his eyes. "Looks like you're gettin' more of a story than you bargained for."

Story. The word strikes like an insult. Once the plane was aloft, the pilot announced that in fact they had themselves a newspaper-man onboard. War correspondent, no less. It was high time the world started paying attention.

They lie silent, listening, watching as the day gains strength and the snow melts off the lip of their lair.

Easley's first trip to the Territory of Alaska was nearly a year ago, on assignment for the *National Geographic Magazine*. He had traveled to the island of Atka, halfway across the eleven-hundred-mile chain, and stayed two weeks in spring, hiking the lush green hills of a place that, from the air at least, reminded him of Hawaii's Molokai. Before this assignment, he was only vaguely aware of these islands' existence. He interviewed shy but welcoming villagers and was invited to go fishing with them. He attended their Orthodox church, breathed in the incense and pageantry. He became fascinated by both the island's natural and human history—the native and Russian braids of the people and their culture. He had happened upon a world little known and far removed.

But on June 3, 1942, just three days before Easley was scheduled to head for home, the Japanese launched a strike from light carriers and bombed Dutch Harbor Naval Base and Fort Mears Army Base, killing forty-three men, incinerating ships and buildings. These outposts on Unalaska and Amaknak islands, near the Alaskan mainland, were the only U.S. defenses in the Aleutian Archipelago. June 7 saw the U.S. victory at Midway. That same day, six months after the attack on Pearl Harbor, the Americans learned that the Japanese Army had seized the islands of Kiska and Attu at the far end of the Aleutian Chain. Eleven days later, the U.S. Navy made a brief statement to the press downplaying events. Easley's original assignment, a natural history article, was quickly set aside. When he finally arrived at Dutch Harbor, the place was still smoldering.

One of a half-dozen journalists working in this new theater of war, Easley dutifully took official dispatches and fed them to eager newspaper editors back home. But then he started interviewing airmen freshly returned from reconnaissance runs. He made notes on what they saw, rumors of how the Japanese were digging in. He carefully edited his own copy, excising anything he believed could compromise the troops, and yet the military censor drew thick black lines through most of the facts. He was left with copy that read: ██████ *enemy encampments at* ██████ *reinforced under the cover of fog.* ██████ *ships of the Japanese Imperial Navy were spotted* ██████ *in the* ██████ *and* ██████ *attempting re-supply. While* ██████ *planes and* ██████ *men have been lost to the aggressor, the biggest threats to our troops so far are the wind, wet, and cold.*

Soon the entire press corps was ordered out of Alaska—even though congressmen were now screaming for news from this far-off stretch of American soil, news other than that broadcast by Tokyo Rose. But news from the Aleutians was now under the intense scrutiny of the War Department, a matter of national security. As the flow of Alaskan information reduced to a trickle, American involvement in North Africa and Guadalcanal served to divert attention. And public information offices were still loudly trumpeting the victory at Midway.

Someone wants this battle fought beyond the view of prying eyes. What were they hiding in the Aleutians? If the Japanese were securing a base for attacks on the mainland, civilians in Alaska, British Columbia, and Washington State had a right to know and prepare. Easley was one of a handful of journalists with any knowledge of this corner of the world. What kind of writer shrinks from such a duty?

A few months later, against the warnings of his editors, friends, and Helen, Easley snuck back in with another journalist as a deckhand with the merchant marine. They never made it to the Aleutians, spending a week on Kodiak Island asking questions before the brass got wind. They were shipped south after a long interrogation and a warning that they could find themselves imprisoned under provisions of the Espionage Act. Next time, Easley would travel alone and hide in plain sight. He flew back in a third time, wearing the uniform of a full lieutenant of the Royal Canadian Air Force—the uniform that had belonged to his brother. He forged documents requesting observer status for future joint operations in the Aleutian Theater. He was meticulous, well rehearsed. He fell into the role with ease.

Easley soon patched together the basic facts as far as the Navy knew them. Upward of two thousand enemy troops are dug in around the tiny village on Attu. Judging by the barracks, vehicles, and roads the Japanese built on the neighboring island of Kiska, there could be as many as ten thousand garrisoned there. The idea that these remote islands could be the breach through which the war floods into North America is something the Navy doesn't want civilians thinking about. They're gambling that this problem can be contained. The plan is to soften up the enemy in advance of an amphibious assault. Regular bombardment of their flak batteries, seaplane hangars, submarine pens, and runways keeps the Japanese busy patching holes. Weather permitting, sorties are dispatched up to six times a day from Adak, the forward base of operation against the enemy positions.

On Adak, he met the pilot of an aircrew who agreed to take him along once Easley explained that no one back home knew what he and his men were facing. Lieutenant Sanchez was a sharp and confident man, about Easley's own age, with a quick and infectious grin. He said the idea that the newspapers were not reporting his war was like a swift kick in the sack. Two days later, Easley was tossed out the hatch of his Catalina flying boat as it sank from the turbulent sky.

Easley crawls out from under the ledge and takes a good long look around. He staggers to his feet, stretches his back, touches tender ribs. The boy joins him, and together they study the Japanese boot tracks in the snow, marveling at the odds of having gone undiscovered.

But the covering snow also mocks Easley's focus on the immediate need to find food, shelter, a secure hiding place. He is confronted by the Big Picture, the fact that—unlike that enemy patrol—the wet and cold cannot be escaped.

For the moment, at least, they have the sun. The glare forces them to squint. To boost morale, Easley declares that, at the current rate of melt, much of the new snow will be gone by dusk.

The boy demonstrates the proper way to repack a parachute. Easley observes the practiced movements, the muscle memory, and the fact that this gives him some illusion of control. When the task is done, they stand with hands on hips, staring at the tight bundle.

THE WIND IS NOT A RIVER

"Let's see what else we got." The boy empties his pockets atop the canvas. He produces a pocketknife, the drowned lighter, a key, a stick of chewing gum, and four crushed cigarettes.

"What's the key for?"

"Front door back home."

Easley reaches into his own pockets and produces only his Zippo and a buffalo nickel. He then tries each of his pockets again but is unable to add to their provisions. The boy holds up the nickel between thumb and forefinger.

"Old girlfriend gave it to me for luck," Easley says, saving the part about the girlfriend becoming the wife.

"So. You get lucky?"

The rush of adrenaline takes Easley by surprise. He considers the boy for a moment: eyes alight with the attempt at levity. Recognizing this prevents Easley from hitting him.

"Didn't think so." The boy tears the gum in half, pops a piece into his mouth, then offers the other half to Easley. "You don't look like the lucky type to me."

"Here—" He flips the nickel back to Easley. "You can buy me a drink when we get off this frozen pile of shit."

AT THE BOY'S INSISTENCE, they spend the balance of the day in search of other members of the crew. Stinging nose and cheeks, throbbing fingers and toes. They arrive back at their ravine famished, dispirited, and—as far as Easley's concerned—disabused of the notion that anyone else from their plane survived. They then split up and scour the beach. Easley hunts for firewood, the boy for something to eat.

Although Easley is better prepared this time around, tonight's fire still gives him trouble. His ribs ache with each breath he draws to blow on the embers. He is pleased, at least, that he has used less lighter fluid.

The boy arrives with a jacket full of fat blue mussels and half-curled mollusks, some bashed beyond recognition and oozing into the fabric. Triumphant, he dumps them on the grass then marches back to the beach. He returns with a flat stone, which he places close to the coals.

"I was wonderin'. How do we know these things are safe to eat?"

Easley looks up and reaches for one of the cracked mussels. He bites the inside of his lower lip to draw a little blood. He then dips a finger in the mussel's gooey flesh and rubs the juice on the sore in his mouth.

"What's that supposed to do?"

Easley sweeps his tongue through the spot a few times, forcing the juice into the cut. "I don't know whether or not they have red tide around here. If your lip goes numb, that means the algae's gone bad. Toxic. If it doesn't, you're safe." Easley waits a few minutes and even pinches his lip a couple of times to make sure. When at last he nods, the boy rubs his palms with glee.

They place mussels on the hot flat stone, watch them open in the heat. The boy presents the first one to Easley, still steaming in its shell. Together, they each extract a morsel of meat and chew, staring at each other over the flames. The boy makes a face, but quickly grabs another.

They spend the better part of an hour roasting and eating dinner. For Easley, this scene, this feeling summons an old sailing trip among the sheltered Gulf Islands with his brother, Warren, the last such trip of the season, the first they were allowed to take on their own. The boat was too small to sleep two in comfort so they spread blankets on a leeward shore. As the eldest, he was in charge of everything that trip—the charts, the sailing, the food. It was not as if Warren, then thirteen, could not share these tasks. He was already an able sailor. Easley kept him from any real responsibility precisely because he could sense his own primacy fading.

The grass around the fire dries out and their clothes lose some of the dampness that has dogged them the whole day. After they've eaten, the boy gets up and goes to the stream for a drink. He returns, wiping his lips with the back of his hand, looking down at Easley.

"Where'd you learn that stuff about mussels?"

"An Indian."

"Where'd you say you're from?"

"Don't think I ever did."

"Well, now I'm askin'."

"I've been living in Seattle the last few years," Easley explains. "Before that, Vancouver."

"Up in Canada."

"That's right."

"Why's that?"

"That's where I'm from."

The boy processes this information silently, like he's busy running sums. He says, "Never met a Canadian before, I don't think."

"Well now you're bunking with one."

"You could've filed your report from Adak. You weren't supposed to be on that plane, were you?"

"Now that you mention it, I don't know much about you, either," Easley says. "Give me the highlights. We can fill out the details as the weeks and months go by."

"There ain't gonna be any goddamn weeks."

Easley sees the failure of his joke and regrets it. The boy stretches out on the opposite side of the fire and props his head in his hand. He studies Easley intently, taking the length and breadth of him.

"How old you say you were?"

"Thirty-eight. What part of Texas you from?"

"That would be a West Texas accent you picked up on. Roan, Texas. Big enough to have two taverns, small enough to know the bra size of every girl in town."

Clearly, this line has passed his lips before.

The boy describes a land that won't support a crop and oil wells that show little or no return. A father he never knew, the constant move from shack to rented shack. Friends who sharked at pool, baptisms in an irrigation canal, cold beer smuggled into a summer picture show. Easley envisions a hot, dry waste that leaves your shirt stiff with sweat.

The boy wanted to play football but, lacking size, discovered his heart had to be twice as big as the next guy's. He figured his wasn't. He did well enough at high school to go off to a semester of college before joining up for the war. When he left for basic training, his mother wouldn't even see him to the door. There she stood, he says, framed in the greasy window with a blank expression and arms folded tight across her dress. Before the truck pulled away, he distinctly remembers seeing the lights switch off and the house go dark.

Easley feels himself back at the edge of that familiar empty space, the gap into which he feels compelled to offer up some private portion of his life. He wants to tell the boy about losing his brother to the war. And now, perhaps, his wife. The boy bares himself intuitively. Easley wonders, why can't I respond in kind?

The boy sits up and pulls out his pile of crushed tobacco. He rests it in the crease of his lap and reaches for a big brown blade of grass at the fire's edge. The air begins to stir again and stars poke through the clouds. There is no hint of the moon. Easley watches the boy place tobacco in the supple blade, then roll it back and forth. He licks it like cigarette paper and tries to seal it shut. It mostly works. He pinches the tips and ends up with a sad little cigarillo. The boy smiles. He pushes the end of it toward the fire, puffs a few times, then exhales in a deeply satisfied stream. He offers it to Easley, who gladly pulls the warm smoke into his lungs. Easley favors a meerschaum pipe, back in his other life, but now finds this sorry roach a little taste of heaven. The boy rolls another, and they lounge warm and satisfied, listening to the surf. It is the first such contented moment they have had since tumbling from the clouds.

When the wood runs low they bury the coals and return to their hiding place. They roll themselves up in the parachute and try to ignore how the sand leaches heat from their bones. At least they are out of the wind. After much turning and shifting of positions, they settle in and listen to the rhythm of the falling tide. Easley feels himself wandering off toward sleep when he hears an almost imperceptible sound, something faint and reassuring. The boy whispers under his breath. He is giving thanks for having dodged the enemy, for the mussels and sticks of semidry wood, for the gift of another day. He thanks the good Lord for the company of one John Easley.

* * *

RAIN DISPERSES THE FOG, increasing clarity. It reveals a monochrome world of varying shades of smoke. They stash the parachutes and strike out in search of food, shelter, signs of other men, the warmth of locomotion. The only creatures they encounter are glaucous-winged gulls wearily patrolling the beach. Easley observes raindrops roll off their feathers in perfect beads, as from the hood of a well-waxed automobile. The gulls appear to be looking back at him the way people might watch a convicted man on his way to the gallows; curious, but unwilling to make eye contact out of respect for the condemned. Easley thinks of how they might taste roasted over the coals of a driftwood fire.

After covering several miles of shore, it becomes clear that the island does not offer up shelter gladly. Beaches curl round coves and end on rocky headlands. Up from the high tide line are rolling fields of rye slicked tight against the land. Then, after some two hundred feet of elevation gain, snow. Neither tree nor shrub worthy of the term. No bushes laden with summer berries. No grazing cattle or sheep, or even deer, rabbits, or squirrels. The only possible sources of protein are also visitors here—birds of the sky and fish of the sea.

The boy, out in front, works hard to stay ahead, his posture betraying the effort. At any moment, they could be spotted from miles away, find themselves the subject of sniper fire.

At the next beach, they encounter a little rise that graduates into a three-story peak of rock. They scan the horizon for friendly ships and the hills for enemies, then scramble up, crouching, careful not to offer a profile against the backdrop of sea. The boy is seized by a coughing fit and is forced to sit and catch his breath. Easley studies the empty land. Nothing presents itself for comment. Only smug birds skirting the shore. More of nothing, nothing more.

As they scramble down, Easley casts his mind back to the plane, the drone of the engines, his quiet, helpless panic after antiaircraft fire ripped through the cabin and wings. He remembers the pale cheeks and frightened eyes of the copilot. How the man methodically double-checked Easley's parachute before tossing him out the hatch.

The rhythm of boots through sand underscores the silence between them.

Eventually, the boy asks, "Why do we want these islands?"

"I'm sorry about your friends. Sorry about Sanchez."

The boy looks back across the sand. "We should walk on the grass as much as possible. We're leavin' tracks down here."

At the end of the beach, they encounter a ravine where a rivulet trickles off the edge and onto a pile of stones. It falls directly past the mouth of a cave, and by the time it has traveled half the twenty-foot drop, it scatters in a steady rain.

The cave is about forty feet deep, maybe half as wide, and opens at an angle to the beach. The rocky floor rises to meet the ceiling in back. Most of the walls are weeping. The back section, at least, is clear of the spray. Like newlyweds inspecting their first bungalow, they exaggerate the positive, ignoring the fact that this is a hole in the side of a ravine.

"It's far enough up from the beach so the tide won't be a bother." Easley sits down on a rock.

The boy wipes his nose on his sleeve. "We could divert the stream."

Easley looks up and sees a determination that could quickly become infectious.

"We could go up top and build a little dike," the boy continues. "Some rocks and a little sand. A few hours' work."

"We could build a fire, but only at night," Easley says, gesturing to the mouth of the cave. He looks to the other side of the ravine then up at the sheet of sky. "The way it faces, no one would be able to see the light, except maybe a passing ship. We're miles from the Japs, they'll never smell the smoke."

The boy scratches his head. "I'd say you just bought yourself a cave."

BY THE TIME EASLEY RETURNS with their parachutes, the light can no longer support colors beyond gray. The boy is nowhere to be seen. The little waterfall that had spilled from the upper lip of the cave has been reduced to a slow drip. Inside, high in the back, a bunk of grass has been constructed. A kind of enormous nest. The boy has done wonders in his absence. Easley had been wary of splitting up, even for a few hours, but now sees the wisdom in it. He makes his way up to the back of the cave, sits on the nest, decides it will serve them well. His gratitude at having shelter, however crude, is tempered by the fear that they will both soon perish here, cowering in the damp and cold as hunger overtakes them.

Helen found their first home by spotting a small handmade sign in a big bay window. The rental market in Seattle had been tight with Boeing working full tilt, churning out bombers and fighters to fill the skies over Europe and the Pacific. She had been searching for over a week.

It was the main floor of a lean little Victorian on Aden Street. The owner wore a matching dark suit, hat, and demeanor. His elderly mother had recently passed and he was unprepared to part with her possessions. He had moved everything upstairs, leaving the lower rooms for tenants. Said he wanted good, reliable sorts to occupy his childhood home. If things went smoothly, they would have the first opportunity to make an offer after the war. When it came time to hand over the keys, the man hesitated in what seemed a spontaneous, emotional response. Helen touched his shoulder, as she would a troubled friend. She told him not to worry, he had made the right decision. Easley watched the man's mood transform utterly.

That first night in the house they made love on the living room floor. Easley knew then that he loved Helen above his own life. In that moment, he imagined the joy and pleasure he took in her body was more complete than any man had ever known. He composed and took a mental photograph—of her, in that light, in that space and time. He had the presence of mind to sense the pinnacle. He felt it in his bones. Beyond this night, his life could not hope to be improved. To Easley, it felt as if they had discovered, *invented* something profound and new. He shakes his head at the ridiculous conceit of it all. He wanted to tell her, but thought better of it. Despite being nearly a dozen years younger, she might laugh out loud at such adolescent delusions.

How, he wonders, have I traveled so far from that night?

The boy enters the cave carrying a jacket full of mussels, loose smile tugging at his lips, proud of what he's accomplished.

"You've been busy," Easley says, glancing up to where the water-fall used to be. "You'll make someone a fine little wife one day."

The boy consolidates his load in one arm, freeing the other hand to offer a single-finger salute.

There will be no fire this night. Even the gray light is in short supply, and there is no time to mount a search for fuel. The wind is picking up. They observe and acknowledge all this without words. They have already begun to develop a vocabulary of glances and gestures.

They crack mussels and eat, listening to the wind whip the shore. Neither is satisfied, having consumed only enough to dull the hunger. The raw, rubbery flesh has already begun to repel them. In this low moment, Easley must find a way to embolden both himself and the boy.

Tomorrow, Easley says, we'll build a proper fire pit. They will cook their food on smaller, hotter fires that require less fuel. The warm rocks will retain heat, some of which will even find its way back to their bunk. Maybe they should rig hammocks. From this cave, they will hide from and observe the enemy until such time as they can signal for rescue from the bombing sorties, or join up with the invasion that's sure to come. The Japanese have already been here for ten months. How much longer do you suppose Uncle Sam will allow such an affront to continue?

The boy nods. For the moment, he seems resigned to reason over rank and protocol. Easley is pleased, because they must come to agreement on each and every decision. They must be of one mind. The peace between them is their only security.

THAT NIGHT, up in the nest, the boy pulls the parachute to his chin. "Storm's blowin' in," he observes. Easley listens to the fury of the williwaw, the signature gale of the Aleutians. It accelerates down cold mountain slopes to the sea. Here, the wind becomes an avalanche, a full stampede of sound and sensation that strips the moisture from your eyes, bullies and casts you to the ground. He too pulls the silk close and marvels at their good fortune of having found shelter in time. As the wind shoves its way across the land, only a slight breeze reaches his cheeks.

"What's the first thing you want to do when we get out of here?" the boy asks. His back is pressed into Easley's.

"First thing?" Easley sighs. "Sit down to a steak and chocolate cake. You?"

"Shower. Plate of ribs. Get drunk and drive around in my truck with the heat blowin' full . . . Man, I'd love to go for a drive."

"Got someone waiting for you?"

"My dog Queenie. She's an old bitch now, but she'll knock me over just the same." The boy rolls over on his back. "What happened to that lucky girl of yours?"

Easley no longer feels any anger—toward the boy for having asked, toward Helen or himself. He considers telling him everything, but the boy speaks first.

"If you're not of a mind to discuss such things, then don't. I don't mean to pry."

"It's all right."

A loud crack and crash thunders down the shore, where an out-sized wave impales itself on the point. They pause and listen to the violence.

"I think we ought'a have a rule around here," the boy continues. "Let's drop the bull and answer questions straight. No tall tales or secrets. No dickin' around. Way I figure it, we owe it to each other.

We might as well be the last two men on earth. So let's do each other the honor of being straight with one another."

"Sounds fair to me."

"Think we'll ever get home?"

"Might take a while." It is as close to the truth as Easley can get.

"Part of me has plans for tomorrow," the boy replies. "Ideas about how we can get meat and wood. Make things better 'til they come for us. Then part of me feels like a ghost. Like we're already hauntin' this place and we don't even know we're dead."

"Listen. We're both strong. We'll find better food. The weather will improve. We're already into spring . . . You had a rule. Now I've got one. I say we each get one shot at this. One chance to complain. The other listens, tells him he's being a crybaby, then we get back to business. This is your chance to whine, so you'd better make it count."

The boy's chuckle turns into a cough, then silence.

HOURS LATER, Easley jerks awake. The wind seems to have died down entirely. Morning can't be far. Out past the beach, over the boom and hiss of breakers, he hears the burble of an outboard motor and the slap of a hull passing through the chop. He props himself up on an elbow and peers out into the gloom. A strong beam of light sweeps across the beach. It flashes past the very mouth of the cave but does not linger. Rescue launch from a U.S. Navy vessel? This first hopeful thought quickly fades. Such a small craft could only have come from the island itself.

A moment later, the sounds and light are gone. The boy does not stir. Easley lies back down beside him.

TWO

S HE IS SINKING—THROUGH HER CLOTHING, THE COT, the floor. Her mind says she's safe, lying in the clinic, but her gut tells a different tale. It's the blood, of course. Lightly pulsing out the vein in tune with the rhythm of her heart. She has an overwhelming sense of déjà vu, and connectedness— knowing that her very life is being pooled and preserved, to be used by someone else, far away. Flowing first into that glass jar, then the veins of someone who needs it even more. Sinking, dripping out and down.

She stops herself from imagining it will ever flow directly into his body. He would have to be gravely injured for that to occur. And he is not injured. No, she imagines it flowing into the arm of the soldier who fought to protect him, to protect us all.

The nurse is all of eighteen, seven years Helen's junior. The girl's head eclipses the light overhead as she hovers, tending the flow. Her confidence affords her a kind of beauty. If only Helen had had some greater sense of direction in school, perhaps she too could have been a nurse. So necessary these days. A nurturing role to be sure, but one that affords a woman real independence. When Helen was a girl, she conceived many possible futures for herself. Early on, it was dancing in the ballet or playing viola with the orchestra. Then, more practically, she imagined a career as a teacher of English literature or French. Now, of course, she sees how her father, her brothers, then John had always been her shelter and shield. She remained untested. But in this dim new world of missing men, she knows her test has come.

Does she feel faint? The nurse wants to know.

"This is my first time," Helen says. "First time in this clinic, first time I've given blood. But I'm sure I've been in this position before. I remember you asking that question."

"It's not uncommon. You blank out for a second or two, but since you're already lying down, you hardly notice. When you come to, the last thing you remember always seems extra important."

"No. I'm sure—"

"We're all done." The nurse removes the needle and presses with an index finger. "But I'd lie there awhile, if I were you. Get your bearings, then go get yourself something to eat. The world will sort itself out again after a little sugar and starch."

SHE GLANCES OVER the top of her menu as he straddles a stool at the counter. He has his back to her. Marking territory, he tosses his hat on the seat beside him, rights the cup on his saucer, nods to the waitress for coffee. The unexpected surge of hope at the sight of him takes Helen by surprise. She holds her menu higher, settles back into the booth, unsure how to proceed.

Tom Sorenson seems physically unsuited to his chosen profession. Helen observes his meaty hand encircling the cup with blunt, mechanic's fingers. She'd always had trouble imagining they could coax a living from the keys of a Smith-Corona. His neck is a broad trunk growing out of low, longshoreman's shoulders. Deep farmer's tan, entirely out of season. Helen stands and straightens her blouse before walking over and placing her palm on his back.

"Helen! Well . . . I'll be."

He embraces her with genuine affection, then holds her at arm's length. "You look great," he says, taking in the sweep of her.

These days, Helen finds it hard to keep up appearances. And yet today, her hair is curled and set. Red lipstick bright against powdered skin.

"Tom . . . I don't know where to begin."

"With me moving over to your booth."

Helen does not know him well, but his connection to John affords them a familiarity that transcends the handful of conversations they've had, the few dinner parties they've both attended. He is a colleague of John's, someone John admires, a friend with whom he shares a professional rivalry. Last night, when she came across his byline in the *Post-Intelligencer,* a story about Tacoma's McChord Field, she knew he must be back in town. She walked to his office directly from the clinic. She'd just missed him, the receptionist said. He was out to lunch, but he has his usual spots.

Her best hope now sits across the table from her, sputtering news through bites of ham sandwich. He had been thrown out of Alaska with John on that second trip—only he had the good sense not to return. He is fresh back from a three-month tour in the South Pacific, filing reports from Hawaii. The war, he says, is an institution they should all start getting used to.

Helen listens politely to his news with a discreet eye on her wristwatch. For the past few years, she has worked downtown at a clothing store to help save for a down payment on a modest house. She's late already, her coworker trapped and unable to escape for lunch until she returns. Interrupting a man telling war stories isn't something one does lightly, but she cannot miss this opportunity.

She reaches out and spreads a hand flat on the table. "And what have you heard about John?"

His posture sags. He rubs his napkin across his lips. "That's exactly what I was going to ask you."

"I haven't heard from him in three months." Helen withdraws her hand. "He was going to try and get back into Alaska again and I—"

"Again? Couple of the guys were talking about going back up. I thought it was just a lot of talk."

"John went."

This news has him reeling. He utterly fails to mask his surprise.

"Do you know where he might be?" There is the flush of anger and shame in revealing that she doesn't know where her husband is, that she is more or less abandoned.

"Haven't spoken to him since we got tossed out in July." Tom chews the last of his sandwich, awkwardly rearranging his silverware. He shakes his head in awe. "Son of a bitch . . ."

She recognizes the primary male instinct: competitive. Even among friends, concern comes in a distant second. He picks up his cup, which she can see is empty. He takes a sip of air just the same.

"Tom, I'm sorry. I'm so late for work. It was wonderful seeing you."

Helen reaches for her purse, but he's already grabbed the bill. She nods her appreciation and slides out of the booth.

"I spoke with his editor at the *National Geographic*, newspaper editors here in Seattle, other reporters. I have called photographers and the wire services. I've tried everything I can think of. I don't know where else to turn." She stands with arms folded tight, then thinks to give him her card. "If you could make a few inquiries, I'd be—"

"Happy to. I'll call you before the end of the week."

Helen embraces him lightly, then turns to go. He stands staring as she rushes past the happy diners, out into the open air.

It's raining again. Helen marches down the sidewalk alongside the buildings, under the shelter of awnings and eaves. She moves as fast as her narrow skirt and shoes will permit. She had invested far too much hope in this meeting with Tom Sorenson. She recites a silent Our Father and Hail Mary, then composes a fresh take on her well-worn prayer for the safe return of her husband. She is interrupted by the sight of a man walking directly toward her. She continues her course, unaltered, until they come to a halt. Helen stares him down until he yields the covered half of the sidewalk and steps out into the rain.

AFTER WORK, she turns up the path to their front door, which is lined with white crocuses and unopened daffodils. The lawn shows wear from the winter past but is greening up with the longer days. She will hire a kid from the neighborhood to mow it when the time comes, or she will do it herself and ignore any pitying stares. The place is not much in the great scheme of things, but it is their first home.

A discreet shoulder check—the houses across the street are quiet, the street empty—then Helen approaches the front door, key out and ready. She unlocks the door, slips inside, and locks it again all in under three seconds. It is a precise, choreographed maneuver. She recently read in a magazine that a single woman is at her most vulnerable upon arrival or departure, especially from home. Inside she hangs her coat, tucks away her shoes in silence.

In three days, her father will arrive for Sunday dinner. All week she looks forward to these visits, which have become essential to her peace of mind. No one else has stepped through this door since John left in January.

The living room is compulsively cleaned and ordered. Magazines stacked, books shelved, dust wiped away. The only thing out of place is the small green edition of *The Sorrows of Young Werther*, which remains on the floor near the wall where she pitched it. The story of a young man's hopeless, extravagant, wholly self-destructive love. Helen had foolishly hoped that Goethe's tale of someone more sorrowful than herself might offer some commiseration or relief.

In their bedroom, she changes out of her work clothes, hanging her sweater in the closet next to John's ironed shirts. Each day she resists the urge to arrange his jumble of shoes on the floor. That's the way he always leaves them.

Over the bed hangs a crucifix, the same one that once hung above her mother's childhood bed in France. On the night table, an enormous abalone shell catches the light with its mother-of-pearl. John picked it off the beach on his first trip to the Aleutians Islands. It now cradles her earrings and necklaces.

Framed photos crowd the vanity. The largest is the portrait of her young mother. A war bride from Normandy, yet her complexion has an almost Latin hue. Eyes so dark the pupil seems lost in the iris. A proud, open smile of strait ivory. She's two months past nineteen. Then Helen and her brothers at Helen's confirmation (she appears as a doll between junior wrestlers), John and his brother at a baseball game, and a portrait of herself and John on their wedding day. But her favorite shot of the two of them, the one she keeps closest to the bed, was taken by a passing stranger on the shore of Vancouver Island, on her first trip north when John "introduced" her to Canada. They hold on to each other and look in opposite directions, smiling as if they've just shared an off-color joke. She realizes she has no proper photo of her father, the only member of her family still present in her life. This is an oversight she has long pledged to rectify.

A second, smaller bedroom became his office despite their family plans. After he left, she thoroughly searched his files for clues as to where he was headed, although she feared she already knew. Now, she rarely opens the door. His makeshift desk is mostly bare, save the handsome toy *bidarka,* the traditional Aleutian kayak. He had placed it on the mantel. She can no longer bear to see it.

There was a time when Helen felt she could sense her unborn children. She could not discern whether they were boys or girls—the shape of faces or the color of hair—but they were a distinct presence to her all the same. Despite passionate, and then increasingly determined attempts, they had so far failed to bring them into being. He said they just needed to give it more time. Looking back, the pressure she brought to bear on them both no doubt encouraged his attraction to work.

In three years of marriage, John had told Helen he loved her perhaps a half dozen times. On each occasion, the noise in her head would suddenly cease, leaving her profoundly centered and serene. Before he left, hearing those words seemed more important to her than anything else. More important than those things he took such care in providing: a home, companionship, security, a future they could build and share. These were the ways he spoke to her. She had not yet learned to hear him.

And then his brother died.

Following the news of Warren's death, John's silence was the sinkhole that appeared at the corner of their lives. She tried her best to pretend it wasn't there. His selfish, self-destructive grief. It ended up cracking the foundation, threatening to pull everything down. Work took him away for weeks on end, and he was distant when he returned. He let his sorrow consume them.

The wind kicked up the night he left, the house creaked like an old ship at sea. They were on the couch, covered in an old wool blanket, when he announced that he'd be leaving again. It felt like she was falling. She fought the urge to reach out and hold on to him. He had no choice, he said, only duty. He must document some part of the war that claimed his brother, the part that seemed to have fallen into his lap.

If someone isn't there to observe and record, capture it on the page, it will be as if it never happened. The sacrifices made on our behalf must be known before they can be remembered, he said. She replied that his family has already given enough. His duty was not to his dead brother, but to the living—to her and their life together. In a desperate attempt to make him understand, she said the words for which she continues to pay.

If you leave now, don't bother coming back. Because I won't be here if you do.

He put his finger to her lips.

The house was cold. He unbuttoned her blouse anyway. He moved his hands down her skin, then pushed the blanket away. Fumbled with his belt in the dim lamplight, his face hard and set. She lay pinned on her back in the crook of the couch as he lowered himself onto her. This had nothing to do with making a child. This was for them. And yet, he avoided her eyes even as she gazed into his. She felt the abandonment again, the passion he kept hidden inside. They moved to the bed and slept back to back. By morning, he was gone.

Raindrops ooze down the glass, distorting the trees and house beyond. Twenty-five years of age and she's terrified her happiest days are behind her. John is fond of saying that words are of little consequence, as cheap as yesterday's news. And this from a writer. Action, he says, is the only language fit for love.

Beside their bed she prays to God, to quell her anger. She prays to the Blessed Virgin, to overcome her despair. She prays to St. Anthony, patron of lost or missing things. She jolts with the telephone's ring.

Tom Sorenson apologizes in advance. He says he hasn't found much, other than having confirmed that John was quietly seeking assignments to cover the war in Alaska. Whether or not he made it, no one seems to know. Were he a betting man, he says he'd lay money on John having made it to "the action"—Dutch Harbor or even Adak. He double-checked with editors here in Seattle, plus Los Angeles and New York and no one's heard from him. He adds that the government has evacuated the native people from across the Aleutian Chain, all but those held by the enemy on the island of Attu. Americans held prisoner on American soil. A story we all need to know. His voice seems tired, weighed down. Perhaps with the realization that John's trail has gone cold, or the thought that he should be there too. In his pause, Helen feels him search for encouraging words.

"I believe we'll all be reading John's stories soon enough," he says. "On page one, above the fold."

She hangs up the phone and marches into the dining room, which has been given over to research. Helen had brought out the table leaves for more usable space. The clippings of the few reports now coming out of Alaska—little more than official Navy bulletins— are laid out chronologically. She picks up the big atlas and lets it fall open to the spread featuring the territory. Graphite smudges mark the page that drew John's repeated attention. She imagines his touch, envisions the squareness of his palms, the scar across the knuckles of his right hand.

Studying the map of this obscure colony, she thinks how much it resembles an elephant in profile. Alaska sticks its head out into polar seas, complete with a tusk reaching west toward Siberia. More apropos, the tusk of a woolly mammoth. She wonders how much land the Japanese now control and just where on this tusk John might be.

The Aleutian Archipelago: fourteen large and fifty-five small volcanic islands, strung over more than a thousand miles. Somewhere there, he's alive. On good days, her faith overshadows doubt. And what is faith but belief *independent* of proof, a conviction that stands on its own. To this, she knows John would roll his eyes. The thought makes her smile.

Had John been a soldier, inquiries could be made to find out where his unit was stationed. She could simply write to him! And she knows he would contact her if he could. Yet there is only silence.

Helen does not know how she is going to find him. She knows only that she must go there to do it.

FOLLOWING LAST NIGHT'S steady rain, the sun's touch is reassuring. Helen wears a floral print dress, lilac and white, an old favorite of John's. It distinguishes her from the gray uniform of that dwindling class of men who somehow manage to stay.

Maxine's Women's Wear sprawls across two large floors in the heart of the city between Sable's Books and Rexall Drugs. Helen's supervisor, Penny, is at the counter, filling out orders for summer stock. She is in the habit of doing this well in advance to gain some measure of security against worsening shortages and delays.

Penny lost her husband in the Solomon Islands. She has no children to soothe her grief or brighten her future. She compensates by being overly diligent in her duties and expecting everyone else to keep up. For this, Helen forgives her.

"Early bird," Penny says as Helen enters the store. Penny looks up with large, brown eyes shadowed by lack of sleep.

"Morning. I wanted to come in a bit early to let you know that, well, I have to leave."

"What do you mean? You just got here."

"I . . . It's John. I . . ." Helen has prepared a speech, making allowances for how her decision might affect Penny, who received the news of her husband's death the day he was buried at sea.

"I'm not sure where I'm going yet, but I have to go," Helen says, afraid she sounds like she's coming unhinged. "I have to try and find him."

Penny studies the counter between them.

"I'll be available for a week or so while I figure this out. I hope it's enough time to find another girl."

"That won't be necessary." Penny feigns interest in the order form. "I'll have a check ready for you Friday. You can stop by and pick it up or I can mail it, if you prefer."

"I won't leave you in a lurch."

"Having someone around who's already decided to leave is bad for morale. Just take the day off and come back for your check on Friday."

"Don't be like this, Penny. Please. At least wish me luck."

"Helen, he'll be okay. He's a reporter—not a soldier."

Helen holds her ground and stares back until Penny is forced to look up. "I'll miss you." This is not what she intended, adding to the burden.

Helen walks around the counter, throws her arms around her boss, hugs her till she relents.

"Put out the sandwich board," Penny says. "I'm going to work you like a dog for the rest of the week."

Helen turns and walks past racks of clothes, whose inventory she knows by heart, past mannequins with which she is on all too familiar terms. The bells jingle as she steps through the door with the sidewalk sign, into the morning light. She opens it, makes a small adjustment, steps back to judge the effect.

Helen glances up as a slight young man rounds the corner, fists pumping as he gathers speed. He dodges people and telephone poles as he closes the distance between them. His head is bare, jacket open and swinging behind him. He glances from side to side, searching. And then she recognizes the fifteen-year-old kid who lives next door to her childhood home. What is he running from, or to? He catches her eye, then picks up the pace in her direction.

"Jimmy?"

"Your dad . . ." He pants out the news. "Something's wrong. He showed up at our place. Couldn't talk. And his arm. He can't lift it. Mom and Dad took him to the hospital."

He grabs her hand. "Let's go."

She steps out of her shoes, gathers them up, breaks into a run.

THREE

THROUGHOUT THE BOMBARDMENT, EASLEY OBSERVES the birds. From inside the cave, he can see only the far side of the ravine and the low gray sky. He watches gulls and terns wheel through the gusts above and pick through the rocks below. The sounds of the Americans hammering the island are distant but menacing. There is the hornet's buzz of planes overhead, the crackle of Japanese antiaircraft fire, the occasional *thump, thump* of ordnance scarring the land. The birds, however, seem oblivious to it all. Throughout one particularly thunderous drop, Easley watches a gull stand poised on a single foot as it preens the underside of its wing.

The boy's beard is growing in feeble patches. Rather than make him appear older, it only calls attention to his youth. It sprouts in sandy wisps, a shade or two darker than the hair on his head. There are gaps between sideburns, mustache, the crop on his chin. Easley wonders for the first time how he himself must appear. He hasn't seen his own reflection for going on a week.

They do not speak during the bombing runs but sit silently on seats fashioned from flat rocks and cushions of sedge. It's not wholly uncomfortable. They have made progress in fortifying the cave. The parachutes have been transformed into hammocks. Anchor lines have been tied to large boulders and the silk hangs a foot or two above the wet stones, the extra material folded in to trap body heat. Each night they take rocks from the fire and place them underneath their hammocks to enhance the perception of warmth.

The fire pit itself is a point of pride. They have built a windbreak to corral the heat and redirect it back inside the cave. The wall is sturdy, curved, and—given the circumstances—would win the respect of a journeyman mason. Its upper lip is used for roasting shellfish, boots, and socks.

A third cluster of explosions can be heard in the distance. This drop has a note of finality. The low cloud reflects, amplifies the sound. Easley and the boy look up at each other, then glance back at the birds—among which there is not even the slightest hint of distress.

They have taken a keen interest in birds. The first one they killed was an exhausted cormorant holding its wings outstretched to dry. The meat was greasy and tasted of the sea, but was a grand improvement over mussels. That night their faces glistened with fat in the firelight. And today, before the bombing run, they were supremely fortunate to kill a ptarmigan. The grouselike bird was caught between its winter and summer plumage with a brown head and back, legs and tail still white. Killing it required little skill. The bird took no evasive maneuvers, it simply froze and hoped the men had not seen it. The boy wound up and pitched a stone at close range, a remarkable shot to the head. Easley retrieved the bird, held it aloft like a prize as the boy jumped up and down until he tipped over in the grass, kicking his feet in the air like a fool. Easley stared into its still shiny eyes. He kissed it square on the beak.

Visibility is too poor to risk signaling planes again. Three previous attempts have been made, with parachutes quickly hauled out and spread upon the grass. All to no avail. The risk of drawing attention from a Japanese foot patrol seems to outweigh the faint hope of being spotted through the clouds. They await more favorable conditions to signal for help, aware that help may never come.

Now that the war seems over for the day, the boy picks up the ptarmigan and begins to pluck. He drops the feathers into the fire pit. Easley looks up at their supply of wood; a few sticks of dry driftwood piled near the boy's knee and a larger quantity of half-dry wood carefully stacked up in the cave. Wood is getting harder to find, and they have become even more precious with its use. Easley decides to check and see if anything new has washed ashore. He grabs his parachute pack and slips it over his shoulders. "I'm going for smokes and booze."

"Don't forget the pie."

Above the cave, Easley can see for miles along the shore. He scans the clouds for aircraft and the horizon for ships, as is his habit, then quickly spins around—he has forgotten to check behind him.

The warmer air of the past few days has pushed the snow line well up into the foothills. While clouds obscure the peaks, he can catch glimpses of the slopes. Then the floaters come back into focus— drifting dust, lint, and gnats. He rubs his eyes, looks again. This time he sees a long black speck against the snow. Easley stares until he sees it move. This is no trick of the eye.

With his face now flat on the grass, Easley waits several minutes before lifting his head again. Like an amoeba under a microscope, the black speck slowly splits in two, moves in tandem across the white. Easley shields his eyes. He quickly rules out bears, goats, or any sizable four-legged beast because none exist on this island— other than tiny arctic fox. These are men, marching single file, several times more than any possible survivors of a flying boat crew.

Easley watches the Japanese inch their way up the slope, then disappear into the cloud.

THE BOY CONSIDERS THIS NEWS like a riddle. He sets the bird aside and stares into the stones. Finally, he says, "And you didn't come get me?"

"Don't be stupid."

"Maybe I have better eyes than you."

"Look. I hit the deck. I was trying to be inconspicuous. I didn't want to give away our position."

The boy sits back and folds his arms across his chest. "What if they were our guys? Maybe they've been hidin' out like us and were makin' their way 'cross the island."

"To?"

"To what?"

"That's my point. To do what? To find what? To eat what? If they're alive, they know as well as we do that the Japs are just over there. They wouldn't be traipsing through the snow, exposing themselves in the middle of the day unless they've lost their minds."

The boy's face turns pink. "Those guys're my pals. You don't know them . . . If there're people wandrin' around out there, I'll decide whether they're Jap or not. *I* hold rank."

"Rank. What horseshit . . . They were Japs and I just hope to God they didn't see us earlier on, jumping around like fools."

The boy looks up at Easley with resolve, unwilling to break his gaze. Finally he gets up and stomps out of the cave.

Easley steps out into the ravine, watches the boy crawl up onto the grass, then lie still on his stomach. Easley follows. Together, they scan the empty hills and mountains. Although the enemy cannot be seen, they are surely there, just beyond the ridge.

"When you're flyin' near the mainland, you tell yourself it's not really so bad, 'cause you could always find someplace to put down if things got too outta hand," the boy explains. "Over the South Pacific? Guys get shot down there they can stay in the water for hours, sometimes a day or two and still hope someone'll come by and save 'em. Out here? There's no hope once you're in the sea. It's a matter of minutes. Your plane goes down here, you're finished."

Perhaps a few minutes longer in the English Channel, Easley thinks.

Forty-seven degrees. That was the water temperature recorded off Plymouth the day his brother's plane went down. Surrounding Attu today, the water is more than ten degrees colder. Did Warren survive his crash? Get free of the plane and tread water? Easley has studied, imagined, obsessed, and grieved over these thoughts for some months now. But unless he explains that a part of himself, his own flesh and blood, has already met such a fate, how could the boy possibly know?

"Well," Easley says, "seems you beat the odds. Let's hope you haven't played your last lucky card."

The boy looks over with a blank expression, then backs up like a badger over the side of the ravine.

Easley rolls over and looks at the lowering clouds, conjuring visions of his previous life—a life that seems increasingly remote. He lies on the grass until a whiff of smoke reaches him from below. He feels a surge of panic and turns around to see. The fog is descending again and the wind is blowing down from the hills, the fire won't give away their position.

Then, an impatient baritone. "Git down here and gimme a hand or I'll eat the whole goddamned thing myself!"

* * *

TWO DAYS LATER, Easley is half a mile down the beach when it happens again. This time, there is no shadow of doubt. He has his trousers down around his ankles, squatting at the edge of the grass. He's gotten past feeling ridiculous, even though the plovers observe him with sideways glances as they dutifully march along like businessmen late for a meeting. The cold air blowing between his legs reminds him just how vulnerable and unprepared he is to survive in their world.

The sound of a plane is upon him almost as soon as he's in position. The moment before he had actually felt pleased with himself, pleased that he had found driftwood, that they have eluded capture another day, that he is at long last able to clear his troubled system. He cranes his neck around to see. When this proves insufficient, he hops around in a squatting position and searches the sky. And there, just past the volcano, he can see a floatplane heading more or less in his direction. He yanks his trousers up over his hips and dives to the ground all in one desperate maneuver. He is reminded of his ribs. The plane drops altitude and flies over the foothills toward the beach.

Easley makes himself as small as possible, tries to melt into the land. He holds his breath, as if the pilot can somehow hear him breathe. He slowly twists over on his back to watch the plane sail past. Single, big pontoon, pair of red-orange dots emblazoned on the wings. He flashes on stories out of the Philippines last year, how the Japanese were said to have starved, beat, bayonetted, and shot their prisoners of war. He searches for signs he's been spotted—a change in direction, a tilt of the wings. He can detect nothing. He thinks of the boy, out hunting for ptarmigan. He fears he did not find cover in time.

The plane flies low over the Pacific on an easterly heading, then makes a gradual bank to the south. It holds its course, then disappears from sight. When the drone gives way to tumbling surf, Easley gets up on his knees. He checks the vacant horizon, then reaches for a handful of sedge to wipe his freezing ass.

BACK AT THE CAVE, Easley dumps an armful of wood on the rocks, grateful to see the boy in one piece, relieved that he won't have to face the future alone.

"Heard it before I saw anything," the boy says. "Ran back before he broke through the cloud."

Squeezing into crevices, crouching behind rocks, traveling in the low lay of the land. These methods hold out hope for avoiding detection by other men traveling on foot, but the view from a cockpit window can offer an unlimited perspective, the ability to double back, circle, and chase.

Easley bends down, empties the smaller chunks of driftwood from his pack, then sorts the pile according to size and dryness. It occurs to him that perhaps the Japanese know they are here. Maybe they've already placed bets on how long he and the boy will survive. He keeps this notion to himself. The one thing they have in abundance is time—time to fashion a thought or opinion from solid stuff, smooth out the edges before handing it over. This care is all very much in keeping with their code of honesty; it helps avoid potential conflict or confusion.

"Found a big log today," Easley says. "Take the two of us to get it back but it'll be well worth the effort."

Not to be outdone, the boy reaches behind a rock, pulls out a fresh ptarmigan, tosses it at Easley's feet. This bird is even bigger than the first. Next, he reaches behind his waist and brings his pack around. He pulls out a handful of small yellow bulbs that seem partially roused for spring. "Go ahead," he says, offering some to Easley. "Tastes like some kinda celery."

Easley tries it and agrees. There'll be a proper feast tonight.

"We'd better stay inside. Watch our backs for a while," Easley says. "Wait 'til dark to light the fire."

The boy wipes his hands on his trousers. Then, with no small measure of pride, he picks up the ptarmigan and walks over to the fire pit. He sets about plucking the bird, then stops and looks up.

"Maybe the young hunter gets to rest while the old man cleans dinner. It's the least you can do for my goddamned birthday."

"Today?"

"Believe so. And here I am stuck in a hole with you."

"Well, that solves it. I'll take care of dinner while you tell me something of your short yet undistinguished life."

The boy retires to his hammock. He climbs in and pulls the extra material around himself until only his face protrudes from the cocoon.

Easley plucks and guts the bird, then, as dusk falls, builds and lights the fire.

Despite improvements, the emotional comfort afforded by their fire pit far outweighs its usefulness for warming skin and bones. Easley waits for the coals to glow. Shadows shift and parry in the honey-colored light as the wet walls refract and reflect their fire, like stars on a cloudless night. How long will they survive when the wood runs out? A week? Two? With the supply on this beach nearly exhausted, they will have to travel increasingly farther afield. He skewers the two chunks of hindquarter and sticks them out over the flames.

The boy is pensive, uncharacteristically silent.

"When I was your age, I was in art school," Easley says, to prime the conversation. "I wanted to be a painter. Still life. Natural history. The new Audubon."

"New what?"

"An artist. Thought I'd travel the world, then hole up in some garret in the city—drinking and screwing. I even grew a little beard." Easley looks over at the boy and catches him in a smile. "Didn't do much painting, though. That was part of the trouble."

"What's the other part?"

The bird's fat bubbles. It runs down the skewer and sizzles on the coals. The smell is overwhelming. It speaks to a part of Easley's being unconnected to mind or soul, something deep and compelling he is only now getting to know. He turns both pieces over to expose a fresh side to the heat. Fat dribbles down his hand, he licks it off like gravy.

"The other part was what my favorite teacher said to me. One day, he took me aside and said that I had just enough talent to torture myself for the rest of my life but not enough to make it as an artist. Said I was old-fashioned. Lacked vision. Showed no real promise of developing a style of my own. He told me to look for something else. It's not too late to be good or even great at something, he said. If only I'd put painting behind me."

"Mean old coot." The boy slowly licks his lips in anticipation.

"He was about as old as I am now."

"Still, couldn't've felt good hearin' it."

"So I became a writer, of sorts."

"But do you have any talent for it?"

Easley gestures around the cave. "Enough to pay for all of this . . ."

"What kind of stories you write?"

"Articles about wildlife, people. Heard of the *National Geographic Magazine*?"

"Yeah, they even have those in Texas. Good pictures."

The bird is not quite ready. Easley sticks the knife into the little thigh and the juice runs quick and opaque. He tosses a few bulbs of the wild celery up into the hammock. "Salad," he says. "Main course will be served directly."

"College wasn't for me." The boy gets out of the hammock and comes down next to the fire. "Too many rich boys for my liking."

"What did you study?"

"History, English, a little chemistry. Had no idea what I was doin'."

Easley hands the boy a hindquarter, puts the other aside for himself, then sets the breasts on to roast.

"When I turned twenty, my friends took me out and got me drunk," Easley says. "Woke up on the floor of a stranger's house. Had no idea how I got there . . . Ended up walking home with no shoes or wallet."

"My last birthday, I was in basic training," the boy says. "I didn't tell nobody. The birthday before that, I had a fight with my mom. She wouldn't leave me alone." He takes a bite of the meat and his eyes light up with the flavor.

"Wouldn't leave you alone . . ."

"My mother ruined my life is the easiest way to tell it," he says. "She ruined me."

Easley bites into his chunk of meat and considers options. Pick up the scent and follow the trail where it leads, risk fouling the day, or gently shift things in another direction.

"We've all got parents," Easley offers.

"No we don't."

Easley stirs the coals as the words hang in the air.

"My daddy left us when I was three. I was the only child. He couldn't stand my mom no more so he just walked away one night. Left everything. All his money, clothes, you name it. Never came back. Well, she couldn't take it. She never treated me right. Like a boy. A son. She always doted on me like something else. Like she needed me too much. She wanted me to sleep with her all the time, keep her company. Then, when I got older and needed my privacy, she couldn't take it. I stayed in my room and she let me alone from the time I was twelve until I was about fifteen. She had a man part of that time. Then he left too. Soon after that, she started cryin' and beggin' at my door."

The boy takes another bite and Easley does his best to keep his eyes focused on the fire. The boy sighs heavily.

"She was on me all the time. She'd buy me little gifts when it wasn't even close to my birthday. We spent every night in her bed. Early on, she'd just hold on to me until she fell asleep, but then she started gettin' worked up. Then one night, that was it. She'd even change the sheets in my old room now and then to make it look like I was sleeping there, in case anyone noticed. I tried chasin' after girls from school, like my buddies were doin', but I felt dirty. Like some kind of criminal." He runs out of steam and pauses, staring into the flames. "I've never told anyone else, but I figured this might be the last chance I get. You don't really want to hear all this, do you?"

"I'll listen to anything you want to tell me."

"I've never had a regular girl. A girl my own age who cared for me and wanted me. I have no idea what that's like. My mother took all that from me. I'm ruined for it."

"So you joined up."

"So I got away from her." The boy takes a bite of meat. "If we ever get out of here, I have to see what that's like. I got to try."

Easley planned to tell the boy more about himself, his home life, which now seems so fortunate by comparison. How he had met and fallen in love with Helen. The surprise of it all when he was just coming to terms with the idea that—at the advanced age of thirty-two—he might be destined to live his life alone. How timing was everything. If he had met Helen a year before or after he would have likely missed his opportunity. How happy they'd been, until the babies failed to come and the war put such notions into perspective. How the memory of having left the way he did gnaws at him day and night. But timing is everything, and this is not the time.

"Karl?"

"Yeah."

Easley sucks the marrow from a tiny bone, then tosses it into the fire. "We're walking through life in the present, changing along the way. The past is something somebody else did long ago. What happens tomorrow is someone else's problem. All that's real is the here and now."

"You believe all that?"

"Sounds good, doesn't it?"

"Yeah," the boy agrees. "It surely do."

THE FIRE FADES to ember glow. Past the pit, the mouth of the cave yawns to the nighttime sky. The boy is already asleep, his breathing shallow and steady. The roasted stones below their hammocks have long since cooled. The cold tests the limits, pacing, creeping up inch by inch. Easley's mind wanders—between Karl's sad story and the nearby Japanese, past huge stacks of tinder-dry wood, then down belowdecks of his father's old sloop.

The summer had been exceptionally warm. He and Helen shared a picnic in the August sun, watching little boats make the most of meager wind on English Bay. It seemed all the world was out on the water that day, but the cabin was theirs alone.

They drank wine and laughed about drifting out past Vancouver Island to Hong Kong before the month was through. She nodded at his tumble of words, enjoying the awkwardness. He stood in the hatchway, trying to keep an eye on the sea. She rose from her seat in the galley, unbuttoned his shirt. Ran her hand across his belly and chest, then pulled him below as the boat turned into the wind.

He has allowed himself the luxury of her remembered presence, the disappeared past. A betrayal of the sermon just preached, it is a comfort all the same. Hiding in the dark and the cold at the edge of the world, are memories all that is left to him?

The wind sweeps down the hills and howls across the lip of the cave. Nose, chin, cheeks grow numb as the coals grow weak and perish.

FOUR

J OE CONNELLY MOVES THROUGH HIS HOME LIKE A
man determined to make a good first impression. He tops
off Helen's cup before she's had three sips of coffee.

"Sit down, Daddy. You're making me nervous."

He is showing off for her, as he did with the doctors. He moves
with care and purpose, anticipates what he will need to carry or lift,
uses his left hand gracefully in the hopes of drawing attention away
from the right. He moves in such a way as to mask any sign of weakness.

Joe was kept in the hospital for two days. Helen felt helpless,
watching him sit up in bed, unable to form words or squeeze his
right hand, eyes wild with confusion. And yet before the day was
through, he was forcing out discernible sentences. The following
day, he was—with effort—able to lift his right arm and extend a
tremulous hand, but admitted the numbness persists. The doctors
were surprised to see his speech return so rapidly. Whether the arm
will follow suit is anyone's guess. Despite medical advances, they
say stroke remains a mystery. He may have another one at breakfast tomorrow, or live to see his hundredth birthday, never having

another stroke again. There is no treatment available, nothing to do but wait and see.

Helen made the decision to break her lease the moment she arrived at the hospital. Hired boys from the high school helped her pack up the contents of the house she and John had shared. She tried and failed to keep them from taking a shortcut through the flowers as they loaded the truck. She stood aside, imagining John's expression, should he return and find another family living in his home. A few hours later, she watched her father step aside helplessly as the boys carried her boxes and furniture down into his basement. She saw him fight the urge to pitch in, do his part, lift, lug, and stack.

From the stowed possessions of her married life, she carried a single suitcase up the rough wooden stairs from the basement. She shut the door and switched off the light.

Upstairs, the hall, kitchen, living room—every surface seems rubbed with the patina of history. It is not so much that the walls or furnishings themselves are particularly ancient or worn, it's more the sense that everything seems to belong to another era—props left over from the first act of her life. She cradles the cup in her hands.

"I hate the reason, but I have to say it's good to have you home."

"Daddy . . ." She is dizzy, from the sudden telescoping of time. Her mind races forward to his next stroke, which she fears will kill him, back to visions of him as a younger man, when she believed he could protect her from all possible harm. Then to where she sits today, being forced to choose between caring for her father, or setting out to find her husband. Forward again—should their grandfather pass before they arrive, how will she describe him to her children?

"You're doing me the favor," she says, "saving me from being alone. Put your feet up. I'll make some supper. Anything in the ice-box?"

"*You* make supper? One hand tied behind my back and I'm still

twice the cook you'll ever be. Don't forget who taught you what little
you know."

He gets back up and disappears into the kitchen.

Even before the stroke, Joe's arthritis had slowed him down.
Regardless, he filled his weeks down at St. Brigid's Catholic church
with light carpentry, maintenance, restoration. He won't take a nickel
for his time. Helen had hoped that volunteer work would afford him
opportunities for conversation and sociability. He chooses instead
to haunt the church early in the week when even priests are hard to
find. He asked only to be allowed to work at his own pace and sees
no reason why this has to change. He will find ways to compensate
for his insubordinate limb.

In both reputation and fact, Joe Connelly has been hard at work
since childhood. He tells of splitting shakes from rough cedar blocks,
dawn 'til dusk, when he was twelve years old. At thirteen, he graduated to cutting shingles with the saw. When the call went out for volunteers for the Great War, Joe signed up immediately—as if it were a
one-time, limited offer. At forty, he was considered too old for combat duty and was trained as a radiotelegrapher instead. En route to
Europe, he shattered his right hand aboard the transport ship during
a storm in the North Atlantic. He spent the balance of the war in a
remote communications post in Normandy. Following the armistice,
Joe came home with a French bride, their two small boys, and a fan-
tastic tale about how he broke his hand on the jaw of a Hun.

Two months after the family arrived in Seattle, Helen was born.
Joe found work in the mill. The year his young daughter started
school, his wife died of cancer. Helen had always believed that it
would have made matters simpler by far if she too had been a boy.
There were womanish secrets and mysteries he spent her formative
years avoiding. She learned the facts of menstruation from a bald and
bifocaled physician. Helen had made the appointment herself because

she thought she might bleed to death and was too embarrassed to tell anyone the location of her injury. Joe made up for these shortcomings in countless other ways.

His sons grew up and moved on years ago, unable to restrain themselves from challenging his supremacy any longer. Together, they moved clear across the country and established a small construction firm in New Jersey, as well as families of their own. The day of Joe's stroke, Helen called her older brother, Frank, who promised to pass the message along to Patrick. He said it was a relief to know that they could trust she had the matter "well in hand."

In the kitchen, potatoes and onion are on the fry. Joe stands at the stove with his good hand stirring the pan, his right hand weighed down like a plumb line to the floor. Helen gently nudges him aside. A pair of chops—probably his entire meat ration for two weeks—sit open on wax paper.

"How did you cut the potatoes and onions?"

"Chop in half," he says, "pin halved potato under a second chopping block. Cut, shift, repeat."

"Sounds like an accident waiting to happen."

He finds himself leaning against the sink. "You stay as long as you want, now. This is your home, especially with John being gone."

"Careful what you wish for."

Potatoes browned, she lays the meat in the pan.

Eventually, he asks, "Got any plans? Other than hovering over me."

She turns to meet his gaze.

"You'll be the first to know."

He glances at the grandfather clock. "*The Shadow*'s starting soon. You listen much?"

"No, Daddy. But you go ahead." She switches on the radio, then moves their plates to the table.

"With all this nonsense I forgot to ask, heard anything at all?"

He refers, of course, to John.

"Not a word," Helen replies. "And you know he would contact me if he possibly could."

"It's a war, sweetheart. He could be out in the trenches right now. Bogged down. Trying to file a report . . . These are tricky times. We have to be patient."

Helen smiles weakly. She asks if they still have trenches. This elicits a scowl.

At the table, she watches as he eyes the meal before him, playing out possible plans of attack. She reaches over and cuts up the meat on his plate. He tries brushing her hand away but she persists.

"Please say a prayer for him tonight."

Joe nods, but the announcer is introducing the program, his attention already drawn away. She observes him negotiate food and fork, his right hand asleep on his lap. She finishes her meal, kisses him on the forehead, and leaves him to his show.

Upstairs she discovers a vase of daffodils on the nightstand beside her bed.

* * *

THE RECRUITING OFFICE of the Women's Army Auxiliary Corps hums with newly directed energy. The address matches the one in the handbill she's been carrying around for over a week. She scans the windows—now covered with posters imploring women to do their bit for their country. She recalls the old placards that hung in the windows of this storefront just a few years ago, promoting voyages to the exotic Orient and sunny South Pacific. Inside, women rush around with file folders and envelopes like they're placing last-minute bets at the track. One of them waves Helen over to her desk.

The woman seems so pleased to see her, it's as if she's been expected. Helen remembers the face from catechism, half a lifetime ago.

"Edith Brown," the woman says, hand stuck out straight from the shoulder. "And you're Helen . . . Corrigan?"

"Connelly . . . At least it used to be. Now it's Helen Easley."

"Have a seat. Can you believe you're the third girl to walk in here today that I already knew?"

Helen flashes back on her father, fumbling with his wallet before they left for his doctor's appointment this morning. How he must now balance it on the wrist of his stiff right arm while he picks through the bills with his left. She has hardly opened her mouth and she already feels like a traitor.

Edith explains the opportunities awaiting women in the WAAC. Helen could become a driver, cook, clerk, messenger, or work in a canteen. Edith herself will be going to England as soon as her papers arrive. Whatever Helen chooses to do, she will be making a real contribution and she will be paid. It all begins with three months basic training in Portland, Oregon.

Three months? Each day since her decision to leave, Helen feels her trajectory falling, the heavy pull of gravity. There must be some way around. "Can I choose where I go?"

"Well, sure. Like I said, you could go overseas. Right now, lots of girls are leaving for England."

"What about Alaska, for instance?"

Edith is momentarily taken aback. "Never heard of girls going to Alaska." She pushes away from her desk. "Let me see what I can find out."

Women crisscross the office in smart uniforms and short hairstyles. It is a hive of feminine determination. Helen can't help but wonder if some of them will wind up getting shot, or blown to smith-ereens.

Edith returns, shaking her head.

"You wouldn't want to go up there, anyhow. Apparently there's been some kind of attack. They've already sent home most of the women and families. They're not set up for women."

Helen picks up her purse and offers her hand. She promises to think it over.

"Take your time—but not too long. You don't want to miss all the fun."

* * *

HELEN WALKS WITH HER FATHER to St. Brigid's, where he is deter-mined to spend the day puzzling over single-handed ways of securing a loose railing. Seeing him so eager to work makes her uneasy, weak with affection, convinced he's hiding something more. She watches him disappear through the door of the rectory, then she continues down the block, and onto the bus downtown.

At the library, she examines the papers for any mention of Alaska. The void she finds is quickly filled with fears of a Japanese advance, a widening and bloody campaign. She chides herself for such undisciplined thoughts, then sharpens her concentration. In the classifieds, she is rewarded with three solid leads for jobs offering passage north: a salmon cannery, an engineering firm, the office of a coal mine.

Months of research have made this much clear: Alaska is not a place offering a wide range of work. Aside from fighting the ele-ments, virtually all labor seems to involve the extraction of resources from the earth, forest, and sea. She makes a list of her meager quali-fications: 1. filing, 2. bookkeeping, 3. shopkeeping, 4. housekeeping,

5. cooking. She notes that her work life thus far has involved much in the way of "keeping." Should she mention her fluency in French, which she learned in honor of her mother? In Alaska, this would be of no use whatsoever. Unfortunately, she's a poor typist. Shorthand might as well be hieroglyphics or runes.

By the time Helen's mother was twenty-five, she had mastered two foreign languages, studied music abroad, and balanced the books of the family dairy. She had given birth to three children, survived a war, and emigrated to the New World. In moments like these, Helen feels eclipsed by her legacy. But if John's absence—if this war—has shown her a single thing, it's that we must reimagine who we are and what we are capable of doing.

Helen pushes the papers aside. What does she want? She makes another list. 1. John home safe and the chance to start a family. 2. Her father alive and well cared for. 3. The end of this nightmare war. She dedicates herself to items one and two while accepting that item three rests in the hands of the Almighty.

In the foyer telephone booth, Helen spreads her notes out over her lap, stacks quarters five dollars deep. Once she arrives in Alaska, she will improvise, somehow find her way out to the islands. All of which means she must unleash a pack of lies.

Three times she is told that no one is hiring women, even in support positions. One man even laughed. The mine foreman says her best bet, her one sure shot, is to find an outfit offering mail order brides.

HELEN STARES UP from her childhood bed, streetlight through windowpanes casting oblong bars across the ceiling. Joe's snore rumbles down the hall. She rolls over on her side, pulls the extra pillow below,

THE WIND IS NOT A RIVER

squeezes it between her thighs. John never snores, unless he's been into the whiskey.

Two more days of dead ends and indecision leave her clutching an old brochure for the Alaska Steamship Company, based here in Seattle. If the government hasn't already requisitioned their ships, she could simply book passage north to Juneau. But why pretend she's going to a job? All it takes is money. Juneau is a long way from the Aleutians, but it is a start. For a moment she allows herself believe her father's claims, that he can manage as he always has, that he has no need of around-the-clock care. She has no real plan—only the will to get closer to John. His continuing silence can only mean that he is no longer undercover but missing. No one else will be looking for him.

She must tell her father of her plans. She must drain her bank account. He will certainly shoot holes in her theories and schemes but would never suggest she remain to care for him. He will have a long list of fears for her safety. Would he attempt to forbid her from going? She must acknowledge, counter, and allay his fears without backing down.

HELEN SPENDS FRIDAY AFTERNOON in the cool spring sun, shopping for long underwear, lined gloves, the heaviest wool coat she can find. She assembles the gear she imagines she'll need, and yet with each item crossed off her list she feels less and less prepared to go. She has done precious little travel, virtually none of it alone. And now she presumes herself ready to sail headlong into the void that claimed her husband?

In St. James Cathedral, Helen genuflects in the direction of the sacrament, then lights two candles, one for John and one for her father. She asks for forgiveness for what she feels driven to do, for leaving her father behind. She prays for guidance and protection, and asks in advance for absolution for the lies and deception she will surely require. She stares at the twin points of light, surrounded by dozens of other wishes flickering through ruby glass.

Twenty minutes later, Helen shoulders through the heavy glass doors of the library. She marches past the librarians, whom she imagines must now consider her some kind of lonely, eccentric spinster. She pulls today's *Post-Intelligencer* and *Seattle Times* off the rack, drops her bags under the table.

She races through each paper twice: first scanning headlines and bylines, then dipping into any possibly related story. Even though it is an active theater of war, neither paper offers news of the territory. On page four of the *Times*, she sees a large photo of a troopship currently docked in port, with an inset photo of Olivia de Havilland. At the bottom of the column is a smaller photo of four women who, the caption reveals, will also be onboard to entertain the troops. Helen's focus drifts to the right-hand corner of the photo, to another face instantly familiar. If her eyes are to be believed, Ruth Simmons is back in town.

* * *

THEY HUG ON THE SIDEWALK outside Woolworth's department store. Ruth's perfume is overly sweet and abundant. Inside, they order ice cream floats at the counter. As Ruth enthuses about the wonders of New York, Helen guesses the cost of her ensemble: green satin dress, fur stole, pillbox hat, silk stockings, gorgeous new pumps. Seventy-five dollars, at least. Helen discreetly straightens her own sweater and smoothes the wrinkles from her skirt.

Helen and Ruth were close childhood friends until Ruth drifted into another crowd. While Helen won a few roles in high school productions, Ruth showed no interest in theater or pageants. And yet, after graduation, Ruth up and moved to Manhattan and had an acting career in no time.

In place of envy, which burned itself out long ago, Helen now finds herself filled with a kind of awe. She never expected to see Ruth again, except perhaps in a magazine, or a small role in the movies. Whenever Helen turns on the radio, a part of her is listening for Ruth's voice in radio plays. Ruth did manage to make her way onto the New York stage, but now finds herself working for Uncle Sam. Aboard troopships, across the Pacific, right up to the front. Helen feels hope rise unexpectedly.

Ruth's individual physical features range from beautiful (hazel eyes and high cheekbones) to ordinary (crowded lower teeth), yet she has always been more than the sum of her parts. Her expression conveys mischievousness, amusement, delight. While she will never be a leading lady, her attractiveness is undeniable. Ruth slurps up the last of her float. She produces a slim silver case, and offers a cigarette. Helen politely declines.

Two young airmen stumble inside. It has begun to rain and their shoulders are splattered dark. They come to an abrupt halt on seeing them but are unable to meet Ruth's gaze. They scan Helen as an afterthought, then slink down one of the aisles like schoolboys caught in a prank.

"Tell me you haven't fallen in with gangsters," Helen says, "or left New York to escape your boyfriend's wife."

"Would it were true. Nothing quite so exciting. But I was getting regular work, until Herr Hitler rained on my parade."

Helen is pleased to see that, despite Ruth's budding success, she still refuses to take herself too seriously.

"How long are you in town?" she asks.

"Not so fast. What about you? Got yourself a man?"

Only now does Helen remember removing her wedding band before scrubbing the pots last night. She had placed it carefully in the tiny bowl on the windowsill. While she feels the urge to relay her astonishing good fortune in meeting John Easley, she is unprepared to recount the necessary and agonizing stories that follow.

"Not at the moment," Helen replies. Instead she offers up her work at Maxine's, the success of her brothers out east, her father's stroke.

When the time is right, she will tell her that, after a string of schoolgirl crushes and two short affairs, she finally met and fell in love with John Easley. At first, there was the physical attraction that made her head spin. She found him kind, attentive, and instinctively honest no matter what the cost. In time she came to realize that he carries within a kind of peace that comes from knowing his own soul. He made her believe such a peace was possible for herself. Once, long before she'd met John, she had asked her father what to look for in a mate. "Find someone better than you," he said. "I know I sure did." This wisdom she took to heart.

Ruth takes a contemplative drag on her cigarette and watches the airmen steal glances. She stares them down until they turn and take their leave. On their way out, they tip their hats as Ruth flashes a victory smile. "Me either. I got *men*."

For Ruth, capturing and holding the attention of men appears to be some kind of game. To Helen, this seems like playing with matches.

"These days my meal ticket is the USO." Ruth gingerly removes a lash from her eye with a precise pinkie finger. "We're heading to Hawaii with a musical review for the troops. There's eight of us. Of course we've been promised Olivia de Havilland to headline, but I'll believe it when I see it. Either way, we get well taken care of. Everyone's getting in. Just imagine the exposure."

"That sounds—"

"Do you still dance? Wait a minute, you had a great voice . . . You should come along."

"To what?"

"Well, we're not rehearsing yet. Just dancing for dimes. Recruits get to put their hands on you and stagger around for a minute or two. But you don't have to dance with anyone you don't want to." She registers Helen's surprise. "It's *patriotic* . . . C'mon, I'm sure I could get you on. Meet me at seven."

Ruth's on a roll. She lights another cigarette and falls into a character from a romantic comedy she was in recently, transforming herself into a nosy telephone operator—to hilarious effect. Helen can't remember the last time she laughed so hard. Ruth seems to sense this and does her utmost to keep the laughs coming.

THE SWEDISH HALL is festooned with Stars and Stripes, crepe paper streamers, posters promoting the USO. The lights are dimmed, the faces further obscured by the fog of cigarette smoke. The wail of a trumpet echoes across the mostly vacant dance floor. In place of the band, a lone girl fingers through records up onstage behind speakers the size of steamer trunks. Huddled near the door, a convention of fly-boys and run-of-the-mill GIs, scrubbed clean, caps in hands, gaze at the selection of hostesses arrayed along the opposite wall. They work up the courage to move.

Helen studies Ruth as she plows around the floor with a sergeant. He is only just her height and has a fat neck that swallows his chin whenever he looks at his feet. There is no grace in the way he moves. But they smile and laugh, and Ruth tosses her hair like she hasn't a care in the world.

Unsure of how to dress for such an event, Helen opted for a modest navy blue dress, hair up. She stands a safe distance behind several other women, wishing she hadn't come. Helen moved from life with her father and brothers directly into her life with John. She has always felt outside the secret intrigues of women, unprepared for the sudden shifts and subtext. It was as if she had been adopted away from her own kind and now finds them peculiar.

About a dozen couples move around the floor with varying degrees of success. After putting it off as long as she dares, Helen finally joins in. She dances for over an hour with a series of partners and a few who come back for more. One unremarkable-looking private, about her own age, clearly knows what he is doing. They dance two songs in a row, jitterbug and Western swing. He leads with his eyes, his body, making it seem as if each step had been her idea from the start.

A few men—those reeking of aftershave or being goaded by their friends—attempt liberties. A squeeze on the hip, the incidental brush of a breast. Chaperones pace the floor, upright Christian matrons. A tap on the shoulder and a wag of the finger puts an end to most shenanigans. A few men are escorted out the door. And then, long after Helen thought he was gone, the private reappears to take her hand.

He leads her through steps she's never seen before and yet she is able to follow his lead. Partway through, she stops thinking altogether. They move so well, others simply stop and stare. When it all comes to an end, he dips her low and stares into her eyes. A slow waltz begins, and they relinquish the floor.

"Hey. That was something!" He wipes his brow with a handkerchief. "I know we're not supposed to ask, but—"

"My husband is in the thick of it. He's a war correspondent."

The private nods to the floor. He takes a half step back, sinks his hands into his pockets. "Sorry. Where'd you say he was?"

"Alaska Territory. They're holding off an invasion."

His eyes narrow quizzically. "News to me." He grins. "We should probably let the yellow bastards have the place—then sit back and watch 'em freeze."

He has no idea. None. And he is not alone. The military is papering over the war closest to home. And now here she is, dancing with strangers. She feels as if she's losing her mind. Helen crosses her arms and plants her feet. Glares until the man backs away.

SHE SLIPS INTO THE BATH with relief, eager to rid herself of any trace of the men's anxious sweat and pomade. The heat of the water penetrates her skin, urging the muscles to release. She reaches down to massage her foot. Downstairs, the murmur of the radio is punctuated now and again with her father's laugh, which she adores. Particularly the laugh he is doing just now, the kind he attempts to hold inside, mouth closed. The kind he would prefer to share if only someone else were around.

In the end, the night redeemed itself with the confirmation of this remarkable fact: all kinds of women are being escorted to the edge of battle. Women like Ruth. There is no need for a lonely boat ride to Juneau to fumble from one lie to the next in the dark. She will let the military take her to John. How can her father possibly argue with such a patriotic endeavor? Helen feels the beginnings of a smile.

F I V E

T HE PAST TWO DAYS WERE SO UNRELATED THEY
seemed born of different seasons. One of bright skies,
driving wind, and aerial bombardment, one of low cloud
and stillness. The birds were unaccountably blasé during the attack,
going about their usual routines, but now seem caught by the dol-
drums, unmotivated, loitering in the grass. Even the sea is calm. Easley had never encountered a place of such profound changeability.

Hunting had gone poorly. It was as if word of their murderous
ways had spread throughout the avian population. Part of the reason,
Easley's sure, was their crude hunting techniques. While the combina-
tion of a diversion and a well-aimed rock occasionally worked on the
incredibly simple ptarmigan, it was far more difficult to bring down
the wily and numerous birds of the shore and sea.

Together they tried pitching stones baseball-style at gulls and
puffins. The boy had superior accuracy, owing to his American
childhood. Easley grew up playing hockey, a sport with no obvious
correlation to hunting, unless the quarry were dark mice scurrying
across a frozen pond. At best, they'd each get a shot or two before the
birds packed up and flew farther down the beach. Mussels and seaweed

are back on the menu. They dispense with the charade of preparing and sharing meals. They simply consume whatever they find, wherever they find it.

Two weeks on the run and Easley's soiled trousers sag from his hips, stiff with salt from sweat and the sea. His ass has gone missing. The speed at which he is wasting away comes as a surprise. Such weight loss is plain on the boy as well: the hollow face, the shrinking neck and thighs. He had much less to lose. And so it is with serious misgivings that they sling packs over their shoulders in the dim morning light.

"Ready?" The boy stands taller than usual. He wants Easley to believe he is up for adventure.

They pause, surveying the meager hole that has served as their home. Easley reaches into his pocket for keys, his instinct to somehow lock it all up before they leave. He covers this embarrassing slip by scratching his groin. They walk out into the fog.

Easley lets the boy take the lead across the barren slopes, through a cold, shallow river, then toward the far ridge—a frontier they've yet to cross. It leads past where they touched down and, they believe, to the village perhaps twelve miles on. Because the fog strictly confines the field of vision, Easley fine-tunes his hearing. After filtering out the familiar sounds—the swish of their own boots through dead rye, birdcall along the shore—he convinces himself that they are utterly alone.

Their plan is to take advantage of the covering fog to approach the village and camp. Since the Japanese occupied the tiny village, they have been busy constructing a system of tunnels and a pier. The boy explains that this had been confirmed from aerial reconnaissance photos several months before. It is anyone's guess what the enemy has done with the villagers. If the fog lifts, they will observe and wait for the cover of darkness. If not, they will return to the safety of the cave.

It isn't long before they encounter patches of snow. Because their footprints will linger for days, they avoid these areas carefully.

After an hour's walk, they come across a rotting post stuck deep in a grove of old wild celery. Weathered gray and spotted with orange lichen, it sticks out four feet from the earth where it has been placed for some unknown purpose. They search in vain through the brightening mist for similar signs. They return to and study the lone marker.

"Think it's some Indian thing?" the boy says, finally.

"Don't know."

"Maybe we should bring it back and burn it. I don't think the Aleutians will care."

"Aleuts," Easley corrects. "They also call themselves Unangan. Not Eskimos, not Indians. These islands you're fighting for belong to them. You should at least know their name."

"I'm fightin' for the U.S. of A," the boy snaps.

They continue on, leaving the post undisturbed.

By midday, the fog shows no sign of abating. They have traveled perhaps three hours around islands of snow, shaky with hunger. The indistinguishable terrain makes them feel as if little progress is being made. Suddenly the boy stops, pulls Easley alongside, whispers into his ear.

"For all we know, this place could be crawlin' with Japs. A whole herd of 'em could be standing over there." The boy raises his finger to point, but the gesture is meaningless. Visibility is less than a hundred yards.

"I say we head down for mussels," Easley replies. "If it doesn't lift in an hour, we'll comb the shore for wood."

The boy shrugs.

On their way down the slope, Easley is again amazed at the seeming proximity of winter and spring. Within a few feet of patchy snow, there is a tinge of eager green. The boy bends down, pulls off a nub of wild celery, and sticks it into his mouth. Easley moves to do the same, but steps into a mossy pit that drenches him to the knee. He has not set foot on a land mine, or booby trap. But as both sides learned in the last Great War, cold wet feet that never dry can pull a man down eventually.

Through thinning mist they spy a colony of mussels clinging to rocks at the edge of the tide. Wanting to leave the fewest tracks possible across the open beach, Easley volunteers to go and get them. He pulls off his boots, then pads across the sand. When a cold wave rolls in, the sting penetrates his bones. Pale and slightly blue, his feet appear to him more naked and pathetic than ever before. He yanks the mussels from the rock and shoves them into his pockets. Just when he thinks he can no longer stand the pain, he hears a deep gasp—then a splash offshore. Beyond the break, the brown head of a Steller's sea lion bobbing in the swell.

Above the beach, they eat without speaking. It is perhaps a trick of the light, or light-headedness, but today the sight of cold, wet flesh on shiny shells takes Easley back to a hotel on San Francisco Bay. He and Helen had a window seat in the restaurant with a view of the setting sun. Between them, a sharp and constant candle flame reflected in her eyes. She had come away with him, clandestinely, soon after they'd met. It was the first of several unofficial honeymoons. She ordered clams and oysters, musing about their reported "amorous" effects. Each mouthful followed by a gulp of wine. Stepping out of the shower the following morning, finding her dancing solo around the room, Easley knew he beheld his wife. He should have asked her then and there, but found neither the courage nor the words—only the fear of chasing her away.

Visibility increases in the falling rain. Easley and the boy rise and continue on.

Soaked and shivering, they approach a ridge overlooking the harbor. In the distance, they see the Aleut village with its white, onion-domed church and simple wooden houses clustered along the shore. Two dozen buildings at best. Smoke trickling from chimneys. Beyond the village, fields of Japanese tents, trucks, gun emplacements. A ship is anchored in the harbor, but no men can be seen. They crouch for a time, scanning the distance, watching for signs of movement. It strikes Easley that, in ten months of occupation, no one else has come so close to the enemy.

"Smart bastards," the boy observes, his breath turned to vapor. "Tucked in next to the fire."

"Let's go. They won't be out in this mess. We should jog back and cut the time in half. Make a fire and . . ." There is no finishing this thought because there is no food to cook, nothing else to do.

The rain turns to mist and a cold, wet wind. Corporal heat is their only defense against exposure. As they shuffle along, Easley can no longer ignore the pain in his mouth. For the third day in a row he has awoken to an aching molar. Today, however, it has graduated to a new intensity.

Easley watches the boy's legs trudging forward, belabored. Like someone struggling upstream.

WITH STIFF, TREMBLING FINGERS, Easley assembles the remaining stock of fuel. Nine pieces of wood remain inside their darkened cave, plus the butt end of the big log they found the week before. With any luck, the fire will be enough to save them. The boy wipes pale hands on wet trousers, then piles up a handful of precious dry grass. Easley snaps the lighter and lets free the flame for a nervous second until the kindling catches. The boy stands and observes, arms and legs quivering like he hears the tune to Saint Vitus's dance. Easley presents his own wrinkled palms to the fire.

In twenty minutes, there is heat from the pit. Within the hour, they have their shirts off, waving them like bullfighters through the smoke and flame. Later still, they dangle trousers directly over the fire, coaxing warm air up the legs and out the waist. Socks and underpants hang on skewers used for cooking. Boots turn white with salt. They expose themselves to the heat until the gooseflesh subsides, then dress again in clothes still damp but steaming.

They push the last of the wood into the coals, pull down their hammocks, then climb up to the nest the boy made the day they arrived. To preserve body heat, they wrap themselves in the silk until they resemble a mummy of Siamese twins. Hungry and spent, the boy is atwitch with dreams as the pain in Easley's mouth grows wilder.

All that remains of heat and hope fade with the coals. Easley turns, settles, then turns again. He wishes for a speedy deliverance—one way or another.

THE BOY AWAKENS in the middle of the night, dysentery bubbling in his bowels. He apologizes in his polite, southern way, untangles himself, crawls off the nest. Darkness is complete. Easley hears him stumble as he picks his way out into the open. He doesn't make it far before he is forced to drop his drawers and squat.

Easley reaches up and touches his face, swollen significantly in the night. The ache bulges out from the right side of his jaw and is advancing up to his eye.

The boy slides back in, apologizes some more, pulls the silk around them.

Easley makes his last thoughts of Helen. He tries to map out her body, every mole and curve. The details already beginning to fade. She has become a series of sensations, the scent at the crown of her head, the taste of sweat on her skin, her thigh stretched over his waist.

But the ache in his jaw bullies all memory. Still, he feels her kissing his cheek, the healing conveyed through lips.

She props the pillow behind his head, lifts a fork full of pumpkin pie to his mouth, ensures that each bite has a dollop of cream. When crumbs fall on his belly, she bends over and licks it clean . . .

She reaches for his shoulder, halfway across the lake. The forced smile cannot veil her fear. He repeats gentle, encouraging words to calm her breathing. Soon enough, toes touch bottom and he bounds ashore, sunburned and dripping, stretches the towel wide open as she emerges, glistening. Even now, there is the coolness of her skin as he closes the towel around her . . .

She leans against him on the park bench, outside the arc of the lone streetlight. The dizziness has been building all day, the news delivered this morning by a distraught comrade who had been especially close to his brother. He twists the myriad emotions into a thick coil of anger. Helen takes up his hand, cradles it in her lap. Away from his mother, his father, the room he and Warren once shared, grief takes hold of his gut, the tightness forcing him to bend at the waist. She rubs his back and waits but the tears fail to come . . .

SLEET BLOWS INTO THE CAVE through weak morning light. Easley watches it cling to the side of their dim fire pit then turn to slush on stone. The boy sits there with knees pulled up under his chin, staring out into the gray. When he sees that Easley is awake, he offers a broad grin.

"You're the ugliest son of a bitch I ever did see." The boy squints. "Hurt much?"

When Easley sits up, the blood pounds as it leaves his head. The pain in his mouth causes his eyes to water. "I have no idea what you're talking about."

"Better have a look. Come out where we got some light."

Easley sits down on a rock and opens his mouth less than an inch. The boy looks down, brow wrinkled, eyes sharp and bright. He puts cold hands on Easley's jaw, pries open his mouth, tilts it toward the sky.

"Swollen and red. Teeth all look the same to me."

"Near the back," Easley says.

The boy sticks his fingers inside. He wiggles several teeth before reaching the culprit. When he does, Easley moans.

"Rotten, most likely." The boy sits down, wiping Easley's drool on the front of his own jacket.

There is no use spelling it out. They have no drugs. No medical equipment—save pocketknife and Zippo. Not even a lousy toothbrush.

"We have to get that looked at," the boy says finally.

"Looked at? What the hell does that mean?"

"I don't know!" The boy folds his arms defensively. "We gotta get that thing pulled. People die from shit like that."

"And how do you plan to pull it?"

The boy doesn't answer.

"We need to get a fire in here or we'll have bigger problems than a goddamn tooth. We need to eat," Easley says. Then, upon reflection, "Maybe you're right. Maybe it's time we discuss our options."

"Options?"

"We don't have to die in here."

The boy bends down and thrusts his face toward Easley's. "We're not gonna surrender, if that's what you mean. You have any idea what Japs do with prisoners? They'll shoot us after torturing us for secrets. Nobody'd know the difference. Everyone already thinks we're dead." The boy steps back and boots a stone. "Trouble with you is you're in over your head. You came to get your story and get the hell out. You're . . . uncommitted."

"Uncommitted?" Easley's indignation is undermined by his ridiculous, ballooning face. "Canadians, Australians—*New Zealanders* fought while you fuckers sat on your hands."

"Maybe so. But what does any of that have to do with you? You're not here to fight. You take notes."

Easley considers enlightening this child about world events prior to the attack on Pearl Harbor. He thinks of telling him about the blood already spilled and that continues to flow in Europe. He considers telling him something he never told another living soul. How, in 1939, he himself presented at the recruiting office of the British Columbia Regiment (Duke of Connaught's Own Rifles) only to be turned away because of an undiagnosed ulcer and what they judged to be an irregular heartbeat. Perhaps he should tell him how, despite Easley's protestations, his own brother was quickly accepted into the Royal Canadian Air Force, only to be swallowed up by the sea. Instead, Easley laughs out loud at the absurdity of it all.

Argument is invigorating. It stirs up something vital. It makes him forget, for a moment, about the dark slide down. Let him rage. Let the boy have his say and let his anger spend itself in words.

"You know what? I'm trained to fight," the boy declares. "Don't go actin' like you make all the decisions and know what's best from the get-go. Leave the war to the warriors."

Airman First Class Karl Bitburg looks like a child dressed up in his father's clothes. A costume hung off a thin frame. A dirty sack of angles: elbows, shoulders, knees.

"Let's just say I'm watching out for you," Easley says. "I've gotten used to the company."

"Is that so." The boy shoves his fists deep into his pockets. "I've told you everything about me. What I want to know is, who the hell are you?"

How long does it take to starve to death or die of exposure? Easley figures the two work hand in hand to hasten the end. Sixteen days in and Easley wonders if half as many remain. And that is if they can continue to avoid detection. If they can stick together.

Easley struggles to his feet, then feels the ground pitch and roll beneath him. He crouches down until he regains equilibrium. The boy watches with interest but is unmoved to offer assistance.

Easley returns to the nest. He crawls into the parachute and listens as the sleet turns to rain.

THE PAIN WAKES EASLEY several hours later. The day is past its prime and the wind sends gravel skittering across the mouth of the cave. He rolls over. The boy, seated below, slowly comes into focus. Karl looks back over his shoulder at Easley in a detached and distant manner, then returns his gaze to the ashes and memory of fire. Easley closes his eyes again.

IT IS THE BOY poking his arm that finally brings him to. The night is well advanced and reflected flame shimmers off the ceiling of the cave.

"C'mon," he says, silhouette in copper light. "Giddy up."

Easley swings his legs over the edge of the nest and looks down at the blaze. It feels as if someone has hammered a spike through his jaw. His stomach, clenched in hunger. Then he blinks in disbelief: scraps of lumber, a small pile of coal, a book lying open on a rock? Easley stares at the little miracle, and then at the boy—who moves back down to the fire.

"Follow the trucks and you find the tools . . . It's all I could get before they started millin' around." The boy removes his jacket and makes a pad on the floor. "Kneel."

Easley kneels down and looks up at coal-smudged cheeks. The boy's beard is coming in properly now. He'll yet make a man. Karl steps closer, takes ahold of Easley's swollen face, pries open the jaw.

"Turn toward the fire."

Easley shifts as directed. The boy's face follows his, staring into his mouth, until the two kneel together. When the boy has Easley facing the firelight, he reaches into his back pocket and produces a greasy pair of pliers. Easley closes his eyes and opens his mouth as far as he can manage. The boy holds the tool in blackened hands and reaches toward the molar. He pins Easley's tongue out of the way with a dirty finger and finally locks on the problem.

"Hold still," he says, rising to his feet. "I don't want to hear no whinin'."

Held like a fish on a hook, Easley's arms go limp at his sides for want of something to do. The boy grips the tooth with the pliers in one hand, presses down on Easley's chin with the other. "On the count of three," he says. "One—" Then he pulls with careful strength.

Easley cries out as the root gives way and moves north a hair's breadth. Tears rolls down his cheeks. The boy widens his stance for better leverage. He tightens the pliers around the tooth, grips Easley's chin, and starts singing.

"So long, it's been good to know you
So long, it's been good to know you
So long, it's been good to know you
There's a mighty big war that's got to be won
And we'll get back together again."

Then he pulls, twists, and sings—all at the same time. The tooth lets go, the boy's grip slackens, and Easley crumples on the ground like he's taken a slug. Karl holds the bloody tooth up to the fire for a better look. Easley lies still, tonguing the gap, blood drooling down the side of his face and onto glistening stones.

When he finally sits up, the pain is such that he can't open his eyes completely. The boy's grin carves dimples as he presents the bloody prize. Easley reaches out and holds the tooth in the palm of his hand. He gazes around at the pliers, the coal, the lumber, the book with Japanese characters, a bright yellow pencil, the carcass of an unplucked gull. Overcome with awe and gratitude, he tries to speak but chokes on blood and spit—then coughs in the boy's smiling face.

Karl pauses. He slowly wipes his cheek, looks at his fingers, then falls on his backside, laughing. Easley isn't far behind.

The relief of laughter is overwhelming. Easley can't look at him without starting all over again. After they mine this particular comedic vein for all that it's worth, the boy sits up, picks up the bird, plays it like a toy—stretching its wing into a salute, making it do a little can-can routine with its cold, webbed feet. He finishes with a ventriloquist act, opening and closing its beak to the lyrics of Woody Guthrie.

"I got to the camp and I learnt how to fight
Fascists in daytime, mosquitoes at night
I got my orders to cross the blue sea
So I waved 'goodbye' to the girls I could see . . ."

Out in the veiled moonlight, they rinse blood, saliva, and coal from their hands and cheeks. Easley lies down and immerses his jaw in the little stream, swirling frigid water through the empty socket. Then the boy helps him up and they stumble back into the glowing cave, arms around each other's shoulders—like drunken sailors back from a night on the tear.

SIX

OWN IN THE KITCHEN, HELEN FINDS THE KETTLE cold, her father's chair tucked under the table—a lifelong early riser. She shrugs and sits down to make a list of questions to put to Ruth, questions that only occurred to her last night as she was falling asleep. Then she sets about making pancakes. Joe will smell the butter in the pan and find his way downstairs. She puts the coffee on to boil. But halfway through the batter, Helen feels suddenly, unaccountably alone. She turns off the burner and marches upstairs, calling out to him, fighting the rise of panic.

At the end of the hall, a gray ribbon of light separates door and frame. Helen pushes through and steps into his room.

"Dad!" she cries again, but his eyelids barely flicker. He is breathing, of this she is certain. How could this fail to wake him? She shoves his hips over and sits down beside him, struggles to pull him up by the shoulders. His head rolls forward, his back and arms are limp. She shakes him violently.

Dear God.

He takes a deep gulp of air and lets it out in a long exhale. He forces open his lids, but the whites of his eyes appear greasy, the color of fat.

"What?" It is more exhale than word.

"What's happened?" she says. "What's wrong with you? Why can't you wake up?"

Another sigh, and he struggles to sit up on his own. His head slumps into her neck. She shakes him again, then he sits up with a start, pulls his left hand across his lips and whiskered cheeks. He manages to meet her eyes.

"I'm tired. Leave me be."

"Get up." She jumps off the bed, scoops up his knees, and pulls his legs round till his feet touch the floor. "Get up and walk with me."

"Why're you crying?"

"Because you're giving me a heart attack." She snatches his pants from the chair and tosses them onto his lap. "Get dressed. I'm calling a cab."

"Where're you going?"

She watches as he gathers himself in slow motion, trying to haul pants up and over his legs with his one good hand. She can stand it no longer. She grabs his shirt and begins dressing him.

"I'm taking you to the hospital."

Again, he says he's tired, nothing more. No need to call the cavalry. But the threat has him scrambling to recover his wits, forces him to sit up like he's ready for work. He runs his fingers through thinning hair.

"Pray with me," she says, "Hail Mary, full of grace." She will get him to follow along, listen for signs of slurred or skipped words, forgotten phrases. But then the telephone rings.

"Calm yourself, girl. I just get tired sometimes. I'll be right in a minute or two."

She stands and wipes her eyes.

"Make yourself useful," he says. "Answer the phone!"

Helen backs through the door, turns, and pads down the stairs. By the time she's reached the bottom step, she regrets her decision to let him out of her sight. And still the telephone rings. She listens for the sound of her father collapsing to the floor up above, but there is only the insistent, determined ring.

She picks up the phone and is met with greetings from John's mother, Margaret. Her quiet, careful voice. But it is immediately clear that Margaret has no news. Helen flashes on her mother-in-law having called Aden Street, discovering the line disconnected. Margaret asks how she is getting on, a preamble, Helen knows, to asking if she has heard from her son.

They're in a terrible rush, Helen explains, no time to talk. Before hanging up, she briefly recounts the stroke, breaking her lease, and now trying to keep her father conscious.

HELEN RECOGNIZES the expression on the doctor's unlined face as patience stretched thin. He is perhaps forty-five and yet only a whisper of gray is woven through his thick, precisely trimmed hair. And the pristine alligator shoes. Helen wonders if he is working hard enough at saving lives. To her numerous questions, he squints and blinks like he's deciphering immigrant English. In her peripheral vision, she catches the roll of her father's eyes. The two of them are commiserating.

"I fully admit that I cannot gaze into a crystal ball."

"You didn't see him this morning."

"Let me summarize," the doctor says. "I see no evidence of another stroke. It is possible, but doubtful. Did he have difficulty waking up this morning? Clearly."

"Extreme difficulty."

"And that can be caused by any number things. Extreme fatigue often follows a stroke. And it may reoccur from time to time."

Joe stands, extends his left hand, and awkwardly shakes the doctor's right. He thanks him for his time. With that, the men bring the conversation to a close.

"I'm starved," Joe says. "Let's eat."

Helen pulls on her coat, grabs her purse.

"Uncertainty is part and parcel of stoke." The doctor wants to end on good terms. "We should count ourselves fortunate. For his age, your father is in otherwise excellent health."

THE FOLLOWING AFTERNOON, a tentative knock on the front door announces the arrival of Margaret Easley. Yesterday two hundred miles and the Canadian border stretched between them. Now Margaret sets her bags and umbrella aside, peels off her gloves. Helen reaches out and gathers her in.

Joe stands and offers apologies for not having prepared for her arrival. Margaret, in turn, apologizes for arriving unannounced, having hopped on the first bus south from Vancouver this morning. To forestall further awkwardness, Margaret declares that she's booked into a hotel for the night. Standing as they are in his big, empty house, Joe won't hear of such great wastes of money. Margaret waves her hand and smiles politely.

"You sounded like you could use an extra set of hands," Margaret says. "I'm here to help any way I can. I don't want to be a bother."

Margaret and William Easley live in one of the well-to-do neighborhoods on Vancouver's west side. Helen and John lived with them for ten months after their wedding while John looked for steady work. John's father, an engineer, is now in Ottawa, "temporarily" seconded from his firm, and life, by Canada's Ministry of

War. Margaret, like so many women in the world these days, finds herself alone.

Helen doesn't need to ask what is on Joe's mind. He has always seen himself as stationed a rung or two down the social ladder from John's "people." Their being Protestants hadn't helped. Plus, there was the issue of the cost of the wedding, which Joe demanded he pay for in its entirety. Unsure of what to do with himself, he gets up and announces he's putting on a pot of coffee. He apologizes for not having tea, knowing it is the drink the Easleys prefer. A refreshment foreign to his palate. It has become for him an indictment against Canadians in general, a people he finds "neither here, nor there . . . neither us, nor them."

Margaret has always treated Helen like a daughter and friend. Shown keen interest in Helen's plans and opinions, although it's often clear she doesn't understand or agree. She attempts to compensate for the absence of a mother or sisters in Helen's life by passing along family recipes and home remedies, the kinds of accumulated experience and wisdom utterly lost on her two sons. She gives gifts of a personal nature, gifts ordinarily reserved for daughters, including her own mother's wedding ring. And as the years began to pass without the appearance of grandchildren, she restrained herself from making inquiries.

Much more than her husband, or even John, Margaret carries in her face the living memory of her youngest son. The full lips, eyes deep-set and steely blue—missing only the look of comic nonchalance that was Warren's alone.

Good things seemed to come so easily for Warren. He never married, preferring to play the field. Before the war, Warren's position—as a pulp trader for a timber company—fell into his lap. He was getting rich selling blank rolls of newsprint while John was getting poor trying to fill them. And he was a shameless flirt, which, to his credit, he refrained from practicing on Helen. He had none of John's quiet self-assurance. In Helen's estimation, being beautiful saved Warren from life's ordinary accumulation of disappointments. But then Warren's luck ran out suddenly, over the English Channel, in the service of us all.

Joe returns, pulling on his jacket, announcing that they are fresh out of coffee and chicory, or much else in the way of hospitality. Helen knows this is only half true but lets him go anyway. He escapes out the back door.

Helen details her father's episode and prognosis. It feels good to give the story shape, relay it to someone who understands what the patient means to her. Someone with a stake in the outcome. Margaret listens intently, asking for a few points of clarification, nodding in sympathy with Helen's worries and frustrations. Which inevitably leads them to John.

"I could guess what happened between you two," Margaret says, "from what little he had to say. But I'd prefer to hear it from you."

Helen remains unused to the presence of another woman in her family, unaccustomed to sharing a space that has long been hers alone. And yet, in all the world, her mother-in-law occupies the closest vantage point to the inner workings of her marriage. Margaret neither sought nor expected this view. At first, Helen found herself resisting this insight, but she has come to recognize just how much she needs it now.

"I told him I won't be alone anymore," Helen says. "I made him choose between his work and me. He made his decision."

Helen recounts their last days together, the hurt and confusion, how she had told him not to bother coming back if he left. How he walked out with no further argument, no word about where exactly he was going, or when he planned to return. She confesses her misery, of knowing that these were the last words she said to him, and the fear that her adolescent dramatics have set in motion something that can't be stopped.

"He came up and stayed a few days," Margaret explains. "He said you don't understand him. I told him no one does. He has his idea of duty and wonders why no one else can see it. I said we all can see well enough, but our family has already given its share. All we want is to have him safe at home."

"I'm sure he's back in Alaska."

"Yes, but where?" Margaret is in the habit of touching her hair when nervous. The grief and worry of the past few years has hastened the fade to gray. "He hasn't written me either. All we can do is wait."

"*Wait* . . ." Helen can hear her own desperation. "If he's been caught again, they could have thrown him in prison until the end of the war, or longer. In which case, he'll need me. If they haven't caught him, then he must be in another kind of trouble. He's not a soldier. If he's been captured or is lost somewhere, no one will even know he's missing . . . I can't sit and wait like you."

Helen buries her face in her hands, regretting her choice of words. Staring back is a woman still reeling over the loss of her youngest son, dismayed over the acceleration of time, fearful of more endings yet to come.

"I won't take that personally, because I suspect it wasn't intended that way."

"I'm sorry . . ." Helen says. "But if I don't look for him, no one will. Waiting is the one thing I will not do."

"Staying here, where it's safe, is the one thing he would want you to do. Just what is it, exactly, you think you can accomplish?"

"Find him. Bring him home. Or, if I'm wrong, find out what happened to him."

Margaret stares at the rug and nods. She gets up and walks over to the door. She returns with a small briefcase and sets it on the coffee table between them.

"He left a few things behind. I tried to squeeze it all in here. Maybe you can make some sense of it."

On top is John's old mackinaw jacket. He must have judged it too thin for where he was heading. Helen is taken aback by her visceral response to holding it again, a sensation that is quickly overcome by the smell of his mother's brand of laundry soap. Below this, she finds handwritten and typed pages, newspaper clippings, and a book each on oceanography, natural history, and the travels of Vitus Bering. She quickly recognizes abandoned notes on Pacific bird migration from John's original assignment for the *National Geographic Magazine*. Mostly, there is research about all things Aleutian. Photographs of natives and their traditional wooden hats. White Orthodox churches. Men pushing fishing boats into the surf.

"Of course his leaving has nothing to do with you," Margaret declares. "He changed when Warren was lost. I think we've all changed since then."

Helen sets the papers aside.

"In '39, John told Warren not to go," Margaret continues. "Said there were important contributions to be made from home. Then we lose Warren and all of a sudden it was John's *duty* to report the war. . . . I remember the last war. My brother fell in the Battle of the Somme. I asked Warren not to go to England. I asked John not to go to Alaska. I told their father not to go to Ottawa. No one listens to me."

Margaret slumps back in Joe's favorite chair. Helen leans forward and begins paging through. She can almost hear the sound of her husband's voice.

Handwritten notes: *Aleuts speak Russian and English, as well as their own native tongue. Traditional culture ravaged by Russian fur traders. Russian Orthodox church now central in their lives.* Circled text from a magazine article: *Today's Aleuts live in modern houses. They fish and raise fox for fur. Aleutian fur can be found warming the shoulders and necks of the natives of Manhattan.* Half an hour of study takes her through the stack and adds little to the sum total of her own research and what John had told her about the islands, save this: *Aleut,* which means "community," was the name the Russians gave them. They call themselves *Unangan,* or "original people."

"You're like John in that," Margaret says, finally. "The concentration." She picks up a newspaper clipping about extreme Aleutian weather, titled "The Birthplace of Winds." After a brief and troubled glance, Margaret drops the clipping back on the pile.

So few people, so far away. This is not the defense of London, or even the shores of Puget Sound. Something Tom Sorensen had said comes back to her again. Last year, the U.S. Army Corps of Engineers punched a road into Alaska through the wilds of British Columbia and the Yukon. Seventeen hundred miles in under seven months. Would they really be wasting manpower and materiel if they didn't fear an invasion?

"Is Joe getting the care he needs?" Margaret reaches for her purse. "We don't have many connections down here, but I do have the name of a cardiologist. I could have a friend of ours give him a call. He's supposed to be the best."

Helen looks up. She stops herself from jumping at the opportunity. Joe will be walking through the door any minute. She can already see her father's jaw tightening at the suggestion of getting some kind of break or special privilege that comes from Helen having married into "gentry." This will require diplomacy, deception, the utmost delicacy.

"I know my being here makes your father uncomfortable," Margaret says. "I won't be staying long. But the doctor. He never needs to know. And you needn't worry about the cost."

AMONG JOHN'S NOTES and files, Helen found no clue but was left with a revelation. She has been overlooking perhaps the greatest source of information about the war in the Aleutian Islands.

The following morning, Helen calls the Bureau of Indian Affairs. The clerk on the other end of the line is less than forthcoming with details about the territory's native population, particularly those from the Aleutians. When Helen says she is trying to locate a relative—the first of what she knows will be many lies—she senses a slight improvement in tone, but still learns nothing of value.

Next she scans the phonebook and discovers the existence of Seattle's lone Russian Orthodox church, named for St. Nicholas the Wonderworker. She likes the sound of that. The secretary tells her that the priest is away until the weekend, but explains that he visits an Aleut family in the hospital. She doesn't know their name, or which hospital, but believes they are still in town. After eight phone calls, and the help of three hospital volunteers, Helen finally tracks them down.

* * *

A MIDDLE-AGED NURSE leads through dim corridors with purpose and precision. She has allotted a couple of minutes to this task and no time will be squandered. She glances over her shoulder now and again to confirm that Helen is still in tow. Helen feels herself nearly overcome by the thought that she might be closer to finding news of John than she's ever been before. She allows the hope to fill her chest and pass through her limbs. After two elevator rides and a disorienting trek through winding halls, they stop before an open door.

"And here they are," she proclaims. "I'll be at the desk down the hall, if anyone needs me."

Inside, Helen discovers a boy of seven or eight, and a man approaching forty. Both have dark hair and eyes. If she had passed them on the street, she may not have guessed they were native. The man appears weak and ashen, but the boy has a healthy complexion. They sit at a table beside a window where a small three-bar Russian cross is perched on the sill. A cribbage board and playing cards are spread between them. They seem chastened, as if unsure how to proceed in the presence of authority.

Perhaps four hundred people live on the eight inhabited Aleutian Islands. On his magazine assignment John visited two of those islands, Unalaska and Atka. The odds are long, but could these people have seen or even heard about him, or have a clue about where he might be?

"I'm Helen Easley." She smiles and steps forward, extends her hand.

"Hello there." The man shakes her hand but does not rise. The pause grows large and awkward.

"I hope I'm not disturbing you. I have a few questions and I was hoping you could help me."

"Nurse said you'd be by. What do you want to know?" The man speaks with a soft, halting accent Helen hasn't heard before.

"I'm trying to find out about the Aleutian Islands . . . What's happened since the war began."

"Well"—he slowly nods—"you'd be the first."

The man turns to the boy and speaks in his native tongue. He clears away the game. After a coughing spell, he introduces himself as Ilya Hopikoff and his boy as Jesse, after Jesse James.

"I imagine it's been tough up there." It's all she can think to say.

Ilya looks up with an empty gaze. She has not been offered a seat and would feel presumptuous taking one.

"The Japs took Attu and Kiska," the man says. "That was in June. By the end of July, Uncle Sam took the rest."

"I'm not sure I follow."

"The Army rounded us up!" the boy interjects. His English is more confident, clearer than his father's. "They made us get on a big ship. They wouldn't let us take our stuff."

"One bag each," Ilya corrects. He nods for his son to continue.

"They put everybody on the ship and wouldn't say where we were going. Then they set the village on fire. Burned it right in front of us so we could see. Said they didn't want no Japs moving in and using our places, so they just burned 'em instead. Said we could bring our fishing boats, so we tied 'em all together. Once we got out of the bay, they said, 'Hit the deck!' Then they shot up our boats with a machine gun. Shot 'em to bits. They laughed like it was some kinda joke."

Jesse sets about building a house of cards in the space where the game had been. Ilya speaks his language for a good long while, then leaves it to Jesse to translate the story.

The people from Attu, he guesses forty-two in all, are either dead or prisoners of the Japanese. Aleuts from the other islands have been sent to government-run "Duration Camps" in southeast Alaska, a place aswarm with biting insects, cougars, and bears—animals they've read about but had never seen. There, the trees crowd out the sky, hem you in, keep you from seeing what's coming or reading the direction of the wind. Jesse declares his fear of forests, having had no previous experience with trees. His people are made to live in an old salmon cannery near Sitka, in broken-down buildings that still reek of fish guts. The government provides store-bought food. Those who are able find work canning salmon, or sweeping up at the mill. A few found work slicing those big trees into boards. But they're not allowed to fish or hunt for themselves. Decisions are made for them without their consent. People are becoming sick in the crowded conditions.

"We know they rounded us up to save us from the Japanese," Ilya says by way of summation. "But they took our rifles. Treat us like traitors. Took us to a place we don't know and left us in the rain."

Jesse explains that they lost his mother to consumption in the camp last winter. When both he and his father took ill, the doctor feared the disease was spreading. They were sent south to Seattle, but it turns out that they only had pneumonia. Things have been much better down here and they are both feeling good again. There are still too many trees, but at least there is some open space in which to walk around and breathe.

The house of cards is now three stories high. Jesse's hand is poised to start the next level, when a coughing fit overtakes him. He steps back and covers his mouth, averting disaster.

Helen is silenced, unsure of how to respond to a story most Americans would find hard to believe. But she is convinced she understands something elemental about the bond between these two. What it means to have lost a mother. What it takes to father a motherless child.

"You heard of the camps?" Ilya asks.

Helen shakes her head. She has read every scrap of information she could find about the war in Alaska. The Japanese invasion was only briefly mentioned, information about the buildup of U.S. forces has been scant. She has come across no mention of the fate of the Aleut people. As far as the newspapers are concerned, it is as if the islands were uninhabited.

"People down here never heard of us," Ilya says. "I gave up trying to explain. You from the church?"

Helen shakes her head.

The nurse opens the door, scans the room, then smiles down at Jesse. "Need anything?"

Ilya shakes his head.

"How about some cookies?" She gives Helen the complete once-over, clearly pondering her relation to the Aleuts. "I'll go get you some. If you ever have a visitor, and you want cookies or milk, you just let me know. I'll be right back." She smiles at Jesse, then pulls the door closed behind her.

"So, what else you want to know?" Ilya asks.

"It's my husband," Helen says at last. "He's gone missing. I believe he's back in the Aleutians and I'm hoping you might have seen him."

As the words leave her lips, she is shamed by the realization of just what a long shot she's taking. She tries to summon that optimism she felt before walking into this room.

"Tall white guy. Skinny . . ." Her pulse trips over itself. "Which island are you from?"

"Atka. Couple of guys came out last summer and poked around," Jesse explains, "talked to some of the elders."

Ilya interjects in his language, then his son continues.

"That tall guy tried to tell the elders they weren't Christians. Said we were worshipping pictures. He didn't know nothing. They told him to never come back."

"Holy Roller," Ilya declares, delighting in the term. "That your man?"

Helen shakes her head. This is what she's been reduced to, wandering hospital corridors, sifting for clues among sick people with troubles all their own. It is now clear that her search hasn't even begun. If she is ever to succeed, she must learn to rein in her expectations, keep her emotions on an even tighter leash.

"John Easley. He's a writer. He was working on an article about the Aleutians. He was spending time out on the land, interviewing anyone who would give him the time of day. Now, he's trying to write about the war."

Ilya shakes his head. None of this rings a bell. Although he admits to having been away fishing with his son and brothers for much of the spring.

"If it's the war he's after, he'll be on Adak," Ilya explains. "The Navy whipped up an airbase out there in no time. Never seen it myself, but they say it's something."

The door swings wide open and the nurse appears with a box of store-bought cookies and a smile. The resulting draft levels the house of cards, and Jesse slaps his knee. "Shit!"

"Pardon me?" Her smile is gone. "Is that any way for a little boy to talk? I'll get some soap so we can wash out that mouth." She drops the box of cookies on the table, one of which escapes the package.

Ilya ignores both the scowling nurse and his son. He reaches out and retrieves the lone ginger snap. Unheeded, the nurse sharply turns and takes her leave.

Ilya offers the box to Helen, then reaches for a pen. He flips over their cribbage score and writes carefully, precisely, then pushes it across the table.

ILYA HOPIKOFF

ATKA ISLAND

TERRITORY OF ALASKA, U.S.A.

"That'll be true again when we whip the Japanese," Ilya says. He speaks to his son in their language, then Jesse translates for Helen. "When you find your man, tell him to send along that article."

She offers her card in return.

Jesse sidles up to Helen and reviews his father's shaky script. He leans into her, puts his arm around her shoulder, as if he's known her all his life. Then he takes up the pen and writes "and Jesse" beside his father's name, admiring the amendment.

THE FOLLOWING MORNING, Helen meets Margaret for breakfast at her hotel downtown. They have just over an hour before her bus home to Vancouver. Once they settle in and order toast, Margaret has an announcement to make. She has been fighting the urge for the past few days, but now feels compelled to say what's on her mind.

She is truly moved by Helen's conviction to find John. She too is convinced he is alive. But if she knows anything about her son, there is nothing Helen can do for him up there that he isn't capable of doing for himself. She will only put herself in jeopardy. John will need her when he returns. And, as a mother, Margaret cannot leave without reminding Helen of a fact with which Helen must be well acquainted, a fact that is now beyond doubt: come what may, Joe will never ask for help.

Helen thanks Margaret for making the long trip down, for sharing her troubles and fears, the arrangements with the doctor, the risk she's taken in speaking her mind. Helen feels unmoved to offer a challenge or a spirited defense of her plans. She cannot make Margaret understand. She feels instead respect and affection for her husband's mother. Along with a kind of pity.

SEVEN

THE UNMISTAKABLE DRONE OF A PBY CATALINA pulls them from the cave. The American flying boat is alone, high overhead, its pilot taking good long looks down through the breach in the clouds. Easley and the boy stumble into the ravine, cupping hands round their eye sockets, making binoculars with their fists. Hair pasted to scalps, an oily sheen covers their faces and necks. Their flight suits dark with sweat, coal, blood. The rest of their clothing, once a representational color of the land, now a part of it. Had anyone been able to see them, Easley thinks, they would surely appear as madmen banished to the ends of the earth.

The plane is gone almost as soon as they spot it. Only the echo remains. It isn't long until they lose it altogether in the sound of wind and waves.

It has not rained in two days. The cloud ceiling is high, the wind manageable after roaring so hard across the land that it was all but impossible to withstand. Easley realizes that this is the driest he has been since landing on Attu.

He tongues the gap in his teeth. It has been four days since the extraction. The hole, clotted up nicely, no longer aches but remains tender and difficult to keep clean. After eating, he sweeps the space with the tip of his tongue, then goes up to the stream to flush his mouth with water. The boy takes a look at it each day. It doesn't appear infected.

"I'm going for a walk," Easley announces.

"You take the high road, I'll take the low road—and I'll be in Galveston before you."

Easley turns and walks south along the beach, away from the cave. The boy marches north on his own.

Their rule about not being out on days of good visibility is observed more in breach than practice. They take chances they would not have dreamt of three weeks ago. Back then, Easley used to feel his stomach sink each time a choice had to be made. Now, such life-and-death decisions are routine. Death itself is no longer an abstract concept, it is an unwelcomed and patient companion.

Now and then, they split up to walk in opposite directions. Although this serves practical purposes—like looking for nonexistent driftwood, hunting for birds and mussels—it also affords time alone. Even if they are viewing the same barren land and sea, it allows space for personal reflection without the intrusion or collusion of the other. This is where Easley frees his longing for Helen, his grief at the loss of his brother. Regrets he otherwise keeps close. Last time, Easley and the boy managed to return with at least an hour's worth of conversation between them. But now he has mixed feelings about the wisdom of solo expeditions. Suddenly he seems unable to face himself alone. He picks up a rock, turns around, and throws it toward the boy. Attention gained, he motions for Karl to join him.

They have made two additional forays to the occupied village since the night of the tooth extraction. The soldiers guarding the anti-aircraft guns spend endless hours staring up into the clouds and scanning out across the harbor and sea. They expect the trouble to come from far away—in the form of the next bombing run, or a shell fired from the deck of a warship. The last foot patrol Easley saw passed by three days ago. The way they sang and shoved one another around, these soldiers seemed more intent on getting exercise than ferreting out prisoners of war. Still, Easley was amazed at the boy's bravado, walking up to a building under no more than the cover of fog or night and simply peering through the windows. That's how Karl found the pliers, the book, and—most critically—the coal. They talk themselves into returning to the village tonight.

The coal dump is located in an old boat shed near the dock. From here, the coal is moved by wheelbarrow over narrow wooden planks to the buildings and tents. The Japanese are so convinced that the island is theirs alone, they do not think to lock up their belongings. Two shovels, a hammer, and empty tin cans can be seen inside. This time, they discover a single boot sitting alone on a shelf above the coal. So small, it seems made for a woman or child. Once standing inside the dark little shed, Easley realizes that this is the first time he's been inside a building since stepping out of the hangar on Adak. The boy takes up his position outside, keeping watch, crouching near the door behind a wheelbarrow.

Easley fills his pack with chunks of coal. They make hollow, ceramic sounds as they disappear into the canvas. He fills the pack until it is solid, then passes it out to the boy—who grabs Easley by the wrist.

Someone is walking quickly over the planks outside. Is the man on his way to alert the others? Easley's heart pounds so hard he begins to wonder if it can be heard beyond the shed. Then, as the footfalls diminish, the man starts singing—some Japanese ditty, which rapidly fades in the wind.

The boy loosens his grip and whispers, "Fuck, fuck, fuck."

Easley shakes his head. He reaches for the empty pack, then fills that one too.

Back in their cave, they warm up with a fire and celebrate their astounding success. They marvel at their proximity to the Japanese soldier, who had no inkling of their presence. Karl mimics the soldier's song. He is convinced that the enemy's arrogance will eventually be their undoing—not to mention the well-known fact that they can scarcely see through those slanty eyes.

* * *

THE COAL HAS LASTED three nights. There is fuel enough for perhaps a fourth night, no more. They will wait for fog before they risk returning to the village. Once near their goal, they will wait for darkness. Easley wonders: What if the Japanese have noticed their thieving and posted guards at the shed? Or what if this cache by the dock has been used up, never to be replenished? Their beach has been long picked clean of driftwood, twigs, and sticks.

Easley hops out of the way of the incoming waves, scanning the foam for anything resembling food. After an hour and a half with no reward, he finally spies something rolling in the tide farther up the beach. It is corralled on all sides by seaweed and complains with an insistent *clink, clink* as the waves shove and retreat. He picks up the pace.

A bottle rolls to and fro in a seaweed nest. Clear glass, with a cork and metal cap, about a third full of cloudy liquid. Easley wipes the sand away and holds it up to the sky. As he grips the cap, he finds his fingers shaking. The act of doing something so ordinary—uncorking a bottle—sparks an unexpected tremor of relief. He holds the bottle up to his nose and inhales. Unsure of the subtle scent, he brings it to his lips for a taste. Sharp, not the least bit rancid. A shocking taste of mint. Then he feels the kick. He lets out a satisfied "Ha!" The cap has tiny Cyrillic letters around the rim. There are no other identifying marks. Vodka. Russian vodka.

On his walk back to the cave, Easley thinks of the Siberian fisherman having lunch on deck, eyeing the reward he's been saving since before he cast off that morning. He imagines the fisherman reaching for the bottle, sitting there on the gunwale, his fingers slick with cheese and oil from smoked fish. He might have cursed as it went over and into the drink, slowly bobbing back to the surface under circling gulls. Perhaps he even watched it float away in the foamy wake of his boat.

The reward will be theirs tonight. Easley will share it with the boy along with the warmth of the fire. After the vodka is gone, the bottle will be used to keep water so they won't have to go out to the stream each time they want a drink. It will make their lives a little easier. With the cave, and the coal, they've bought themselves some time. The wind has died down, and it doesn't seem quite so cold. For a moment, it is possible to count blessings, to realize that they have eluded capture for the better part of a month, to believe in the possibility of survival. Easley considers all these things as he rounds the point and bounds down the ravine toward the cave.

THIS IS NO MINOR FRACTURE, the break appears complete. If even gentle pressure is applied to the top of the foot, a lump appears on what should be the smooth front of the shin. A point of bone edges up, turning the skin pink, then white with the force. The boy moans when Easley touches it, covers his eyes to hide the tears. The boy's hands and knee are also cut and bleeding. He explains that he crawled and crab-walked back to the cave through a buzzing haze of pain. Easley removes his jacket and places it behind the boy's head, stretches him out, ensures the broken leg is higher than his heart, tries to make him as comfortable as possible. Time and again, the boy says he's sorry.

Puffins had been arriving in squadrons. Some had even begun building nests in crevices on a nearby cliff. Although it is probably too soon—and impossible to tell from the ground—the boy had wondered if a few might have already laid eggs.

He approached a growing colony on the cliffs at the far edge of the beach. Most were too high up, impossible to reach, except one nest on a tiny ledge about thirty feet off the ground. The boy climbed up to have a look. As he approached, the birds made a god-awful racket. This told him he was on to something. When at last he reached the nest, he found it empty. But the signs of a second nest, still farther up, came into view. He considered attempting this further ascent, thought better of it, and decided to climb down. But an early slip had robbed his confidence, left him shaking. He stopped and tried to gather his courage. He tried feeling his way down—fingers in cracks, hugging the wall—but his boot could find no purchase. He hung there, suspended for what seemed like an age, contemplating where he was, what had brought him to this place, this predicament. And still the birds complained and harassed. He came to the conclusion that his odds were better if he chose his moment and landing site. Finally, he let go. The bone snapped on impact, sending light bursts through his brain.

The constant drip and trickle of water is amplified.

Easley's first instinct is to cuff him across the head. How could he have been so foolish? But the boy has gone gray with shock. Easley gathers him up in his arms. He steps with care away from the dark fire pit, finally laying him atop their nest. Easley covers him in the parachutes and gently props up his leg. He loosens the laces of Karl's boot but does not remove it. It will help retain body heat.

Once more, he runs his fingers along the shin where the point of bone threatens to poke through. Then he pulls the pant leg down so they won't have to see it.

"I'm going to make a fire," Easley says. "Then I'm going to find a splint."

"They'll kill us both if you surrender."

"Surrender? Who the hell said 'surrender'?"

"Just sit here with me awhile. Talk to me."

Easley considers the boy. The dark, bruised smears at the hollows of his eyes, skin pale and greasy.

"Let me make the fire."

Down at the pit, Easley assembles a little pile of coal, dry grass, and sticks. He holds the lighter in position. Three turns of the striking wheel fail to produce a flame. The fourth try is the charm. The grass catches fire and Easley pushes more nourishing blades atop the heat and light. It travels down stems and under the sticks until finally the coal itself is aflame. For the moment, they ignore the fact that the lighter has likely given its final performance. Easley arranges more coal around the little blaze until it can stand on its own. It is then he recalls the vodka. Easley pulls the bottle from his pocket and scrambles back up to the boy.

"Look what I found. It's not whiskey, but it'll make you feel better just the same." He uncorks the bottle and holds it out to Karl, who first wipes his mouth on the back of his hand. After a tentative sip, he tilts it in the air.

"Once you're warm and comfortable, I'm going to get a splint. Then I'm going to set that leg, and—"

"Sit with me."

Easley sits.

"I'm tired. I just want to sleep, but I'm too cold. And afraid."

"Karl."

"I haven't been much of a Christian." The boy's eyes bloodshot and shiny. "You know, much of a believer. I wouldn't blame the Lord for not believing in me."

The boy twists knuckles in his eyes as Easley looks on, ashamed of his own uselessness.

"You're not alone," Easley says.

He gestures to the booze. The boy finishes it off and holds out the empty bottle.

All at once, Easley is certain of two things: that the boy is still falling, and that he will do whatever it takes to catch him. He also knows that this is not a sentimental or unselfish devotion—it is an act of self-preservation. It is as much Easley's leg cracked and useless, as much his own soul stunned and reeling.

"There's still a few hours of light," Easley says. "First I'm going to get you a splint and set that stinking leg. Then I'm going to scare up a couple of blue plate specials"—their term, of late, for mussels.

EASLEY RUNS ALONG the beach in the failing light, straining to see farther along the shore. It is the want of simple things like this—a long, straight piece of wood—that makes him hate this place so perfectly. He runs past the spot where he found the bottle of vodka. The day is too far gone to risk a trek to the village and back. When he reaches the cliff at the end of the beach, Easley feels his eyes welling up, the heaviness of having let the boy down. And then he remembers the post.

He jogs a steady pace. He arrives at the site as the setting sun flashes through a rent in the clouds, illuminating the ceiling of sky. Because the beach faces east, he cannot see the sun itself, only its remarkable effect on the day left behind. It shines up shades of copper and pink so dazzling it makes him stop. He imagines it filling his lungs. He pulls in all the beauty and light for the boy. If need be, he'll bring it back to the cave and breathe it straight into him.

They had assumed the lone post might have marked a grave or some pagan place. They agreed they would respect it. Now, Easley falls to his knees and seizes it with his hands. It is about as thick as the boy's ankle. He grips the base and pulls for all he's worth. It breaks free of the earth and Easley falls back on a patch of wild celery. He scrambles to his feet, inspects the wood, and finds that it is rotten. To test its integrity, he pulls it across his bent knee—it crumbles into uselessness.

Easley drops the post and holds his face in his hands. He stumbles around in a rage and stubs his toe on a pile of stones. He curses the blushing sky, then scans the distance to see if anyone has heard. He backs away from the broken post, the pile of stones, the bitter celery. He stumbles back toward the cave.

The gap in the cloud widens, allowing stars to poke through. They offer the only illumination on Easley's approach. He picks his way down the ravine and through the rocks by touch and memory— the way he would move in the dead of night through his childhood home, or the house on Aden Street. Inside the cave, only the faintest glow lingers around the ashes and coals. Easley calls the boy's name but hears no reply. In the absence of light, he feels his way up to their nest. He startles when his hand glances the boy's shoulder.

"Hey buddy." Easley squats down.

All is darkness. Easley touches the boy's shoulder again, but feels no response.

"Couldn't find a splint, but I'll get one in the morning."

The boy's head rolls forward.

"Karl."

Easley puts his ear to the boy's nose to sense if he is breathing. He feels the boy's neck. Cool—and still, without a pulse.

"Karl."

When Easley reaches for the boy's hand, his own fingers come back sticky. He brings them to his nose, then his tongue.

"*You . . .*"

Easley locates the wrist, then the seam that's been opened there. He moans out loud. He searches the other arm and finds a matching wound. Easley works his hand into the boy's jacket and through the shirt. He finds more stillness there.

Easley cradles Karl's head and shoulders. He rocks back and forth, and cries for the loss of a friend he never let close enough to know him. He cries at his failure to find a splint in time and for the mistake of having left him alone. He cries as never before. He cries with fear—not of death itself but of the wait he must now face alone.

* * *

EASLEY FOLDS EACH filthy garment removed from the body, left modest only in stained underpants. The diffused, midday light reaches through the cave to cold, waxen skin. A hint of jade where veins once flowed. The overall effect is marble. Easley raises his head from the task at hand to watch the birds turning in the mist. Thin fog softens every edge and line.

The wait for the turn of tide has finally come to an end. Adrenaline has been replaced with the kind of nervous, twitchy exhaustion that can only be solved with a big meal and a sleep of several days.

Bloodstained trousers, shirt, undershirt folded and stacked, as if destined for a drawer. Socks draped over the wall of the fire pit, boots paired up near the coal. I will have to wear them soon, Easley thinks, in order to avoid going mad at their sight. He must claim them as his own.

He tells the boy that he will be missed, that he will make good use of his things. One day, Easley vows, he will drive to Texas. He asks the boy to forgive him if he can. Put in a good word with the powers that be, if Helen is right and there is indeed a heaven.

Do not haunt me, my friend. Leave me in some kind of peace.

Easley scans the hills, sky, and sea. Seeing no enemy, he carries his burden to the beach. He lays Karl's body on a bed of flattened rye. He removes his own boots, socks, and trousers, then gathers Karl up again.

The surf—tugging at his legs—is so cold it seems to burn. It would pull them both out to sea. Easley wades up to his waist, then turns his back on an incoming wave. Once it passes, he kisses the boy's forehead and turns toward the deep. He lays the body in the foam as the spent wave slackens and begins flowing out again. It floats heavily toward the next set, then tumbles back with the following break. He keeps watch until his legs beg mercy and he is forced back to land.

Easley dries himself and dresses again, not once giving in to the urge to turn. Only when his boots are laced, jacket zipped, does he permit himself one last look.

Sandpipers and plovers scurry along the edge of the tide, giving him the quick double take. He scans near and far, but the boy is already gone.

EIGHT

S HE AWAKENS WITH A START. HELEN HAD FALLEN asleep so easily after supper, drifting off to the sound of heavy rain lashing the windowpanes, coursing through the gutters above. Only two hours have passed. Her muscles are stiff, her skin damp with perspiration. She swings her legs over the side of the bed, stands, gathers her sense of place.

Helen stops unnoticed at the top of the stairs with a view to the living room below. Despite the late hour, the light is still on. Her father sits at the little card table, shoulders hunched, the space for three other players gone wanting. His good hand glides in careful, rhythmic motions as he deals the cards. A game of solitaire stretches out between a bottle of rum and a nearly empty glass. Unaware of her presence, he surveys the upturned cards. He takes another sip, the ice clinking in his glass. He places it back atop the coaster and rests his forehead in his hand.

Joe isn't a heavy drinker, just a regular one. He'll have two rums before going to bed. Helen doesn't think it does him any harm and she's never seen him drunk. It's like baseball, radio programs, or mass on Sunday mornings. A small comfort in a world seemingly designed to deny them.

He flips over cards, three at a time.

Since moving back in, Helen hasn't spent as much time with him as she'd planned, as she told herself she would. Instead she's been deceiving him, telling him she's been out searching for work when all the while she's been preparing for her departure. And now she feels a great swell of tenderness, looking down at her diminished protector, her first love, her oldest and truest friend. She reaches for the railing, a slight creak issues from the old fir floor. Joe glances up and sees her standing there. He runs fingers through thinning hair.

"Sweetheart, what's the matter?"

She doesn't know where to begin.

"Come on down," he says, looking around for another chair. He spies one folded and leaning against the wall by the bookcase. He nearly trips in his eagerness to get it.

Helen descends the stairs and resists the urge to help him as he shakes open the chair for her. He pats it twice. She takes up the seat—along with her father's glass.

"You don't mind if I have a sip, do you?"

"Let me get you a fresh one." He starts to get up, but Helen tugs his sleeve.

"I'll just have a taste of yours."

Joe scatters the solitaire, stirs the cards around in lieu of shuffling, then—with one hand—deals a game of Crazy Eights. Helen pours two fingers of rum over the pebbles of ice. One sip and the alcohol glows at the back of her throat.

A stroke, she has been told, is caused either by a blockage of blood flow to the brain, or the opposite, a hemorrhage in the brain. A drought or a flood. It is unclear which occurred in her father's head. While the recovery of his speech was rapid, his arm has been a different matter. In the first week there were slow gains, but now the gains have stopped. She has lost hope that his right hand will ever be of much use to him again. Helen picks up her hand of cards. He slides his seven cards to the edge of the table, lifts them up, attempts to spread them into a fan. A three of clubs escapes and falls face up. He lays his hand back down, retrieves the fallen card, and tries to spread them into a fan again—all the while stifling the curses she knows he keeps behind clenched teeth.

"How's the job hunting?"

"Actually, that's what I need to talk to you about." This is the moment. She will deceive him no longer.

"Well good," he says. "But before you do, I was thinking . . . I'd like to clear the air."

He gestures to the discard pile. She should continue the charade of the game.

"Honey, you know I am not a sophisticated man. But I've lived a good life. The few regrets I have involved letting myself be talked out of doing what I know I should have done."

"Daddy, there is something I have to tell you."

"Even with your brothers. I don't regret the way I raised them. Your mother thought I was too hard on them. I was hard, but fair. Maybe too quick to punish or scold. But look at them, they're strong, successful men. They don't like me too much, but I believe that's the price I had to pay."

"I can see how much you're hurting," he continues, "not knowing where John is. If he's safe. I also know that you want to go and chase after him. I don't think that's a good idea."

He stares into her eyes with that expression of finality she grew up dreading.

"But none of that matters," he continues. "If *you* think you need to go, then go. What *I* need is to make sure you're not spending your life tiptoeing around here, waiting for mine to end."

The man sitting across from Helen still appears to be her father, but now she wonders if his judgment has also been impaired by the stroke.

"I've been hiding things from you."

Joe chuckles. "Tell me something I don't know."

"I found a way up. A *safe* way, through the military, that will get me close to the places he's likely to be. Now, please just hear me out before you say anything." Helen raises her hand. She must play this out carefully. "I have a chance to join a touring show. Ruth recommended me. She cashed in all her favors. An outfit called the USO."

"USO . . ."

United Service Organizations she explains, quoting from memory the pamphlet Ruth had passed along. Catholic and Jewish groups, the Salvation Army, all teamed up to bring comfort to the troops in the form of comedy, song, and dance. Entertainment. Patriotic duty. Joe responds with a blank expression that says he's paying out just enough slack for her to wrap around her neck.

"To boost morale," she concludes. "The girls go wherever the troops are stationed."

"That Ruth takes too many chances," Joe says. "I'm surprised she's not already knocked up. Or smoking opium."

"What an unchristian thing to say!"

"In my day, we had a different sort of female entertainment on offer. A time-honored tradition."

"Thank God your day is done. And we're talking about a highly respected organization. Do you read the papers? Ruth has already completed a tour and has nothing but good things to say."

Joe takes a deep breath then sighs, theatrically.

"You haven't seen much of the world, honey, so let me paint a picture. Hundreds, thousands of men forced together, a long way from home, no women around. Then you and your girlfriends show up, *parade* around, whip them into a frenzy? You're dangling raw steak in front of a pack of wolves."

"Last year, they sent Bob Hope and Frances Langford to Alaska," she says as a kind of proof. "Rehearsals are starting in Los Angeles. Most girls will be heading out to Hawaii after that. Ruth'll be based in California and fly out to aircraft carriers."

She brushes a lock of hair off her forehead and meets her father's gaze. Joe takes a sip of rum and considers his daughter, carefully.

"One group is scheduled to go north." She speaks in a measured tone. "I'll get close, but I'll be safe. Surrounded by soldiers and airmen who will *protect* us. Men John might have met . . . I know something's happened to him. I know he needs me. This is my only chance."

"You think you're going to track him down in a battlefield while he's trying to report on the war? What if he's in jail? What if he's hiding to keep from *going* to jail and doesn't want to be found? Have you thought about that?"

Helen stands and glares down at him, determined not to cry.

"Yes. I've thought of that, along with everything I risk by leaving you here on your own."

Joe's expression softens into the same confused look he'd have when, as a girl, she'd throw tantrums. The more emotional she became, the more helpless he'd be.

He gets up, walks into the kitchen, and returns with a box of cornstarch. He takes his seat, opens the box, and shakes a pile of bills atop the scattered cards.

"There's got to be eight hundred dollars there, a bit more in the bank."

He pushes the money toward her.

"Take it. You might need it. And I'll feel better if you have it."

She sits back down.

"Your mother . . . In those last weeks before she died, she didn't want you kids anywhere near her. She didn't want you to remember her that way. I have to admit that a big part of me didn't want to see it either. Part of me wanted to run. I've never told anyone that before. But the truth is I could hardly stand being away from her even to take a meal. I knew without a doubt where I needed to be. Even she couldn't have changed my mind."

Helen moves her chair over, sits down beside him. She takes up his useless hand.

"You don't have to admit it to me," he says, "but you'd better admit it to yourself. You have no idea what you're getting into. Remembering that fact now and then will help keep you out of trouble."

Helen nods, dutifully.

"John may be dead," he says. "You need to hear that from me. You also need to hear that if he's gone, you will survive it."

*   *   *

THE FOLLOWING MONDAY MORNING, Helen unfolds a map sketched out by the mother of the Los Angeles family with whom she's been billeted. It soon becomes clear that she will be forced to hike the last quarter mile beyond the reach of the bus, in the bright sunshine, through a neighborhood of small, single-story bungalows, unpaved and littered streets, below teetering power poles and the odd palm tree. A dog trots past and down the sidewalk with purpose and direction. Helen tucks the map into her pocket and follows his lead.

When Helen told Ruth about John, and her plans to find him, Ruth rose to the occasion. She spent the better part of a week reviewing her previous USO show for Helen, breaking down—step by

step—the various numbers and routines. Helen tried her best to imi-
tate Ruth's dancing, the way she delivers a song, the way she moves
across the stage. Ruth offered practical critiques, words of encouragement where appropriate, demands of more work where required.
She examined Helen's dancing from every angle. Of course each
touring show will be unique. Their goal was to deliver Helen to her
own rehearsals with as much "stage presence" as possible.

Helen's childhood ballet classes came back to her; the impossible
height of the barre, her father sitting patiently near the door of the
studio with the other mothers, thumbing through a fishing magazine.
Even as a child, Helen suspected she had no innate talent, no resident
grace. And yet, under Ruth's tutelage, she threw herself into this new
role without reservation. Progress was uneven, but they were making progress all the same. Then suddenly Helen found herself on a
train bound for California.

By the time she reaches the high school's gymnasium, Helen has
worked up a sweat. The place appears abandoned this Saturday morning. The only light comes from the stage at the far side of the gym,
behind the wings. She removes her shoes, not so much a conscious
decision to save the hardwood floor, but a conditioned response from
her own student days. She stops just past the free-throw line, where
she catches a whiff of smoke. She hears a snap, then metallic clatter
as something hits then rolls across the floor. "Goddamn piece of . . ."

A man steps out from behind the half-open curtain with a pipe in
his mouth and a rope in his hand that disappears up into the rafters.
He wears a herringbone blazer, cream trousers, shiny black shoes.
He tugs the curtain aside. The light strikes the man and his smoke
from above, making him appear as a character in a play. Then Helen
catches his eye.

"This was ruined long before you or I ever arrived," he says, looking up into the lights. "I'll be damned if I can't get it to move."

She approaches the stage then stops, unsure how to proceed. The man tosses the rope away, wipes his palms, then smoothes down his wavy black hair. He bounds down the stairs at the corner of the stage, pipe stem clenched in bright white teeth, hand stuck out before him. Helen shifts her shoes to free her right hand.

"I'm Stephen Brooks."

"Helen Easley."

"Pleased to meet you. Long way from Broadway, aren't we?"

"Well, actually—"

"And this is Carnegie Hall compared to where we're gonna be performing."

He looks around the place, and Helen feels she should too.

"Am I early?"

He glances at his watch. "Right on time. The others are late. C'mon. Let's check that piano."

Helen follows him up onstage and helps remove a canvas cover from a battered upright piano. Stephen pulls out the stool and cracks his knuckles. He plays a few scales, and then launches into "Daisy Bell (Bicycle Built for Two)." After the first verse, which he sings alone, Stephen turns toward Helen, raises his head and eyebrows, nods when it's time for the chorus. She feels the flush in her cheeks.

She shakes her head and shrugs her shoulders, as if she doesn't know the words. He continues solo until she tentatively joins in. Halfway through the song, his voice trails off, leaving Helen to sing it alone. Her voice is tremulous at first but gains strength. He purses his lips approvingly.

Four women stroll into the gym. They take the stage as if it has been in their family for generations. They slip out of sweaters and pile handbags atop the piano. None of them have bothered to remove their shoes.

Stephen spins on the stool and introduces himself. Each woman gives her name, where she's from, and her résumé as an entertainer. Judith, a "resident" of Hollywood, has hair in the style of Ingrid Bergman, cascading in big brown curls around her cheeks and shoulders. The effect is diminished by thin lips and a lazy eye. She's had three small roles in movies Helen has never heard of but stands out for her confidence and winning smile. She's worked with Stephen before. Sarah has a somewhat solemn disposition, along with plucked eyebrows and bleached hair approximating Marlene Dietrich. She hasn't quite managed to launch an opera career in San Francisco. Jane, a chain-smoking mouse of a girl, has sang back up for both Peggy Lee and Woody Herman. She hopes this ticket out of Los Angeles will help ease an aching heart. Gladys seems the most pleased to be here. A gangly stage actress from Chicago, she's dramatically overdressed in a pink linen skirt and matching jacket and has clearly had her nails done. Perhaps she thought this was an audition.

It doesn't appear as if they know each other—despite their communal arrival—yet they behave as colleagues, like they have earned their right to be here. As Helen's turn approaches, she says a silent, preemptive prayer for forgiveness.

So this is it. This is how she abandons her father and searches for her husband in a shooting war in the North Pacific. With showgirls and a string of lies. But how many teenage boys have left their local bar jacked up on draft beer and whiskey, pledging loyalty to one another and revenge for December 7? At the recruiter's office they're allowed—*encouraged*—to lie about their age. Adolescents, the military, Roosevelt himself—as the war rolls on, who hasn't bent the truth?

Helen introduces herself and her invented accomplishments. She is originally from Seattle, she says, but worked at a theater company based in Vancouver, most recently in a production of *On Your Toes*, the lesser-known Rodgers and Hart musical she made a point of studying at the library, a show that shouldn't be familiar despite its famous composers, a show she prays they haven't seen. She chose Vancouver over Seattle to avoid any possibility of encountering someone familiar with the Seattle theater scene. Vancouver, she was sure, would be well beyond anyone's experience. Her great fear is that they might ask for details or, god forbid, a song or a couple of lines. She is met with blinking eyes and vacant nods.

Stephen congratulates them on their patriotism and bravery. The opportunity to entertain the troops is an honor, an experience they will relay to their grandchildren. He says that, unlike the fascists, who believe soldiers must concentrate exclusively on annihilating the enemy, Uncle Sam wants his men to take a well-deserved break now and then. The chance to have a couple of laughs or to see a flash of milky thigh spurs them on to victory, reminds them what they're fighting for.

Helen is reminded of her father's warning. She masks her reaction to this description of their assignment, telling herself that Stephen is only exaggerating for effect.

Everything is moving fast, he says, everyone's under pressure. With more tours going in every direction, there is less of everything to go around, especially time. They will have ten days—ten long, working days—to put a show together. They will have to work harder than ever before. They will create a musical review with some as yet unnamed star to build it all around. They probably won't learn who it is until they're ready to pack their bags. Certainly a recognizable star, but suffice it to say, there will be no Bob Hope this time around. Songs, dance routines, a skit or two, jokes and comedy throughout. Their dresses will be made by volunteers, who will take the girls' measurements tomorrow. Stephen will choreograph and play the piano. He will direct the production and manage the tour.

Stephen has broad shoulders and is well built, aside from what appear to be bandy legs. Lips, full and rosy. Handsome. Within ten minutes of meeting him, however, Helen begins to suspect why he's not on the front lines, serving his country in a more conventional role, why he might be a safe choice to chaperone five women from base to base, living and working in close quarters.

It's nothing overt. It's more in the way he looks, or rather doesn't look, at them. He is a man with little interest in women. He takes a turn dancing with each of them, and by the end of this exercise, there is even less room for doubt.

Stephen plays piano and they all sing along to "I'm Nobody's Baby." *Each night and day I pray the Lord up above, please send me down somebody to love* . . . The second time through, he groups the girls together according to vocal type and pulls a little harmony out of them. Helen intuitively follows his conducting style of looking directly at a girl, nodding his head, and fine-tuning with his eyebrows— narrowing them when he wants her to sing lower, raising them for higher. The big, toothy smile means he is pleased, closed eyes signal the opposite. As naturally as she follows his lead, Helen is inclined to trust her instincts about the quality of his character.

Lunch is brought in by volunteers, and they eat leaning against the piano. Stephen takes the opportunity to review the schedule. Immediately following rehearsals, they will be flown north, take a layover night in Seattle, then up and into the territory. For security reasons, they won't receive their itinerary until after they're in the air. He takes a look around. As soon as he's convinced that everyone is finished their sandwiches, he calls them back to rehearsal.

At the end of the day, Helen pulls on her sweater while every-one else is still laughing, trading gossip and boasts. There is talk of an icebreaker dinner downtown, away from this dingy locale.

Everyone agrees this is a fine idea. Unfortunately, Sarah, the Diet-rich devotee, has a previous engagement. Helen knows she should probably go, to make a good impression, but she has told Joe that she would telephone him tonight at seven. She doesn't want to give him any extra grounds for worry. The others walk out, laughing and singing across the basketball court, leaving Stephen and Helen to cover the piano.

"At least I know who I can rely on," he says. A fog of dust rises from the canvas. "I'm sure the other girls wish they were heading to Hawaii. They pulled the short straw and ended up with me. If I remember correctly, you asked to go north."

Whether he's already guessed she has something to hide, or is simply making conversation, remains to be seen.

"I've been to Hawaii," Helen says. "Overrated." She aims for sophistication but fears she's come off like a spoiled child.

Before this trip, she had been as far south as San Francisco, as far north as Vancouver. It makes her light-headed to concoct a new life on the fly.

"I see," he says, giving it some thought. "No. Actually, I don't. But I suppose your reasons are your own."

He holds the door open for her and switches off the gymnasium lights, allowing her the grace to escape.

"I've wanted to go to Alaska since, forever," she says feebly.

"Well . . ." He searches his pocket for the keys, then locks the door behind them. "Let's see if we can make that dream come true."

AT A QUARTER PAST SEVEN, Helen sits alone in her host family's parlor after having said good night to Joe. Her father was never any good on the telephone. He seemed stumped for conversation and offered little more than one-word answers to her questions. His interest was piqued, however, with her report of the California weather, which they tell her has been unseasonably warm.

Helen rests in the shadows, perspiring, listening to a record playing in the background. If it's this hot in springtime, how do they stand it in summer? Her thoughts drift to Seattle's cleansing rain, her scramble to procure enough warm winter clothes for Alaska.

That first winter they were married, Helen had been secretly admiring a red coat in the window of Leahman's department store. John was between assignments at the time, and money was tight, so she only window-shopped when she was alone. The coat was gorgeous, finely cut and tailored, with three oversize buttons. Elegant simplicity. She tried it on twice and would stop by now and then to admire it. One day she dropped in to see if, perhaps by some miracle, it had gone on sale. When she saw that it was missing from the display she felt strangely relieved. Either it was gone and she could put it out of her mind, or it was inside, hanging on the discount rack. The salesclerk informed her that the last one had indeed been sold. Helen turned to leave but the woman called her back. "Are you Helen?" She reached under the counter and pulled out a garment box tied with a bow. "A gentleman was in last week . . ." Had he been watching her? Had he asked one of the girls at work? Half an hour later, when she strode through the door at home, John looked up and broke into applause. "It's about time," he said. "I was wondering when you'd fall into my trap."

During the day, the memories come in waves, in social situations and when she's alone. Sometimes she fails to even conjure the specifics of his face. The guilt makes her clench her teeth. Other times, she can feel the dent in the air beside her, and the memories rush back so fast and warm she almost forgets to breathe. When the sun goes down, his absence is even more acute.

Helen stares at the telephone a moment more, then turns out the light.

* * *

FOLLOWING TEN CONSECUTIVE and exhausting days, Helen is dropped off in front of an immense open door—the biggest she's ever seen. Inside the empty hangar, a volunteer from the USO hands her a box, half again as big as her single piece of luggage. It is identical to the boxes now being given to the other girls. Each is packed with items they are told will be in short supply or unavailable where they are going: cigarettes, makeup, stockings, tissues, tangerines, chocolate, cotton batting, powder, soap, shampoo, cream, handkerchiefs, needles and thread—many of the things Helen had planned to pick up herself on their layover in Seattle.

Stephen claps his hands and gestures for everyone to gather round. He wants them to take a moment to appreciate his achievement. They have worked hard, he says, and he has molded their individual talents into a cohesive and pleasing form. He claims that one hour of rehearsal for each minute onstage should more than suffice. Altogether, they've had one hundred hours to build and polish their show. Curtain-to-curtain, their act comes in at just over ninety minutes. By his estimation, they are now overqualified. If only Helen could allow herself to believe him.

A crew of airmen arrive. They gather up the boxes and luggage, load it all onto a trolley, push it out into the stark morning light. Helen follows Stephen and the girls across the pavement and toward a waiting plane. At the bottom of the gangway steps, Helen feels compelled to reconfirm just how much time they will have in Seattle. Will they still get the full twenty-four hours they've been promised? There's been a change, he explains. Seattle's out. It's overnight in Portland, along the coast of British Columbia, then points north and west. A small detail that appears to have slipped his mind.

"I just found out myself," he claims, reading the expression on her face.

Helen pictures Joe preparing for her arrival. He's swept and mopped, put fresh flowers on the dining room table and in her room. Filled the icebox for the one meal they had planned together. He glances at the clock with increasing frequency.

This was to have been a kind of dress rehearsal, a trial run for her father to be on his own before she finally took off for Alaska. Time to assess how he was getting on with the household chores and his work at the church, time to check back in with the new doctor, and Mrs. Riley next door. Time to finally say good-bye.

She must find a telephone as soon as they arrive in Oregon. She will tell him how much she misses him, how terrible she feels about this sudden change of plans. Remind him that she will be thinking of him each day, that she is counting on him to be careful, sensible, and patient with himself—for her sake if not for his own.

As she steps up and into the plane, Helen tells herself that she will find her husband and she will return to her father in just over six weeks' time. She has made the right decision for her family. She will bring them together again.

NINE

ASORTIE OF B-24S AND P-38S SPLITS THE SKY. Strangely, no bombing ensues. Instead the American aircraft fly over the island then turn around, as if the pilots have suddenly changed their minds. Easley draws comfort from the hum of the engines, the man-made, manufactured silhouettes sailing above land and sea. But when they're gone, the awareness of isolation grows more acute. He tells himself that he is not the only one. There must others like him, hiding from the enemy all over Europe, north Africa, China, maybe even here in the Aleutians. At first this thought gives him a lift, but it soon conjures images of people taking cover together, in pairs and even in groups. But as he now knows, this form of hiding bears almost no relation. They are not alone.

Easley removes the boy's dog tags from around his own neck, where they have hung for four days. He holds them in the palm of his hand and reads aloud:

"KARL A BITBURG

12870763 T41 A

ANGELA BITBURG

242 BORDEN ST

ROAN TEXAS P"

He guesses the "A" near the hole is his blood type, he assumes the final "P" stands for "Protestant." Easley has no doubt that the key in his pocket will open the door of 242 Borden Street. He did not divide the pair of dog tags, place one in the boy's mouth, as he once heard he was meant to do. Nor did he bury the body. In this matter, he has no regrets. He didn't want the Japanese finding it, and more important, he didn't want the boy becoming part of the island.

The past four days were spent with the book Karl had liberated along with the pencil, pliers, coal, and wood. Easley no longer wondered what information the book might contain. He turned it sideways and stopped seeing the alien spider words for the white space in between. He has passed the days inside the cave transcribing his memories of Karl. Impressions, conversations, the times Karl had made Easley laugh. He hopes that by recording these things, and carrying them into the future, he would remember Karl as completely as possible. By remembering him, Easley hopes to honor him. Karl's story will become part of Warren's story, part of Helen's and his own, then be folded and tucked into the narrative of this unknown and expanding war. He has filled nearly thirty pages with this tribute and now he is hungry. Easley puts the dog tags back around his neck. They clink as they settle against his skin.

He wears everything at night. Karl's clothes underneath, because they are smaller, then his own trousers and shirt over top. In the absence of coal, this has made some difference. Now, in the light of day, Easley removes his jacket and walks outside.

The fog has lifted, and the sky is alive with the confetti of descending birds. To the west, where the clouds have opened above the sea, the water is a deep, alluring blue. This is the most dangerous time of day. If the enemy is hovering above, or shuffling across the land, they will surely see him. Outside the cave, there is no place to hide. His mind calculates the risk, but his body won't be denied the promise of light, the opportunity for movement, the hope of warmth.

He takes comfort in the great cacophony of ducks, geese, gulls, and terns. These and other birds have begun to arrive in unimaginable numbers. He is reminded of the assignment that first brought him to these islands, a profile that was to include the annual avian migration from the Pacific Northwest, California, the Sea of Cortez. Journeys from warm paradise to dank exile. Now he is grateful for the company—and the promise of meat. Easley feels the strongest kinship for the uncatchable albatross because they, like himself, are solitary travelers in an indifferent world.

He ate a dozen raw mussels in the morning, a frond of kelp midday, but now hungers for more. Among the exploding population of birds, Easley has trouble finding ptarmigan. He left the cave with high hopes of success, but as the day matures and the raft of clouds drifts back in, his desperation grows.

Easley throws stones at the gulls strolling the beach. The moment he winds up for the pitch, however, they are already on the go—a running hop and then into the air. He strikes one in the belly but the stone simply bounces off. The gull lets out a loud squawk, shimmies, as if trying to shake water off its back, then continues on its way. Easley sits down to rest. Tonight, when it comes time to face the mussels, he will attempt to mute the taste of the sea by calling up the fading memory of deep-fried chicken.

An unknown raptor circles above a chevron of geese. Thick golden beak, black body, white shoulders and tail. It is the biggest eagle Easley's ever seen. Perhaps blown off course from Asia, a victim of unfavorable winds. He watches it bank sharply to the right, then dive down into the prey's formation. The lead goose doesn't see it coming, the others hold their course. The eagle strikes one near the back of the line and it falls flapping from the sky. Easley rises to his feet. The goose fights for control, but all it can do is tumble onto the grassy hill. The eagle swoops down directly. It travels so fast Easley thinks it too will crash. Then, at the last second, it pulls up and comes in for a controlled landing. Easley begins to move. The quarry still attempts flight with its remaining unbroken wing. This only pushes it in circles on the grass. The eagle loses no time jumping on the goose's back, talons outstretched. It even attempts takeoff, but the payload proves unwieldy. Easley picks up the pace.

Desperate to get up and into the air, the eagle flaps its wings so hard that feathers fall away. It swings its head around and sees Easley approach. In one desperate move, it lifts the goose fully five feet off the ground, then drops the heavy load. The eagle swoops down and towers, panting over its kill.

Easley closes in. He swings his leg. The eagle spreads its wings to make itself appear even larger and more forbidding, then plunges its beak at Easley's boot. Easley swings again and forces the eagle off the goose. The bird complains so loudly, Easley is sure every soldier on the island will come running with bayonets drawn. He backs in toward the goose, grabs it by the neck, and takes a few bounding leaps toward the beach.

The eagle takes to the air and flies low over Easley's scalp. Planting his legs in the grass, Easley wields the goose like a sack of stones, daring the eagle to try again. It circles twice, then takes another plunge. Easley swings the goose aloft the second before the raptor arrives— the startled bird flaps and turns away. It flies back to the site where its prey first came down and searches for signs of a meal. Finding no stray morsels, it stands there, glaring at Easley as he skips toward the beach. Some hundred yards away, Easley switches the goose from one hand to the other. He turns toward the eagle and bows.

A short-necked Aleutian Canada goose, it is smaller than the familiar variety but still much larger than any previous bird he or the boy has been able to kill. The coal is long gone and he hasn't seen a stick of driftwood in days. It must be eaten raw. Dead wings unfold as it is carried downslope.

Easley sits and stares at the prize for a time. Beak half open in silent protest, hematite eye glazed with sand. He unfolds the boy's pocketknife.

The meat glistens when exposed to the light. Each muscle clearly defined. The flesh is soft and pliant in his teeth, the flavor faint and not unpleasant. It is a shame not to be able to roast it, to crisp and darken the skin. Because the meat will go bad within a day, the job is to consume as much of the bird as possible. Easley tosses the entrails on the sand, and the seagulls are quick to respond. After consuming the breast and legs, he belches, takes a break, then goes back at it again. He cracks bones for the marrow. His head feels clearer by the minute.

All this time, the eagle circles above, watching. Easley can ill afford another foe. He keeps track with peripheral vision.

At last he stands, cheeks smeared in blood and grease. He abandons the feathers and carcass to the gulls. Scrubs his hands with wet sand, splashes cold surf in his face. Then drowsiness overtakes him.

Easley finds a ribbon of green near the edge of the beach where spring has come ashore. He lays himself down, hands clasped over full stomach. All around, new shoots of sedge inch toward the light, cradling him. He imagines himself lying next to Helen. He recalls how she'd often hold his hand while dozing off, the way her arms and legs sought him out, even in sleep. He can feel none of these things. Easley strains to picture her eyes, recall the sound of her voice. He finds that he cannot. Now, cut off from all human contact, memory quickly betrays. He falls into a heavy sleep.

Easley walks empty streets until at last he reaches the park. A warm summer day, there should be people about, traffic in the streets. Instead there are only birds shuffling past on the pavement, in a hurry to get someplace else. They gawk at him, then turn to whisper to one another. He passes playing fields and looming Douglas fir until he sees a single vehicle in the parking lot. An old Ford pickup. Could this be Karl's truck? There appears to be people inside. Easley steps around and over murmuring birds as he closes in on the cab.

In the side window, he can see the bare head and shoulder of a man. As Easley draws near, the man moves into shadow. As Easley reaches the truck, he peers inside and sees a woman atop the man. She grips his shoulder above what appears to be the smear of a tattoo. But it is not Karl. It is Warren who reaches up her thighs and hips, kneading the skin. The woman's hair is draped across her eyes until she tosses it back, revealing herself to be Helen.

Easley sits up and blinks at the sky, head throbbing with the beat of his heart. The sun has abandoned the island and now reaches through distant clouds to the sea. Two hard shafts of light, as in religious paintings of old. They set a patch of ocean ablaze with the promise of something better.

Long before he met Helen, when he was twenty-two, Easley brought home the only other girl who had ever meant anything to him. He saw the problem with his brother almost from the start. The way Warren turned on that smile, told stories out of turn, made her laugh, and laugh, and laugh.

It wasn't that his brother was consciously making a pass at the girl. Warren was simply born to charm. Yet watching it happen right in front of him, with a girl Easley had chosen, loosened something terrible inside. When he confronted him, Warren simply laughed at the ridiculousness of it. Claimed he could get a dozen better girls if he'd

been so inclined. Easley hit his eighteen-year-old brother so hard and
fast, Warren didn't even have time to raise his hands. Laid him out flat
in the hallway of their parents' home with a broken cheekbone and a
gash below the eye.

Easley hadn't just wanted to put his little brother in his place. He
had also wanted to hurt him. Specifically, that handsome face. He
wanted to leave a mark. Years later, when Warren met Helen, he made
a point of ignoring her—until Easley told him to stop.

Back on his feet, Easley sets an ambitious pace. He must keep
moving. Movement means survival. He soon finds himself at the site of
the rotten post, the broken splint. He stops and surveys the spot once
again. The only man-made marker encountered outside the village.
What is it doing here?

The post lies in pieces, where it was tossed on Karl's last night.
The impression of Easley's own body remains in the wild celery where
he tripped and fell. There is a shallow indentation to the left of the
marker where last year's weeds are especially thick. A grave? If this
is the result of a collapsed coffin, then why are the stones piled twenty
feet away? Don't Aleuts bury their relatives in the Russian church-
yard? Easley circles the pile, looking from stones to weeds, then back
again. He falls to his knees.

The little pile itself is only two feet high. Unless someone was
looking for it, it would likely go unnoticed. It hasn't been here long.
After removing the stones, he digs with his hands. The soil is soft,
perhaps recently disturbed. He's dug barely a foot into the earth when
his finger snags on something metal. He sucks the finger, spits red mud
on old blades of rye.

Easley excavates around what appears to be a small metal box
wrapped in sheets of tinfoil. It hasn't been long in the ground. Tea tin?
He shakes it and hears a dull thump inside. He turn it upside down,

inspects it from every angle. Easley clutches it to his chest and scans vacant land and sea. He pushes soil back into place, tamps the earth, then reassembles the stones much as they were found.

At the mouth of the cave, where the light is still of use, Easley gingerly removes tinfoil as if it were fine Christmas wrapping. Upon reaching the can itself, he smiles at the sight of the familiar red letters on gold and green, his first suspicion confirmed. Nabob Pure Indian & Ceylon Tea, Kelly, Douglas, & Co. Limited Vancouver, B.C. 3 lbs net. He pops the lid, pulls out and unwraps a length of red flannel concealing the point of an ivory harpoon. Exquisitely carved, complete with barbs and a socket for a shaft, it is nearly as long as his hand. Packed beneath the harpoon point is a small, framed photograph of a young native woman in a dark wool coat casting off on a voyage. She stands at the rail of a ship, waving a gloved hand down at whoever holds the camera. Her smile is quiet, her posture unsure.

He studies the image a good long while, then wipes a fresh spot of mud from the glass with the least offensive part of his sleeve. Below the portrait lies an icon of the Madonna and Child adorned in gold leaf. Russian, presumably. Next, a roll of cash held tight with a red rubber band. He counts 373 U.S. dollars. Encircling the other contents is a folded rectangle of bright-white linen embroidered with buttercups and fireweed. It is a shock to see its purity in the gray scar of the ravine. Easley holds it in cold, filthy hands as if it were the Shroud of Turin.

At the bottom of the tin is a folded piece of paper amid a trace of black powdered tea. Easley removes the paper with one hand, sucks his free index finger, then rubs it clean on the front of his shirt. He presses it into the tin, then to the tip of his tongue. He holds the flavor there, pressing sweet dust against soft palate. He closes his eyes and smiles.

A gust of wind bends the paper back over itself, then Easley shakes it open. There, in elegant blue script:

August 10, '42

My Dearest Love,

You have found me gone and our things hid safe.

They came to the village June 7 and we fear they will take us away.

I will wait for you. Think of your promise to me and remember, the wind is not a river.

Yours,

Forever,

Tatiana

Easley rereads, then carefully folds the note and returns it to the bottom of the can. *The wind is not a river?* He replaces the cash, the linen, the Russian icon, the ivory harpoon tip, then secures the can on a shelf high in the back of the cave. He flattens and folds the tinfoil for some future use unseen.

He sits holding the photograph, straining to see the girl's vulnerable face in remnant light. He feels something shift inside.

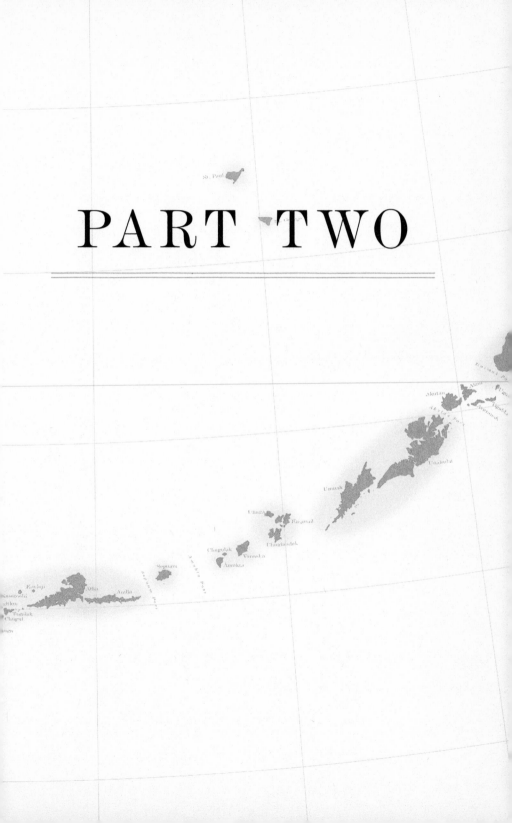

PART TWO

TEN

ELEN SITS SANDWICHED BETWEEN STEPHEN AND Judith, whispering an endless loop of Hail Marys into the constant wail of the engines. Sarah and Jane are strapped in their seats along the opposite wall, legs crossed, clumsily flipping through the latest issues of *Life* and *Look* with gloved hands. Over their flight suits, they wear new parkas zipped to the top. Gladys, having grown up in Chicago, has the most experience with the cold. She's on the far side of Sarah, head tilted back, sound asleep. The rest of the space is filled with a cargo of desks, filing cabinets and chairs, colossal black tires, canned carrots and beets. It's the third leg of Helen's first airplane journey. This dim, unglamorous scene bears no resemblance to her previous notions of air travel.

They touch down seven hundred miles north of Portland at the Royal Canadian Air Force Station in Prince Rupert, British Columbia—a place that seems newly hacked out of the otherwise impenetrable forest. Snow is still on the mountains, but beyond the pavement the grass is greening up with the promise of spring. They have lunch on the grass by the edge of the taxiway while the plane is being refueled. They eat egg salad sandwiches out in the sun, wax paper balanced on knees, while men run around as if there is some sudden, unseen of emergency. A uniformed member of the RCAF Women's Division greets them with coffee, which she pours into thin paper cups. Helen soaks up the heat in her hands. When it's time to go, she stands and performs a set of jumping jacks to stretch her legs and back. The other girls join in, and soon they are all jumping up and down, waving their arms by the side of the plane.

On the final leg of the flight, they belt every song in their opening set over the persistent A-flat of the engines, then huddle at the window and watch the sun disappear in a purple and orange sky.

Each of these women has the same dream: to somehow make their mark in show business. Gladys considers this gig a leg up, a chance to be seen and appreciated beyond Chicago, an opportunity to gain much needed exposure. Judith, with her movie experience, sees it as a step down, a necessary place to exercise her skills while waiting for more worthy opportunities and the end of the war. Jane and Sarah are grateful for the work. All have someone they care about serving in uniform and believe they are being of service in the Cause, a part of history in the making.

Late at night the plane bounces, then careens down the runway near the city of Anchorage. It is colder here than in Prince Rupert, but not far below freezing. The wind is cold and wet against Helen's cheeks as they move from plane, to bus, to barracks in the dark. A thin crust of spring snow covers the ground beyond the slivered headlight beam, except where the earth has worn through in twin, muddy tracks. No one speaks. The airplane's roar has been replaced by a ringing in their ears, and now the bus's lumbering whine.

They lurch to a stop in front of the last in a row of Quonset huts, which resemble enormous tin barrels toppled over and half-buried in the earth. A solitary bulb hangs over a door marked #17. The driver shuts off the engine, then glances back over his shoulder and flashes a star-struck grin. "Well, this is it!" he declares.

Judith has fallen asleep on Jane's shoulder. Jane is in no rush to finish her cigarette. Gladys and Sarah whisper in a private conversation as Sarah ties a scarf over her head. Someone has to move. Helen makes her way to the front of the bus, thanks the driver, then steps down into the mud and is reminded that her boots are still in her bag. These were one of her two good pair of shoes. Ignoring them for a moment, she looks up into the sky to catch a glimpse of the aurora borealis, which she's read so much about, but clouds obscure the view. Her relief at having made it this far is quickly overtaken by the thought that John might be out in some thin walled tent, shivering through the night.

The other girls quit the bus with limp hair and sour looks, pulling parkas tight at the neck. Stephen shakes the driver's hand, then steps down as the door swings shut behind him. He looks at Helen and musters a smile.

"Weaker girls would not have survived," she says, rewarding him for the effort.

Inside the Quonset hut, Helen discovers a large open room with a dozen canvas cots. A warm coal fire glows in the center stove. The girls stumble in behind her. Even their most sour expressions melt at the discovery that a single paper rose has been placed upon the pillow of each immaculately made cot. On a table near the stove is a bright bowl of oranges and a white layer cake with WELCOME TO ALASKA, USA inscribed in cherry red icing. Beside the cake, a hand-made card stands at attention, crammed with welcoming signatures. The girls smile and coo over the card as Stephen cuts the cake. Helen is standing near the stove, warming her legs, when a song suddenly erupts outside.

Helen is the first to the door. The other girls press at her back as she is met with a chorus of over a dozen men singing and swaying in the dark. They hold flashlights up to their young faces, which makes them look like kids in a Halloween stunt. Voices turn to vapor above their heads as they sing "I'm in the Mood for Love." When their song is through, the girls clap and cheer and yell "bravo!" The men wish them sweet dreams and want to know if there is anything they need to make their stay more enjoyable. *Anything,* they repeat.

"Thanks for comin' by," Judith says for them all. "Tomorrow night we'll give you boys something to dream about."

This draws whistles and groans of anticipation. The men wave good-bye and turn back down the road, singing and shoving each other around.

Sarah soon declares that it's time to call it a night and summarily switches off the lights. Helen undresses in the dark and settles into her cot.

Now that the constant motion has finally ceased, her fears gather round. The unbearable emptiness she experienced high above the wilderness, where so few signs of civilization could be seen. The unending expanse of the North Pacific. The knowledge that John must be in a place more desolate still.

In her prayers, Helen includes the flight crew that safely brought her north, her weary companions, and the unaccountably sweet and joyful men who did their best to make them feel at home. She wonders if John has such good company as these men seem to be. These are the thoughts she tries to hold as she lies in wait of sleep.

THE FOLLOWING MORNING, Helen carries a tin tray to the edge of the empty mess hall and slides in next to Judith. The girls are seated at the first of several dozen sets of long table and benches. The place is remarkably clean and well ordered for having just accommodated hundreds of hungry men. On the opposite wall, a USO poster features the disembodied head of Teresa Wright throwing her hair back in some kind of musical ecstasy, phallic microphone shining in front of too red lips. Under the name "Teresa Wright" appears "& the USO Swingettes" in smaller, humbler type.

The USO failed to inform the men that Miss Wright won't be performing. Stephen only broke the news to the girls two days before their departure. This led to a tantrum, in which Sarah called into question the professional ethics of Stephen and the entire United Service Organizations, and to Judith's smoldering, cinematic exit. Unmoved, Stephen simply puffed his pipe and declared that the songs Miss Wright was supposed to sing would have to be divvied up among them, the more difficult tunes going to Judith, who was no longer present to protest. Let there be no mistake, the show would go on.

The coffee is bitter from having sat too long on the stove. Helen chases corned beef hash around her tray with a fork, failing to uncover the appetizing bits. She takes refuge in toast, which she butters and dunks into her coffee. It is half past eight in the morning and the sun is already climbing in the sky. The men have long since disappeared to the airfields and hangars, otherwise occupied with the business of moving planes, men, and materiel from the States out to the Aleutian Islands. There is an excellent chance that John passed through this base on his way west, took a meal in this very same room.

"They're making an announcement today," Stephen assures them. "They'll know long before we show up that Teresa isn't here. Trust me. They'll be falling all over themselves to see you girls. You'll see."

"Put yourself in their shoes," Gladys says.

"It's like ordering filet mignon and getting a lousy frankfurter instead," Judith snaps. "How happy would you be?"

Jane, who recently ended her relationship with a married doctor, declares, "I wouldn't say no to a hot young frank." She smiles and blows steam from her coffee.

"I didn't hear that," Stephen says. "And don't let any of them hear it either. They get the slightest inkling one of you is in heat and we'll have more trouble than the Japs."

Judith unsuccessfully attempts to conceal the fact she is picking hash from her teeth. "You can't drag us all the way up here, then push us out onstage when the boys were expecting a star," she says. "It just ain't fair."

"Who promised you fair?" Stephen folds his arms across his chest. "There's no fairness in this world and it's our job to help these guys take a vacation from that fact for one night a year."

The girls glance at one another, then look to Judith.

"*For cryin' out loud* . . . This isn't Forty-second Street!" Stephen pauses, then quickly collects himself. "These guys will love you. We'll knock 'em over."

"I'm talking about *communication* . . ." Judith says, tension rising in her voice.

In eleven hours, they will be onstage. Helen feels her nerves constricting both body and mind. A year ago, if she'd asked herself where she thought she'd be now, Helen would have imagined pushing a carriage around the park at Green Lake with John, breathing in the delicate fragrance of apple blossoms, trying to figure out how to successfully mother an infant without the benefit of help or advice from a mother of her own. But she knows everyone on this base should be someplace else. How many millions of lives have been diverted by this war? Unlike the tally of ships, dollars, or casualties, there is no math for personal losses, losses quiet and unseen. No restitution for what could have been.

Helen stands with her tray and backs toward the door. She dumps her uneaten meal into the garbage and sets the tray on the counter. A kid in a white apron intercepts it and asks if there is anything else she wants. Bony, drooping shoulders. Adam's apple sharp to match the chin. He appears all of seventeen. Turn him sideways and he'd be five inches wide. The only thing to recommend him is a pair of stunning green eyes.

"Lookin' forward to your show," he says. "We're real pleased you're here."

"Teresa Wright didn't make it. It'll just be us girls tonight."

"Heard yesterday. We got word from the boys in Prince Rupert that she wasn't on the plane. I never believed she was comin' anyhow."

"You don't care?"

"She don't even seem human to me. At least you girls seem like the real thing."

Helen wants to tell him that this is the nicest thing anyone has said to her in months. That his words give her courage. She says, "That's one gorgeous set of eyes you've got."

The resulting smile surprises and incapacitates him, transforms him utterly. He looks away, then backs off a few steps. He brushes a hand over a head of short-cropped hair, makes a sound meant to resemble a laugh, then disappears into the kitchen.

* * *

BEFORE THE APPLAUSE DIES AWAY, Helen flees to their Quonset hut through the dark, splashing slush halfway up the inside of her thigh. She can't get away fast enough. She pulls the door closed behind her, then stops—her pulse racing to catch her. At the stove she finds the embers glowing still. She tosses in a scoop of coal.

Helen sits with crossed arms and legs, considering the disaster of her performance, the shame of having let everyone down on opening night, the danger that being found a fraud will pose to her chances of finding John.

Up onstage, it began with a confused, sideways glance from Judith at the top of their third number. As the other girls each took up a verse from "Don't Sit Under the Apple Tree," Helen somehow missed her cue. It was a small thing, really. Gladys tried to give Helen a lift with a big, encouraging smile. The men didn't seem to mind, they cheered wildly each time one of them turned around, shifted position, or—heaven help them—bent over. But Helen's throat had already tightened with nerves. That first mistake grew into a dark cloud that seemed to shadow her every move. Try as she might, she never really recovered.

Halfway through "Cow Cow Boogie," Helen's harmony truly went south. On the first verse following the musical interlude, Judith looked back over her shoulder. Stephen glanced up from the piano—eyebrows raised, then lowered, then narrowed in frustration. Undaunted, he tried again even bigger, making it a part of the act. Despite this comic direction, Helen couldn't find her way to the note. Eventually Stephen just smiled and blew her a kiss.

Helen had hit her mark consistently during rehearsals. Tonight she was forced to abandon singing harmony altogether and silently mouthed the words for the remainder of the song. She sang faintly on the easier melodies, and felt a little more secure with her dancing on "Chattanooga Choo Choo." But when she looked to Stephen for reassurance, he tugged the corners of his mouth and aped a grin. Throughout the entire second half of the performance, her goal was sheer survival.

Helen gazes up at the arching ribs of the ceiling overhead. What is she doing here? John will be as close to the action as possible, and that is still over a thousand miles away in the Aleutian Islands. After Anchorage, their itinerary calls for shows in Fairbanks, the better part of a week spent, before finally heading out to the islands. Stephen confirms that they will be performing on Adak, halfway down the chain, the forward base of operations for the ongoing assault on the Japanese. Of all the places on Earth, this is where John is most likely to be. Once there, she will have only four days to find him. But as Helen has learned, itineraries change. What if suddenly they're sent not west, but farther north or south? What if the Japanese advance and they are ordered out of the territory altogether?

The door opens and Stephen steps in, stamps the snow and mud from his shoes, unravels his scarf. He whistles the tune to "Tangerine," the encore number of their show. He stands next to Helen, contentedly gazing into the fire as if nothing were the matter. As if everything had gone according to plan.

"I feel like Santa Claus," he says. "Or the owner of a strip club. Someone who spreads cheer."

"I had a case of nerves." Her prepared remarks are barely audible. "It won't happen again."

He unbuttons his collar and loosens his tie.

"We were all a little shaky," he says

"No, we weren't. *I* was."

"Okay, you're right. You were. And you looked like someone was holding a gun to your head. But at least you didn't fall into the audience."

"I kept expecting you to get the hook and yank me offstage."

"Forget it," he says. "We have plenty more shows ahead. Everyone has an off night or two. You just used one early."

She is unsure whether he is trying to rally what's left of her confidence, or just going easy on her in advance of the storm headed her way.

"Where are the girls?"

"Still signing autographs."

"I haven't been in front of an audience since . . ." Helen searches her memory for the lie. "Vancouver."

Stephen pulls a flask from his jacket and offers her a drink, which she declines. He helps himself to a taste, then squats down and checks the fire. He smiles and nods his head, as if reliving the highlights of the night. Helen is struck with the urge to trust.

"You knew I was a fake. Didn't you?"

Stephen gets up, grabs a chair, and sits down next to Helen. He props up his feet on another chair and studies his flask before tilting it to his lips again.

"You made great progress in rehearsals. You've a beautiful voice, as good as the rest of them. You just need to spend some time in front of an audience."

"You knew I lied about my experience."

"You came recommended, and I liked you from the start." He shrugs his shoulders. "I wanted to see if you could pull it off."

"Stephen—"

"Who hasn't lied to get themselves where they want to be? You think I haven't invented a few accomplishments to get steady work in Los Angeles? Look. This business is all about perception. You know how you get hired to direct a three-act musical, with orchestra, and cast of twenty in Sacramento? Tell 'em you've done it in New York. Then you move on from there. Producers don't ask you to swear on a Bible. Perhaps they should start."

He takes another swig. Not long ago, Helen would have judged him for being so casual with the truth.

"People don't care about what you've done," he concludes. "They only care about what you can do for them. Is this all really news to you? Sweetheart, come on."

"I don't want to disappoint you."

"Then don't. Just learn to hear your own sound coming through.

Then find the melody and tail it. It'll pull you along. And *smile,* for God's sake. Don't stop smiling. If I don't see you smiling every second of every song, I'll throw something at you. Smile at the other girls, smile at individual guys, smile at the audience in general. Make eye contact and tease."

Judith arrives alone. She hangs her jacket on a hook, then staggers over, shoving Stephen's feet off the chair before sitting down. The cloud of gin isn't far behind. "That was the sexiest thing I've ever done and no one even touched me."

"Congratulations," Stephen says. "Need a cigarette?"

Helen is relieved that Judith has arrived to pull the spotlight in her direction. If she's waiting to deliver a damning critique, it's not the first thing on her mind. The other girls push their way through the door together, swinging hips so wide they almost knock each other over. They drop coats on cots, kick off shoes, slip on thick wool socks over silk stockings. As they gather round the stove, Helen's sense of isolation grows. Her stomach tightens as they circle in, boasting over who gave the most autographs. When the chatter subsides, Helen looks over at Stephen, who winks. She gestures for his flask. When the whiskey reaches the back of her throat, she has to fight the urge to cough. Instead a single tear escapes and begins to roll down her cheek. She instantly wipes it away and clears her throat. "My God. I was a disaster. I couldn't sing to save my life and I'm sorry." Helen holds up the flask again as the girls focus in. "Maybe this will help." She takes another drink.

"Oh, boo hoo," Judith says. "I blew it on 'Just Squeeze Me,' Jane went flat on 'A Good Man Is Hard to Find,' and—if you can believe it—Gladys farted on 'All of Me.'"

"I did not!" Gladys feigns shock at the accusation.

"I nearly burst a seam," Judith says. "You learn that at Julliard? Or whichever schools they have in the wilds of Illinois."

They pass the flask and take their time scrutinizing the tiniest nuance of each and every song. No one is spared.

When the festivities show signs of winding down, Judith lets fly about secret parties she heard about while on a show in New York. Parties where husbands and wives come in masks and end up with strangers. Parties where people wear masks and little else. "I haven't seen it myself, of course, but you'd be shocked to know who's involved. I mean big names."

The girls take turns guessing the names of actresses and actors but must take a swig with each guess made. The game continues until the whiskey is gone. But then a bottle appears in its place and continues the established rounds. Soon, half the stars of the silver screen are ensnared in Judith's tale.

Deep in the night, Helen lies down and picks a bolt in the ceiling above and stares at it to keep the room from spinning. She has only been drunk like this once before. This time, she has no regrets. She has been pardoned, accepted by a group of women determined to look after their own. Worldly women with little thought of starting a family anytime soon. The kind of women Joe would warn her about, the kind of women Helen would have otherwise avoided. Helen recognizes this as a gift she does not deserve. She falls asleep thankful for their kindness—and the grace it affords on her way to finding John.

THE FOLLOWING MORNING, Helen finds herself in the mess hall, gazing into the emerald eyes of the skinny dishwasher, who now blushes hopelessly over a tray of reconstituted eggs.

Men. Despite the unsettling wave of testosterone she felt barreling toward her onstage last night, Helen pities their weakness. Here, among soldiers rallied for war, she is embarrassed by her inordinate power—a power derived entirely from her gender and appearance. She and the other girls are the fleeting reflection of their hopes and desires, a temporary release from their worries and fears. If she had encountered John, her own brothers, or her father at this age, in such a state, how would she want them treated?

With Stephen and the girls distracted at their table, Helen gestures for the boy to approach. When his shiny face is within reach, she takes it in both her hands and plants a kiss on his cheek—then turns and walks away.

ELEVEN

THE RAIN HAS CEASED BUT THE SEA CONTINUES TO boil. The wind whips up to astonishing speeds. Easley wonders if the island is being hit by an arctic hurricane. The strongest gusts force their way into the cave, but stumble and wear themselves down by the time they reach his cheeks. Easley lies entombed in parachutes. The blackest time of night.

The edges of the little frame are smooth in the palm of his hand, the glass flat and cool. Easley has stared at the image for so long now, he no longer needs to see it. He sometimes thinks that she is more than her photograph, more than a real, living woman—that he can feel the brush of her wings in the cold heart of night. Do angels take on human form when they descend into the lives of men? His mind warns him to fight such thoughts, but his soul does not hesitate to embrace them. Tatiana encourages him, gives him strength to carry on.

Suddenly, the wind ceases altogether.

Get up. Time to go.

THERE IS NO NEED to see when traveling this beach. He knows every boulder and gully, can hear the surf rushing up to knock him over and pull him into the deep. Walking in the dark, arms out-stretched, gives him the sense of flying.

He has been without coal for nearly a week. His last incursion into the village was cut short when he noticed three Japanese soldiers fixing something in the low spot near the shed. Jammed machine gun? Land mine? They were there for what seemed like hours. Yet by diverting his course he discovered where kitchen slop had been tossed behind the camp. Under the cover of fog, he found a half-rotten onion and some rice, which he consumed on the spot. It was only when he had finished eating that he noticed a wad of bloody bandages mixed in with the scraps.

Now, through his boots and ears, he reads sand, then grass, then sand again. Blindly marching on in the dark.

"What's come over me?" he wonders aloud, startled by the sound of his own voice. Falling for a snapshot of a woman he can never know. And Helen—the guilt of having let her down. Hungry and exhausted, he must fight to keep his wits, avoid indulging in philosophy or fantasy. But the question grows and crowds out other thoughts: What if Tatiana is the last person waiting for me?

THIS TIME AROUND, his approach is marked by shades of dawn. Sentries should be posted, but Easley can detect no movement. The village now appears abandoned, the camp itself tightly battened down. And then he sees them, a group of six, setting out from the tents together, arms swinging as they set a respectable pace. Easley has seen this before, a show for their superiors. As soon as they are beyond the camp, they will shuffle through the motions, stopping now and then to peer up at the clouds above or out to sea. Having easily subdued the island's few inhabitants, the Japanese are convinced they have Attu to themselves. Easley cautiously makes his way to the ridge in the dim, colorless light. From there, he waits and surveys the blight of more than a hundred tents, which appear as a vast Hooverville. Hopeful no eyes are staring back, he cautiously approaches the dump.

Upon arrival, he sees that the birds have picked the litter clean. Among the rocks, there is nothing to eat. Easley gawks at the emptiness for a time, forcing down the hunger and the fear. He scans the ground for anything resembling food. Even the eggshells that had once been here have disappeared. Only the loneliest grains of rice and a congealed pile of grease remain. He is ready to turn and leave when he sees it—the bright, battered rind of a lemon. He picks it up, brushes off gravel and sand, slips it inside his pocket.

The clang of what he imagines is an empty pot issues from one of the tents, perhaps a hundred yards away. Easley crouches and holds his breath. After a long pause in silence, he rises and cautiously retraces his steps back over the hill.

The most important thing now is to fill his pack with coal. Circle around the hills behind the camp and village, then top the rise to get a good look at the shed. Easley pokes his head above the rocks and sees the houses and church, but the shed is gone. His bowels constrict, the bile rises in his throat. He scrambles around the back of the hill, then makes his way to where the shed used to be. Between the rocks, wet coal dust is all that remains. Easley is unsure of what to make of the despair he feels welling up inside. With a trembling hand, he pulls out the lemon rind and sticks it in his mouth to keep himself from crying.

And now the sound from the camp is unmistakable: a generator's *clunk* and *whir*. Men. Machines. Food and warmth. Easley sucks on the rind, considering—then walks straight toward the village.

The first house is silent. He peers through the windows at the shadows within. Where chairs, a table, and beds should be, he sees only emptiness. The walls devoid of pictures, calendars, or lamps. He walks around back of the small wooden home and tries the door. There is no lock. Carefully, he turns the knob, takes silent steps inside. A glance around the corner reveals only the top of a jar and some scattered papers. He pulls the door closed, presses his back against a wall as the wind tears through the cracks and seams. What happened to the people who built this home? Are they still alive somewhere? Were they relations of Tatiana? He slides down the wall until he's sitting on the floor.

EASLEY WAKES to the sound of a truck rumbling down the road. He holds his breath as the vehicle passes the house and continues onto the beach below. Falling asleep in the enemy's lap? Karl would be sorely disappointed. When Easley hears only wind, he rises to his knees and peeks through rippled panes. He sees no movement, save the distorted image of a lone soldier walking away from the village toward the camp. The man carries a large empty sack, his free hand moving to his lips every couple of strides. Cigarette.

Since the truck is on the beach, he will have to escape directly over the hill. He steps out the door and sees several bulging sacks near a large tank at the rear of the adjacent house. He pulls back against the wall.

Easley keeps low to the ground as he moves between buildings. When he reaches the second house, which is much like the first, he listens for signs of life. Hearing none, he opens the first sack. Heavy canvas with a metal clamp on top, Japanese characters stamped down one side. When this war is done, will we all be forced to learn Japanese? He pulls out a pair of trousers and a sock falls onto the grass. He reaches in for another sock, then shoves the pair into his pocket. He rifles through, finds a pair of trousers that might possibly fit, and stuffs it into his pack. He closes the first bag and opens the others: shirts, underpants. Easley grabs two of the latter, then puts the sack back the way he found it.

Roads. Houses. Other people's clothes. Despite the danger, this feels better than being left alone with his thoughts in the cave. Here, the immediate danger makes the world seem brighter, more alive somehow, the line dividing the real and the imagined more clearly defined. And yet the protective pull is strong. Tatiana is all alone.

As he moves beyond view of the village, Easley can sense he's being followed. Instead of fear, there is a warm surge of relief. And so this is how it ends. Unfamiliar with the customs of surrender, left with neither the desire nor a place to hide, Easley continues walking away from the harbor. They will shoot him in the back, or call out and he will raise his hands in the air. When neither happens, impatience rushes in. He reaches a ditch carved by a little stream. He drops down, hides behind the rise of grass and stone.

When at last Easley raises his head, he finds himself staring at the muzzle of a dog. It neither cowers nor barks. Instead, it sits on its haunches about six yards away, staring back at him. As it yawns, its ears pull back and its tongue curls out in a long, pink hook. Easley looks to see if the dog has betrayed his position but finds no sign. He gazes into the dog's inquisitive face. "C'mere."

The tail wags on approach.

"You speak English." Easley extends his hand in greeting. The hand is given a sniff, then the dog returns to its original position six yards away. Unsure of what to do next, Easley considers his companion—a small shepherd cross—but it gets up and turns to leave.

"Hey, boy. C'mere!"

The dog returns as requested, hindquarters swinging side to side. Easley is able to pet the dog this time; it clearly relishes the attention.

"Who sent you? They take you prisoner too?"

The dog sits down, allowing its head to be stroked. Around its neck is a thin yellow ribbon with some charm dangling at the chest. It turns out to be a coin with a hole punched through the middle. Japanese. The dog rolls over on its back, baring its belly for a rub.

Easley scratches and strokes. The dog rolls on its side and Easley buries his face in its fur. Sour. Dusty. Deeply comforting. The dog looks around at him with something like affection. For the first time in weeks, he feels almost human again. Then he feels the gnawing emptiness and his hands begin to shake.

The dog wriggles and scratches its back in the gravel. Easley reaches for his pack. He retrieves the parachute cord and measures out a length. He ties a slipknot, makes a loop at one end, then passes it over the dog's head. Easley rises to his feet with the rest of the rope in his hand. He looks back toward the village, scans the ridge, but finds no sign of pursuit. Satisfied, he bends down, cups the dog's face in his hands, then kisses the top of its head. Good boy. A deep sigh, a swift jerk on the cord, and the dog writhes like a fish on a line. It is all he can do to hold it out and away from his weakened body.

To end it, Easley jerks up again with all his might. The dog tries to cry out but the sound is cut off in its throat. It tries to bite the cord that remains beyond its reach. All of Easley's strength is required to hold the dog off the ground as it kicks and paws for air. Easley gives two more swift jerks and finally breaks its neck.

The dog's muscles relax as its rump is stuffed into the pack. Only half the body fits inside. To keep it from spilling out, Easley sits down and slips his arms through the loops of the pack, then pulls the cord over his shoulder so the dog's head—still tight in the noose—stays next to his own. He stands up, adjusts the load, then starts back the way he came.

Easley's strength is fading. The load is heavy and he is forced to rest several times. The forepaws work their way free and reach straight into the air. When Easley stops to repack the load, he avoids looking the dog in the face. Once he has the pack on his back again, its head lolls in time with his stride.

Soft fur teases his neck all the way back to the cave.

TWELVE

HEY WANDER THE STREETS OF ANCHORAGE IN search of souvenirs. Judith buys a fur hat that makes her look like a Cossack. She begs the other girls to try it on, but no one wants to ruin their hair. Helen buys postcards of Mount McKinley framed by a sky supernaturally blue. The cashier explains that the real mountain—North America's highest—is usually shrouded in cloud and that this is the only view she's likely to get. They are lucky to have postcards at all, the cashier says. The military confiscated most of the other landscape postcards for fear they might provide clues for the enemy.

Earlier this morning, they packed up and left Fort Richardson, made the short trip into town, and now find themselves with several hours to spare. As a treat, they all buy tickets to a matinee of Hitchcock's *Shadow of a Doubt,* which happens to star the elusive Teresa Wright. The theater, brand-new, has an art deco facade, which already seems hopelessly out of fashion. The carpeted lobby is surrounded in wood veneer. Framing the screen are towering copper reliefs of heroic men and machines extracting Alaska's natural resources. Helen leans back in the velvet seat. On the ceiling above, dim lights shine in the shape of the Big Dipper and North Star, as featured on the territorial flag. She finds herself in an unexpected oasis of civilization.

Fifteen minutes into the unsettling show, the projector jams, the film melts in two, and the screen goes blank. The girls sit in the dark, critiquing Wright's performance, awaiting further instructions. Eventually the house lights come up and an aged usherette props open the lobby door. They all get their money back and make their way to the train station.

As they listen for the all aboard, the girls take turns dancing with one another, each finally donning Judith's Cossack hat before taking the lead. The other girls stand bolt upright, chin out, trying to move in a very determined way, but it is Gladys who really pulls it off—better than most male leads. Helen takes her turn, then marvels at how seamlessly they all move between and with each other, for the benefit of no one beyond the oversize ravens preening themselves on the platform outside, glancing in through the windows.

THE TRAIN DEPARTS in the late afternoon. Remarkably, they are the sole occupants of the passenger car at the front of a long line of empty coal cars heading north to Fairbanks, the opposite direction of the Aleutians. Either a hawk, or some sort of eagle, makes lazy circles over hills that grow in size with each passing mile. John would know which bird it is.

There was no news of him at Fort Richardson. Helen's careful enquiries were met with crinkled brows, shrugged shoulders, the shaking of heads. Regardless, she continued to stick out her hand and introduce herself to everyone, hoping to meet pilots who had flown to the Aleutians, or knew men serving there. In lieu of the truth, she invented a cousin to ask after. She hasn't seen him in years, she says, but heard that he's stationed in the islands. Having carefully built her biography of lies, it is both easier and necessary to lie again.

After their second performance, a pilot came up and introduced himself. An unkempt man of perhaps thirty years with shadowed eyes and a week's worth of beard. He was on his way to Idaho on bereavement leave and wanted to personally thank her for the show. It had lightened his load in ways she can't imagine. When he told her that he had been stationed in the Aleutians for over a year, she caught her breath and pulled him aside.

Helen asked about her imaginary cousin. He gave it some thought, but then shook his head. He'd never heard of a Connelly from Olympia Washington. But between Dutch Harbor, Umnak, and Adak, there were thousands of guys out there. Wherever he was, the pilot assured her that he was most likely safe—for now.

Then she pressed: What about journalists? She had a friend who was a member of the press. Had he ever run into a reporter? His expression soured. In fact, he had run into a lady in Dutch Harbor who called herself a journalist. She took endless notes, asked questions about the welfare of the men. He told her that morale was low and insubordination on the rise. But when her story hit the wire services, it was a whitewash, he said. Made everything sound practically jolly. She must have been working for the Navy. He won't waste his time again.

Outside, day gives way to a cold, clear night. Among black spruce shadows, white paper birch reflects dim moonlight. As they pass a marsh, Helen sees a moose raise its rack and stare back at the passing train. Although in silhouette, this is the first moose she's ever seen. She feels the urge to jump up, point it out to Gladys, but they're past it in a blink. Beyond the tracks and telegraph line, there is no sign anyone has ever been in this place before. She turns and glances back to the end of the car, where Stephen buttons his sport coat as he pulls closed the lavatory door. He smiles and checks in with each girl, but chooses a seat next to Helen. In no time, he's sound asleep on her shoulder.

In the seat ahead, Sarah pulls out a pen and begins writing a postcard on a book spread across her lap. They have been warned not to mention the war in their correspondence; anything to do with their location, destination, facts about the soldiers or bases they've seen. They should limit their news to the weather, the songs they sing, how happy everyone is to see them. Soon, everyone's bowed over writing.

Judith suggests the girls draw pictures. She passes around her postcard, which features a flattering cartoon of herself belting out a song, surrounded by everyone else in something less than supporting roles. The bust of her self-portrait is out of proportion with reality by a factor of two. By the time the card makes its way back to her, someone has written "A Girl's Gotta Dream!" in a little marquee up above with arrows pointing at the voluminous breasts.

Helen takes comfort in the warm physical presence leaning into her, the scent of tobacco and aftershave. The weight, the heft of him is the most satisfying part. She considers his long legs, the knees pressed up against the back of the seat in front of him. For a moment she feels disloyal, then she catches herself. It is a strangely liberating sensation to have a man occupy such an intimate space without being a lover.

She reaches into her bag and pulls out a postcard. She pauses to think for a moment, then chooses her words carefully.

Dear Dad,

How I miss you! You would find Alaska fascinating. Big enough to be its own country. I've only met a few people actually from here, but I pity anyone who would attempt to fool with them. You can bet these folks know their way around a rifle. They don't think much of outsiders telling them what to do. I have the sense that, if things heat up around here, they could all just disappear into the bush and cause havoc 'til the end of time.

You would be impressed with how much we do with so little. The girls, and Stephen, somehow light the stage up each night. I can't tell you how much I miss you. I will be writing again soon with good news about having found our mutual friend.

Love,
Helen

She writes a second postcard to the parish priest at St. Brigid's, thanking him for checking in on her father once a week. To ensure he remembers his promise to her, Helen underscores her gratitude for his pastoral care and his many prayers for her family throughout the years.

And then she puts the postcards aside. The car gently shimmies and sways as the train makes a long bank to the east.

She is ambushed by the question she'd become adept at avoiding. Why hasn't John contacted her or his parents? No telephone call, letter, telegram, or postcard. No word sent through someone else. Silence. Of the dreadful possibilities, she prefers military stockade, but surely she would have been notified by the authorities. There is the reoccurring thought of him being taken prisoner by the Japanese. Beyond this, she will admit no further speculation without evidence. He is alive until proven otherwise.

THE TRAIN STOPS at a place called Curry, but no one is there to meet them. One by one, they step into the sharp night air and walk a short gravel path to a silent hotel that would serve as a set for Hitchcock. It is well built and brightly lit, but made ominous by the unbroken sea of night extending for hundreds of miles around. Inside, an adolescent bellhop sets his comic book aside to belatedly help with their bags. Behind the check-in desk, a man old enough to be his grandfather stirs to life and smiles mechanically as the girls approach. It is as if these two have been waiting in silence for months, putting off this inevitable disruption until the last possible moment.

They discover they each have a room to themselves upstairs, complete with proper spring mattress, washbasin, and towel. Luxury. Everyone agrees—this is more the style to which they hope to become accustomed. Helen closes the door, paces her room, then sits on her bed, wishing she had a thick Russian novel.

STEPHEN IS IN HIS UNDERSHIRT when he cracks open his door. Although it's midnight, it is clear she hasn't roused him from bed. His eyes are bright and the light is still on. He peers out from behind the door, hiding his lower half. "Can it wait 'til morning?"

"It's nothing, really. I just wanted to . . . This is silly. Good night."

He pulls suspenders up over his shoulders and looks both ways down the corridor.

"Forget it," he says. "Come in. Sit."

The solitary chair has his sports coat draped over the back—likely the only sports coat between here and the North Pole. She rests her hands on her thighs and sits forward to avoid crushing the collar.

"Everything all right?"

"I just wanted some company, that's all."

He reaches into his pocket and produces his flask. "You want a shot?"

She declines with a wave of her hand.

"I prefer not to drink alone, but I drink either way." He sits on his bed, unscrews the cap, and takes a sip. Then he twists the cap back in place definitively, as if he's just had his fill for the night.

"Do you mind if I sit for a while?"

"If you're willing to risk the rumors."

They sit across from each other for a few uncomfortable moments, at a loss for what to say. There is a stillness in the room, the hotel, and, it seems, the surrounding wilderness that makes her wonder if the end of the world has passed them by but they're simply too far removed to get the news.

"Okay," he says finally. "I'll start. Can I ask a question?"

Helen nods.

"Why're you here?"

She feels the blush bloom across her neck and face. "I told you I need the company."

"Up here, I mean. With us. For springtime in Alaska."

"To find someone . . . and bring him back."

"I hear you've been asking questions."

She pauses, holding back for one last moment, then finds she can no longer bear it. "I'm here to find my husband." How pathetic she must sound, abandoned, unaccepting. She takes a deep breath. "There's something sad about the way love boosts your confidence. You fool yourself into thinking you can do anything, but then . . ."

Stephen unscrews the cap again and takes another swig.

"He was always committed to his work," she says, feeling the cliché in a complaint that must echo across the generations. "But after his brother was killed in Europe, he took it up like a cross he had to bear."

Stephen offers her the flask again. This time, she accepts.

"His name is John. He's a writer. He used to write about wildlife and nature. Now he writes about war. He was in the Aleutians when the Japanese attacked, and he's one of the few journalists who could find them on a map. He feels he has a duty to get the story. He is the most honorable man I know. I also know he's somewhere in the Aleutians right now and he must be in trouble. All I want is to bring him home."

Helen tips the flask. She crinkles her nose at the harshness of the whiskey, wishing instead for a taste of her father's sweet rum. She watches Stephen sort the information, reconciling this new person with the one he knew before.

"You're married . . ."

"I'm sorry I didn't tell you. I was afraid that if the USO knew what I was up to they'd never let me come. Or that you would think I was some hysterical, jilted wife."

Stephen nods slowly, chooses his next move with care.

"Was there another woman?"

She shakes her head. This suggestion is dismissed with such swift assurance that Helen suddenly realizes it is a gift. Not once has she questioned whether she is the only woman in John's life.

"So, he left you for his work . . ."

"It's more complicated than that."

"Always is. Let me get this straight. You think you can find him in the Aleutians, convince him to pack it in and go home with you because you've come all this way."

"You make it sound so hopeless."

"Hopeless? I *know* it would work on me."

Helen studies his eyes and finds sincerity.

"So, tell me what he's like."

What's been long packed deep inside wells up with such force, she's barely able to get her hands in front of her face in time. At last, she weeps. Stephen gets up, grabs a clean undershirt from his bag, nods for her to take it.

"He's determined." She wipes her face, takes a breath. "He is kind and loyal to a fault. He can concentrate on one thing to the exclusion of all else. Once you've been the object of that kind of attention . . ."

"Sounds possessive."

"Devoted. You'd think he's quiet if you met him, but once you got to know him . . ." She brushes the hair away from her face. "And here I am in a musical review, chasing after him. I feel like a fool . . . He would have contacted me if he could. I need to do this carefully."

"Your secret's safe with me."

Stephen stands and extends his hands. Helen gently places hers in his. He helps her up and holds her in his arms.

"Sometimes I wonder if anyone will ever feel that for me," he says. "I've felt it for other people, but it never seems to come my way."

Stephen releases her with a kiss on the forehead, then fetches his wingtips, shoe brush, and polish. He sits down and sets about shining his shoes. It occurs to Helen that in relaying her story she may have triggered some memory for him.

"Stephen, is there—"

"It's late."

She nods, hands back his undershirt.

"You've seen how frantic they are up here," he says. "This war could change in a heartbeat. And we'll be heading toward the front . . . I just hope this guy deserves you."

* * *

THE SKY IS ASWARM over Fairbanks. Helen is so distracted by the roar and purr of aircraft flying in formation, circling overhead, landing in turn, she has to force herself to look down now and again as she walks along the airfield. One after the other, the planes bounce, then taxi down the runway. They park in haphazard rows near the edge of the pavement and the forest of stunted black spruce beyond.

Some of the pilots have to be lifted out of their seats and carried by other men. Others exit their plane on their own power, but then stumble after a step or two, grabbing hold of the ground crew for support. When Helen enquires what's afflicting these men, she's told no more than that they've been aloft so long that their legs have gone numb and useless. But at a dinner in their honor that night, Stephen is pulled aside and informed that it's all a part of Roosevelt's plan to send thousands of planes to the Soviets, quietly delivering them through the back door, from Montana to western Canada, then here to Ladd Field at Fairbanks. This is where the Soviets take over and fly them on to Siberia.

The following morning, the temperature plunges to minus ten degrees. Helen has never experienced air so cold that it burns her nose or causes her lungs to ache. Under her coat, she bundles up in several layers of clothes, covers her face with her scarf, but sees the Russians wandering between the airfield and barracks in relatively light coats and jodhpurs, trousers flared at the hip and tight at the knee. These are older, hardened men who, the Americans say, have considerable experience killing Nazis and seeing their own people slaughtered. To Helen they seem suspicious, ill at ease. When they catch sight of her and the other girls, they don't respond with the usual wide grin or comic flirtation. These men leer and stare. They whisper to one another and blow thin streams of smoke through bad teeth while sizing up their quarry.

In Helen's search for her invented cousin, she hears of American and Canadian pilots passing through on their way to serve in the Aleutians, but none coming back in this direction. There are about two thousand enlisted men and nearly as many civilians at Ladd Field. They are busy getting planes refueled and on their way west, constructing hangars and barracks, and conducting cold weather aeronautical research for arctic warfare. The men boast they've had perfect conditions of late. This past winter was one of the chilliest in memory, with drops to minus fifty-two degrees.

Their three-night run goes remarkably well. The show has gotten sharp and tight even as Helen feels her search unraveling. But then a thought occurs to her up onstage, staring out at the crowd of uniforms. A winning idea that has her flushed with hope again. What about that other organization with personnel in the islands, and around the world? Men who are bound and dedicated to helping their fellow men? That organization in which she is a lifelong member.

A CROSS HAS BEEN NAILED to the front of the last in a row of bleak Quonset huts. Icicles hang from the crossbar like feathers of out-stretched wings. A red candle glows inside the window, signifying the presence of the Blessed Sacrament. The pile of snow outside the door is pockmarked with discarded cigarettes. Helen knocks twice. Hearing no response, she lets herself in.

Rows of benches lead to a simple wooden altar at the back. The arching walls are unadorned, the room bare and utilitarian— practically Presbyterian, she thinks. Not a church, but a chapel. It is meant to welcome soldiers of every faith. She walks up the aisle and genuflects. As if freed by this gesture, a chaplain emerges from behind the screen. But he seems taken aback when he sees her. Like most men she encounters these days, he is unaccustomed to seeing a woman dressed in something other than a nurse's uniform. Under a heavy green cardigan, he wears a black shirt and white collar. He is perhaps forty-five, but exudes an air of authority and weariness that makes him seem far older. He fumbles with bifocals when Helen presents her hand. He introduces himself as the local chaplain, Father Michalski, and apologizes for the cold. The place never really warms up 'til it's packed full on Sunday.

"Father, I need help and I don't know where to turn."

"Well, with God's help let's see what we can do." He pulls a hand-kerchief from his sleeve, blows his nose, and stuffs it back down his wrist. "You're in the show tonight?"

"That's right."

"It's a great comfort to the men. But I'm sure I don't have to tell you that."

She smiles. "It's always nice to hear."

He studies her, tilts his back head for a better view.

"Having something to look forward to makes all the difference . . . Don't you think?" He doesn't wait for an answer. "Where's home?"

"Seattle. St. Brigid's parish."

"*Seattle*. The word's starting to sound nostalgic." He removes his glasses and pulls out the same handkerchief. He uses it to clean the lenses, then inspects the result. "What can I do for you?"

"Well, it's a private matter."

"You want a confession."

"No. But I was hoping to speak with you . . . in confidence."

"I see." He crosses his arms and cocks his head, preparing—it seems—to dispense judgment.

She's an adult, married woman, twenty-five years of age. Yet nothing changes. Perhaps he doesn't intend it, but the priest's gaze makes her feel like a nervous child. He gestures to the front pew, and they sit down together.

"My husband's a war correspondent. He was working in the territory when the government ordered them all out. But he came back."

"I see."

Again, he "sees." For Helen, this exchange has none of the release that comes from a good confession. It's as if he doesn't want to get involved.

"No one's heard from him in months."

"Well, if he's up here, against government orders, there's a good chance he's been caught. There's a great sensitivity about information, as you can understand."

"I believe he's in the Aleutians. Most likely, Adak."

"That's a long way from here."

"Well, I was hoping you might know someone out there. A fellow priest or pastor? Maybe you could contact him and see if he's heard anything about a reporter being captured, or . . ."

An airman enters the chapel and removes his cap and gloves. He meets the priest's eyes for less than a second, then sits shyly on a bench near the door.

"Mrs. . . . ?"

"Easley." A name she hasn't claimed in months.

He considers her expression, perhaps recalling what it was like to minister to women. Remembering a time when he was one of several priests in the rectory sharing the load, when he did not have to perform emotional triage on men regularly risking their lives.

"You must know there are other men missing." He lowers his voice. "Men in uniform. Now, I have a young airman waiting for me."

"People have a right to know what's going on up here, if this war is coming their way. This is American territory."

"Let's trust our president about what people should and shouldn't know." He puts a hand on her shoulder in a perfunctory manner that lets her know he's done it a thousand times before. "Can we arrange a time later?"

"Father, that's just it. I'm running out of time."

Father Michalski lifts a purple stole from a shelf next to the altar. He kisses it, places it over the back of his neck, then turns to face Helen again. "I'll make a call to the chaplain on Adak. I don't know if it will do you any good, but he has a feel for what's going on out there. Come back and see me tomorrow morning after breakfast."

Helen turns toward the man in the pew. Receding blond hair, the hunched shoulders of the condemned. He musters the strength to go in and face the priest.

On her way out, Helen glances down at his hands. Dark yellow stains begin at the bandaged wrists and disappear under the sleeves of his coat. In that moment, the man reaches out and gently touches the hem of her dress where it protrudes from under her coat. Stunned, Helen does not flinch or step away. The man neither looks up for permission nor moves closer to her leg. He simply traces swollen fingers underneath the hem, then lets it fall back in place again. Navy blue, with small flowers yellow and white. She glances back to see Father Michalski watching silently from the altar. The priest meets her gaze for only a second, then turns and disappears behind the screen.

The airman rises and Helen steps aside. He walks up the aisle, genuflects to the altar, then bows behind the screen. There is nothing left to do but pray. At first, she sits on the bench where the airman had been, but rises as soon as she senses his lingering warmth.

On her knees, she feels remote—from God, other people, herself. Regardless, she gives thanks for this new, slim chance.

At the door, she instinctively reaches a finger into the holy water font and finds it turned to ice.

THE FOLLOWING DAY, Helen returns as instructed to find the chapel locked. She bangs on the door until she's certain no one is inside. She marches to the office next door, where a plump airman is seated behind a desk. It's only midmorning, but he already seems weary. He forces a smile. The chaplain is in town ministering to the Indians, he explains, and won't be back until supper.

"He told me to meet him here this morning." Helen measures her tone, but leaves no mistake about her frustration. She never expected the priest's coldness toward her would develop into a complete rebuff.

"The last twenty-four hours have been difficult." He leans back in his chair. "His schedule's all shot to hell. We got word yesterday that a plane lost a month ago was finally found. Crew of six, still strapped in their seats . . . The chaplain was up all night waiting to receive the bodies."

"I'm so sorry."

The clerk hands her a folded slip of paper.

"He said you'd be by."

Dear Mrs. Easley,

Like myself, the chaplain on Adak works hand in hand with the chain of command. He makes it his business to keep track of the comings and goings from the island. He has no knowledge of any journalists visiting Adak. Reporters are not welcome at this time. My advice to you is to return home and await your husband's return, or notification through official channels. I wish you God's blessing. I will pray for you and your husband. Please pray for me.

Yours, in Christ,

Francis Michalski, Chaplain, Captain, USAF

THIRTEEN

THE STONES HAD BEEN SELECTED AND HAULED UP from the beach by the pack load. Easley dumped and sorted them at the mouth of the cave. The renovation project has been under way for two days and the end is now in sight. Karl would surely have been pleased.

The wall was a grand idea. The best he's had in weeks. It has given him something to think about—other than the fact that he can count his ribs, that his legs have withered to sticks, that he questions the difference between the real and the imagined. Still, he is feeling revived. For this he has the dog to thank. Seeing the wall take shape gives him the feeling of progress. He picks up a flat capstone and sets it snug in the new wall. He takes a step back into the mist and says, "Shoulda been a bricklayer!"

Easley speaks to himself as a reminder that he was once with other people. He sings to himself, recites poetry, puts on accents like actors in amateur Shakespeare. He has taken to describing aloud everything he does, so as not to lose track of what the point is supposed to be. Mostly, he speaks to the woman in the picture.

The wall rises clear to his chest. A narrow opening provides

access. It will help keep out wind and rain, make the most of the
fire within. Easley thinks it gives the place the look of one of those
ancient Pueblo cliff dwellings in Colorado, a little Mesa Verde. How
it might appear from the beach below, should the enemy happen by,
concerns him no more.

When finished, Easley changes out of his own filthy clothes and
into the new Japanese underpants, trousers, and socks. To celebrate
the completion of the project, he allows himself an extravagance
of coal. Easley never did find where the Imperial Japanese Army
moved the little coal depot, or locate another, but he did manage
to find a small cache inside one of the empty Aleut houses. Enough
perhaps for two meager, or one bright night. He now gathers a handful of dried grass and kneels to light the fire. When it becomes clear
the lighter won't work, he slides it back into his pocket. Although he
knows the lighter fluid is long gone, he had hoped for one final spark.
He covers his face with trembling hands.

Easley collects himself and stares down at the pile of kindling and
coal. He stretches out his hands, imagines the flames, the pinpricks in
his fingers and palms as the skin begins to thaw. Conjures the smell
of smoke, the loosening of muscles as the warm air swirls. Moves his
leg back a safe distance because the heat soon has these new trousers
too hot to touch.

If he turns and looks just now, will he find his shadow enlarged,
cast up on the wall of the cave? Then there would be two of him. A
kind of company.

There was a lecture in university. Plato? Prisoners in a cave,
chained in darkness their entire lives, held facing away from a fire kept
burning behind them. A parade of animals and people pass between
the fire and the prisoners, but the poor wretches see only the flickering
images on the back of the cave. Do these men perceive the difference

between real life and the shadows on walls that imprison them? Once released from the cave, shown light and life, they turn back to the cave because shadows are all they've ever known.

Better not sit with these thoughts too long. Best not turn around.

COME MORNING, Easley finds himself staring at the picture of Tatiana. He has memorized every fold in her coat, the way her black hair brushes her neck, the number of rivets in the wall of the ship. An old man stands behind her, his back turned to the camera. Easley cannot see his face but envies his proximity. And then it reveals itself: the pearl earring. Japanese pearl? How could he have missed it? She never fails to show him something new. He lifts the image to his lips.

NIGHTFALL BRINGS A LIGHT but steady wind. Sparking stars hold out hope of a few hours without rain. Easley pulls on the pack, slips the picture in his breast pocket, then marches out to meet his fate.

On the rise overlooking their camp, Easley counts three discernible sources of light coming from the tents below. It is astounding how so many men can remain so quiet. He can identify where the barracks are, as well as the big guns, a hospital, and, at the water's edge, what appears to be pens for submarines. Haphazard rows of tents, mounds, and the mouths of tunnels where they must hide from the reoccurring hail of bombs. All connected by muddy tracks and wooden planks. From hours of close observation, he can guess where they keep the food.

One of the lights blinks out and now there are two.

His night vision is well developed. He takes careful steps, keeping to the short grass to avoid the swish of boots through taller blades. As he walks toward the tents, the first blush of aurora borealis appears in the sky. He takes only a moment to look up at the gathering pink, then moves toward the outer perimeter of tents.

Each step demands a decision. Each new sound calls for rapid reassessment: the murmur of voices, peal of sudden laughter, the scrape of a file against metal. When Easley rounds the corner, he sees the calf and boot of a man disappear behind a tent. Shuffling steps melt into the distance. The snap of a tent flap opening. Easley cocks an ear next to the canvas of what he imagines is a mess tent, listens to the rustle of wind. He hears no movement inside. Silently, he lies down and rolls under the hem.

Inside, it is impossible to see. He bends his knees, holds his hands out in front, moves cautiously across the gravel floor. He runs fingers along the outline of a low table. After losing his way, he decides it is best to skirt the edges of the tent where there are fewer obstructions and, if need be, he can quickly lie down and roll outside again.

He breathes in meals that have been here before. The odor of cooked meat is overwhelming. Beef. Pork. Fish. Meals forgotten come roaring back as if he's tasting them again. The power of old smells. He searches with fingertips, discovering pots and pans. Next to the stove is a large metal trough, like those found in barnyards. Next, a crate with dozens of tin bowls nestled one inside the next. Despite this careful search, he finds nothing to eat.

The stove is large and low. It catches his pant leg above the knee. When he reaches down to free himself, he cuts the heel of his hand on a flange. His blood tastes of coins.

Men walk past, boots heavy on the path, in the throes of an argument. One man, trying to convince the other of something, speaks in a beseeching tone. The second man interrupts angrily. This puts the conversation to rest.

If they find him, they will thrown him to the ground, boot him in the ribs. Once they see that he is unarmed and starving, they will put their weapons away and beat him. This will soften him up for the interrogation sure to follow. They'll want details about where he's from and what the Allies are doing; how many planes they have, their plans in general and specific. He will tell them all he knows, transposing the crucial details. Then they'll beat him for lying.

Down in the gravel, on hands and knees. Maybe one of them dropped a dinner roll. Do Japs eat rolls?

Back at the stove, bits of charred fat are stuck to the grill. Picking them off, licking fingers clean, triggers memories of summer barbecues, of his father laying steaks over leveled coals. Potato salad. Corn on the cob. Butter and salt. Salt. He'd kill for a lick of salt. His mother wanting to know if he can eat another dish of ice cream.

"Yes, please," Easley whispers.

He holds the grill in his hands, listening. The murmur and laughter are gone; only the rustle of wind remains. He closes his eyes for a moment, then attempts to fit the grill back in place. It won't go willingly. When he tries an adjustment, it clanks against the frame.

The conversation flares up again. The men shout over one another, trying to make a point. Easley winces, as if the words were meant for him. Someone else walks past at a fast clip. Easley lies down on his belly, slowly lifts the hem of the tent, peers across the gravel. A few more men can be heard rushing past, but he sees no boots. Then the sound seems to die away. He crawls free of the tent, hears bootsteps closing in. Easley stands, brushes dirt from his jacket, shoves his hands into his pockets in the hopes of blending in with the random silhouettes in the dark. He can think of nothing better to do. A man walks past, gazing up at the sky, oohing and ahhing in equivalent Japanese. Perhaps five foot six—they all seem undersized. Surely this man's aware of the looming presence, but he never looks into Easley's face. Easley turns and walks away.

Men emerge from tents, mouths agape, heads tilted back like chicks in a nest. Following their line of sight, Easley looks up and sees a neon curtain of green and red rippling across the sky. An astonishing display of Northern Lights. As it passes overhead, individual blades of light stab down toward the earth before pulling back again.

This is the moment, the distraction that will allow him to pass undetected. Allow him to avoid capture and beating in exchange for dying in the cold alone. Could this be Tatiana's doing?

Someone steps out of a tent and lights a cigarette. The lighter's flash reveals dark eyes and a young Japanese face. Now in silhouette, the man takes a steady pull on the cigarette and appears to look directly at Easley. Then, like having caught the eye of an acquaintance he'd rather avoid, Easley turns and walks away from the man without haste, pretending he never saw him.

Easley listens for the shout that fails to come. He travels fifty yards before allowing himself a quick shoulder check. The sky ablaze like Dominion Day, or the Fourth of July. The soldier stands in silhouette by the tent. Easley puts his head down and carries on.

* * *

TWO DAYS ON, Easley is picking mussels in the midday fog when he hears their approach. Fingers stiff and numb, and yet he's managed a sizable batch. When he realizes what's happening, he quickly slides the pack over his shoulder and wades around a boulder. Waves rush into his boots and up his thighs—water so cold it feels as if his feet are aflame.

There are four of them. They appear on the ridge, one following the next, less than half a mile from the cave. This is the closest they've ever come. They move like men lost, stopping with hands on hips, turning their heads every which way. They pass the beach where Easley is hiding and continue up into the hills.

He eventually dries off, changes into the Japanese socks and the boy's drier boots, but it will take the balance of the day for the ache in his feet to subside. Following another quick check for intruders, he cracks and eats the mussels before returning to the cave and falling fast asleep.

A PLANE BUZZES THE BEACH in the late afternoon the following day. The fog has lifted, the temperature has dropped. Steel wool clouds press down toward the land. The pilot makes the most of the space in between. When the plane passes overhead a third time, Easley thinks about running out with his hands up in the air. Instead, he peeks around the lip of the cave and sees twin blood suns underneath the wings as the plane banks out over the sea.

When the drone of the engine fades away, Easley is left with firm conclusions. Hope and fear are worn out from overuse, only facts remain. Fact One: everything dies eventually. Fact Two: dying is preferable to living alone with the silence and cold and a mind that betrays. Fact Three: he is too much of a coward to die. Fact Four: the smallest victories can rush like a drug through the veins.

Easley reaches for the tea tin high up on its shelf. He pries open the lid and unfolds the note. He reads it again, and again, and again—reveling in the fact that he still remembers how to read.

The wind is not a river.

He puts everything else back inside the can and sits down at the fire pit. He tears bits of paper from around the edges of the still dry note, leaving the words intact. When he finishes, he holds the margin-less note in one hand and a pile of small white petals in the other. He puts the note back in the can, returns the can to its shelf. He takes out Tatiana and props her up on a rock so she can see.

He flips open the empty lighter, pulls the wick away from the casing, presses it against his cheek. Still damp. To beat evaporation, he quickly places it in the bits of paper. With his thumb, he flicks the wheel until he gets a spark, but it is too far from the wick. He tries again, but the spark won't come. The flint is worn to a nub.

"Help me."

Easley quickly takes the guard off the striker and uses his thumbnail to bend the flint closer to the wheel. There's almost nothing left. He kneels down over the drying wick and turns the wheel again. The spark jumps from his hands, to wick, to paper. The flame spreads from paper to grass. It isn't long until the coal is aglow.

Easley holds his palms out over the fire, reminding himself of the pope in newsreels, blessing the multitudes at Saint Peter's Square. When it is clear the fire will survive, he presses his hands together.

His shadow on the back of the cave is sharply defined. It expands his frame into something large and threatening. But this fire is no illusion. The heat reflecting off the newly constructed wall allows him to dry his clothes and boots. It is so warm that he removes his jacket. He looks up at the little picture of Tatiana, reflected firelight flickering at her feet. When he holds it just so, the glass becomes a mirror. Staring back, he sees a pair of deep-set eyes he does not trust. Mangy beard on sunken cheeks.

He removes all of his clothes. He stands dangerously close to the flames.

THE LIGHT OF DAWN reveals a fresh delivery of snow. Although wet, and a mere two inches deep near the beach, more significant accumulation can be seen at higher elevations. And this is the month of May. Having just stepped back inside after surveying the scene, Easley pauses when he hears the crack and rumble of an avalanche in the mountains above. He hustles back out into the open to see if danger is headed his way.

He looks up to see the small avalanche expend itself below a man skiing across the slope. The skier makes elegant arcs, pausing on the lip of one bowl before sliding down the next. This isn't about moving efficiently across newly fallen snow, it appears as if the man skis for pleasure. Easley watches from the beach for a few moments before hustling up the hill and out of the line of sight. The snow comes alive with floaters.

The shallow creek is a black scar in the fresh white face of the land. To avoid leaving tracks in the snow, Easley sacrifices his boots and feet to the cold water, tracing the creek upslope. Half an hour later, when he reaches the top of the hill, he crouches down and scans for more intruders. Seeing no one else, he keeps low, stalking through the snow on all fours, until he sees the Japanese soldier standing some two hundred yards away. The man holds binoculars to his eyes, focusing down on the beach.

Easley's stomach twists as he backs away from the edge. He takes a few deep breaths. To ensure his mind is not playing tricks, he risks a second look. But he finds himself alone. Easley makes his way over to where the clean tracks came to a halt, where the soldier's skis and poles made a mess of the snow, then he bounds down into the bowl. With flagging energy, he trudges up the other side and peers out over the edge in time to see the graceful, swaying turns as the skier closes in on the cave.

RAGE AND POSSESSIVENESS clamber up over Easley's fear. In the face of recent ambivalence about his own fate, the force of it startles him. Of this godforsaken island, that hiding place—its memories and treasures—are his to preserve and keep.

By the time Easley descends to the top of the ravine, the sun's burned through and the air is warming up. On south-facing patches down near the beach, he notices the snow is as thin as lace. There is snow enough, however, to show the parallel tracks that stop near the low edge of the ravine. There, the intruder abandoned skis and poles, and continued on foot. He is inside the cave.

The click of stone on stone issues from within. The thought of the enemy reaching the back of the cave, handling Tatiana's photo, her clean white embroidery, causes Easley to buckle at the knees. He pulls back from the edge and searches the snow for a rock of suitable proportions. From the dike Karl made, he removes one the size of a cantaloupe. He carries it to the edge and holds it in unsteady hands.

A pate of black hair emerges some three stories below. The target stops, turns round, glances back inside. Easley makes swift calculations, lines up, then lets the boulder fall. Dull thud on impact. The man collapses like a marionette. What a surprise, how easy this is.

Easley scrambles down the slope, to where blood now bubbles from the intruder's mouth in bright red foam. From his throat comes a clicking noise that doesn't sound human. Easley stands over him, watching him die, wondering how long it will take. Suddenly, the man lets go of the fur hat clenched in his hand. His elbows push back in an attempt to sit up again. It is the deep, reptilian part of the brain telling the body to jump up and run. It too has been irreparably damaged. The man's arms flail at his sides, unable to make sense of gravity.

Easley crouches in the snow beside the intruder and puts his arm around the man's neck. The body still tries to mount some kind of escape. Easley grabs the back of his head with one hand, the forehead with the other—black hair oily to the touch. One swift snap and the struggle comes to an end.

The hat is still warm when Easley pulls it over his ears.

He steps through his new stone wall, waits for his eyes to adjust. First, he looks up to the tea tin, which is still snug in its place on the shelf beside the book with the memories of Karl. The nest is undisturbed. And there is Tatiana in her frame. Although her eyes have witnessed the enemy intrusion, she seems unmoved by the crime or Easley's response. Finally, he sees a box in front of the fire pit.

Easley missed it at first because it is nearly the color of stone. Shallow and square, like a box of chocolates. Japanese characters on top. He removes the cardboard lid and finds the box packed with sardines, a ball of rice, hard yellow candies wrapped in clear cellophane. A note, in English, written on the back of the lid:

Brave Yanqui
I see you on night of lights
Come to give yourself in and you will be OK
With honor
Sgt. Major Uben Kubota

Easley stands over the body, perhaps twenty-five years old. He notes a pistol holstered on the belt. He takes it up in his hands. Even their guns seem smaller.

He studies the face of Uben Kubota, the same face he believes he saw reflected in the lighter's flame. What is beyond doubt is that whoever saw Easley that night could have easily shot him then and there. Why allow the escape? Treachery, pure and simple. Why else show up on a ski holiday with a box of sardines and candy? What is this, the Welcome Wagon? An attempt to soften him up, make him feel like the Japanese aren't so bad after all. Perhaps a little warm rice wine when he turns himself in. Just a few details of what the Allies have in store and everyone can part friends. Pen pals, even.

"Fuck you, neighbor."

An officer won't return to barracks tonight. A search party will leave at dawn's first light. Perhaps it is better to save everyone the trouble. A swift slug through Easley's own temple would solve problems that now seem entirely beyond his control.

He watches the wind tease the thick black hair, then looks to the horizon.

Some men have the great misfortune to stand at life's continental divide and see that the land beyond is barren. There is no hope of turning back. What does one do with this view?

It takes the rest of the day, but then the answer descends on him like a revelation. Easley's eyes open wide, he stands to greet its arrival. It is the phrase, the riddle he has been repeating like a prayer. It is, of course, Tatiana.

The wind is not a river.

Her chain of islands that dares to separate the North Pacific from the Bering Sea. A chain through which the wind whips into some of the world's most fearsome storms. One minute it's a hurricane, the next a breeze. But rivers! Rivers flow throughout the seasons—under bright summer sun, plates of winter ice—morning, noon, and night. Wind rises up and fades away, but a river flows endlessly.

And our suffering? This too shall pass. The wind is not a river.

FOURTEEN

I T IS KNOWN AS THE "ALEUTIAN STARE," THE WAY THEY gaze into the distance unfocused, unspeaking. To Helen, it appears like a kind of dread. Three men afflicted with the condition wait at the side of the runway as Stephen and the girls step down off the plane on Adak, at last. The men wear canvas straitjackets and stand alongside the military police. When it comes time to board their plane, the MPs help each man navigate the steps, gently pushing his body up through the hatch. These men are being removed to a stateside mental asylum.

"Sorry that's the first thing you have to see." Sergeant Cooper combs his black hair with his fingers, but it's so short this effort makes no perceptible difference. He's beaming. The idea of escorting women around the base clearly gives him a charge. Above his broad smile is a pencil thin mustache, which has gone out of fashion due to its popularity among the fascists.

Helen takes a moment to recover some shred of the soaring hope she felt on first sighting the island through the clouds, her palpable sense of proximity to John. Despite the chaplain's note, she remains convinced that this is where he's most likely to be.

Adak is six hundred miles west of the mainland, two hundred and fifty miles east of the Japanese on Kiska. Attu is farther still. It's not nearly as cold as it was in Fairbanks, and this comes as a surprise. Four empty jeeps are idling, each covered with a canvas top to protect occupants from the driving wind and rain. The troupe and its luggage are divided among the vehicles. Helen slides in back next to Gladys, who reapplies makeup as their bags are loaded.

Tracks of land have been recently cleared of what appears to be rolling fields of barley. Fifteen thousand men are stationed here and the place looks like an open quarry. Through the jeep's mud-splashed windshield, Helen can see neither tree nor bush of any description. From the towering fir and hemlock of Prince Rupert to the stunted spruce of the Alaskan mainland, she has watched forests and trees shrink in size until they disappear altogether. On this island, it's as if no living thing above waist height stands a chance against the wind.

The airfield is vast. At the moment, it might not appear as hectic as Ladd Field at Fairbanks, but as Sargent Cooper explains, that can change in short order. "We are the main base of strike operations against the Japs. From here, we fly bombing runs to Kiska and Attu. We aim to pound the daylights out of them until they scurry back into the sea."

The "runway" is unlike anything they've seen before. Instead of concrete or gravel, it consists of identical sheets of metal grating cinched together in a vast quilt stretching hundreds of yards atop the saturated sand of a recently drained lagoon. Shallow ponds of rainwater form throughout. Cooper pulls over and they all watch another plane come in for a landing. The metal surface buckles in rolling waves as it touches down, tires sending up great plumes of spray, as if landing on a lake.

Then they all stare as the plane with those three bound and broken men skips and splashes before leaping into the sky.

Sergeant Cooper drives with his face near the windshield, hands together atop the steering wheel. He tries and fails to avoid potholes so deep they make the engine hiss. Given what Helen has seen so far, he seems inordinately happy to be here. Stephen sits beside him with his hand braced against the dashboard.

A city of pyramid tents and Quonset huts has been built between wind-whipped puddles. Smoke flies wild from the tops of the tents. Men shuffle between shelters with shoulders hunched, picking their way through the quagmire. Dogs gambol about, seeking and finding affection from any one of innumerable passing masters. Everything is the color of hay, smoke, and khaki green. The red of Gladys's lipstick stands out from its surroundings like a desert bloom.

There are hangars, warehouses, offices, recreation buildings, mess halls, and countless tents separated by fields of mud. Some of the buildings are connected by wooden planks or boardwalks. The power lines strung along the roads are the tallest features on the landscape, aside from distant hills and peaks. Sergeant Cooper points out all of this with a kind of civic pride that makes Helen feel sorry for him.

"There was next to nothing on this island eighteen months ago," he says. "The place was uninhabited. We built this all from scratch."

Gladys feigns genuine interest in the sergeant's commentary. She sits at the edge of the seat with her head bobbing up and down. Helen leans back and stares out at the men walking muddy paths. They stop and return the gaze, wondering if they can trust their eyes.

"You'll be attracting plenty of attention," Cooper observes. "We have a saying out here: 'There's a woman hiding behind every tree in the Aleutian Islands.'"

They are greeted at their quarters with the news that Judith has been ill. Queasy on the plane, the jeep ride finally did her in. Forced to skip the driving tour, the other girls arrived at their quarters before them. The Quonset hut they've been assigned is ordinarily reserved for visiting officers. It has a dry wooden floor—a luxury on Adak, where most residents are forced to camp on bare ground. The room is half the size of the one in Fairbanks and is designed for a single man. Six cots have been brought in and lined up side by side. Judith sits at a little table beside the window, head in her hands, muddy shoes splayed out before her. Helen thinks she can see a little blob of vomit on the tip of Judith's shoe.

Judith lifts her head. "A little morning sickness," she declares. "Nothing a good scotch can't cure."

Helen appears to be the only one who doesn't find this amusing. She turns and seeks out the kettle. Before the water boils, she's rounded up a stash of tea, a bucket, and the last of her own saltine crackers. She wets a towel with some of the hot water and hands it to Judith, who wipes her face gratefully.

The other girls busy themselves unpacking. They exchange knowing glances, hoping they won't catch whatever Judith's got, wondering how they are ever going to perform with their lead in such a state.

Stephen lights his pipe and leans up against the door. "It was a bumpy ride," he says. "Good night's sleep and she'll be rarin' to go."

Everyone hopes this is true. Stephen fetches a length of rope and hangs wool blankets to separate Judith's cot from the rest of the room. As he works, he declares that this is being done for Judith's sake, for her peace and quiet, but it's clearly aimed at quarantine. Finally, Stephen slings his bag over his shoulder and sets out to find where he'll be lodging for the night.

THE WHINE OF ENGINES warming up on the airfield begins before dawn. At 06:10, Judith wakes the entire room to go outside and wretch. An hour later, Stephen arrives to collect Sarah and Jane to view the stage and take the piano for a spin. At half past eight, Helen and Gladys take their turn visiting the hospital.

The air inside is warm and moist, having circulated through the lungs of thirty-two patients in this ward alone, perhaps hundreds more throughout the facility. Helen and Gladys remove their coats as each open eye gazes back at them with a kind of wonder. Gladys takes a step closer to Helen and whispers, "They're undressing us in their minds."

Gladys wears her royal blue dress and white silk scarf with a rhinestone brooch in the knot, the brooch her mother gave her for good luck on this journey. Having never met her own father, having grown up under the tutelage of a strong woman on the outskirts of Chicago, Gladys has honed many of the feminine skills Helen feels she lacks. Gladys knows how to read the ever-shifting social winds, build consensus in her favor, lead without the appearance of leading. She is fluent in a language Helen never had a chance to learn.

This morning, Gladys's flaxen hair is curled back over her forehead and collected in a snood. Her nails have a fresh coat of red, and Helen thinks Gladys looks about as good as a woman could a thousand miles from the nearest salon.

The doctor is all of twenty-eight years old but carries himself like a surgeon general. He takes great pleasure in announcing the girls to his patients. Helen is pleased to see a few female nurses on hand, and yet as Helen and Gladys approach, they shrink into the background. There is a general stir as the men hike themselves up into seated positions, cover exposed limbs, square shoulders, smooth down cowlicks, close open robes. Those who are able, applaud.

Pinups are tacked in great collages over their beds. There are the standard-issue Betty Grables and Rita Hayworths, but also snapshots of mothers and girlfriends representing a remarkable range of sizes and orthodontic predicaments. One boy has a picture of his horse.

Helen feels moved to touch. She holds hands, strokes arms, brushes hair off their brows. The urge to comfort and protect. This, and the constant awareness that each man might have met her husband.

They declare their name and rank, tell her where they're from, describe their injuries. When they announce that they have sweethearts back home, Helen nods but can't help but wonder how many of those girls are still waiting. The part that moves her the most is how forthcoming they are about their commitments. As if Helen's presence at the side of their bed calls for uncommon chivalry. As if she needs to be reminded that, at present, it would be improper to allow romance to blossom between them.

There are burns and broken bones. One patient has a tube running out of his chest into a jar of puss, another has his neck in a brace. The doctor explains that the bullet wounds were all received from antiaircraft fire erupting up and into the backsides of airmen on bombing runs over the Japanese stronghold on Kiska. Some of these men flew back to base with dead comrades seated beside them. Two have been miraculously pulled from the sea. Most, however, are victims of exposure. So far, the weather has claimed more casualties than the enemy.

One boy, with rust-colored hair and freckled cheeks, reclines atop the covers, flipping through a tattered sports magazine. His legs are crossed at the ankles and one foot taps out some unheard tune against the other. Helen learns that Petty Officer, Second Class Michael Kenny threw his back out unloading planes. He did it once before, but this time it's much worse. Might be a slipped disk, he explains in an Arkansas drawl. They give him morphine for the pain and the promise he'll be assigned lighter duties once his condition improves. He apologizes for the unglamorous nature of his injuries. Helen asks how long he's been here.

"On Adak, just over a year. In here, three days."

"That's quite a while. Must drive you crazy." She immediately regrets the choice of words.

He shrugs. "Some folks, I suppose."

"It's a shame people back home don't know the first thing about what you boys are going through. The newspapers hardly ever mention it."

"It's the blackout. That'll change when the movie comes out."

"Movie?"

"They came up here and shot a documentary picture. Filmed bombing runs in Technicolor. John Huston. I helped his crew shift their gear all over the place. I flew with them on a sortie out to Kiska, helped their cameraman keep his tripod from falling out the hatch. When the censor releases it, everyone'll know."

This is as close as she's come. This place, these men. She can feel the distance narrowing. "Have you heard of other reporters, journalists, coming through?"

A slight wince mars Kenny's face as he shifts position. "They all got kicked out ages ago. This place is tighter than a drum. You should see what they do to our letters. Any news you read about this place comes straight out of Washington, D.C."

All at once, her doubt is unleashed. Maybe John isn't here. Maybe he never even made it this far.

Gladys approaches from the other end of the ward, swinging her hips, waving at the men along the way. She smiles down at Kenny and motions for him to shove over. She makes herself at home on the cot, her hip pressed against his thigh. "This man looks perfectly fine to me," she declares.

Kenny blushes, sits up a little straighter.

Gladys glances at her watch. "We'd better make a move. Stephen will be getting antsy."

They wish Kenny luck, then pay quick calls on a few more

men—leaving lipstick on as many cheeks as possible. Before they leave, the doctor thanks them and tells them what wonderful work they're doing, lifting the spirits of the men. Wishes he could bottle it, he says. Best kind of medicine there is.

THE GIRLS SIT in the mess hall awaiting the big announcement. They have the place to themselves, except for a squat, aproned man stacking mugs on a shelf along the far wall. On Adak the officers and men take their meals together. Helen has noticed a loosening of protocol on this far island, longer hair and scruffy beards, salutes rarely seen. Now it appears as if the man is stacking, moving, and restacking mugs just so he can ogle them a while longer. Helen feels the hours available for her search draining away.

At last Stephen arrives, packs his pipe, and tells them what they already know—that Judith will not be performing. Long sighs and pouts all around. Judith is the foundation upon which the show has been built. In the absence of Teresa Wright, Judith sings the lead on most of the songs in their repertoire. With neither star nor understudy, should they cancel tomorrow's show? Pack it in and go home? Stephen is building toward inspiration.

Sarah wastes no time knocking him down. "Absolutely. There is no 'show' without Judith."

Helen feels a tightening inside.

"Not so fast." Stephen rests his foot on the bench and leans in. "We *postpone*. We divvy up her songs and spend the afternoon in rehearsal. We get the show ready and perform tomorrow night. If Judith gets better, we put her in. If not, we press on without her."

"*If* we agree, who gets what?" Gladys lights a cigarette. She sees the opening but waits for it to come to her.

"Well, for starters, you get 'One for My Baby' and 'Time Goes,'

Sarah gets 'Don't Fence Me In' and 'Tangerine,' Helen gets 'The Nearness of You.'"

No one speaks. The distant rumble of bombers returning home. Helen knows she must act. This cannot be allowed to spin out of control, threaten their presence on Adak.

"No offense," Sarah says, glancing at Helen, "but why don't you just drop 'The Nearness of You.'"

Gladys's eyes grow large. She turns toward Jane, in search of another ally.

"It's not Helen's fault." As Sarah digs in, her mouth goes tight and small. "That song is trickier than it seems. It calls for perfect pitch and timing. Maybe we're better off getting out while we're ahead."

"Maybe I'm in charge of this goddamn show." Stephen jumps to his feet and nods, agreeing with himself. "Maybe I should get a little credit for knowing what I'm doing."

Sarah crosses her arms. "Am I the only one who remembers what happened back at Fort Richardson?" Now she's up on her feet, too riled to sit. "I mean, we have to be honest with one another. Helen's fine with backup and melodies. She can dance better than I can, but you're putting her in a position—"

Stephen raises his hand. "That's enough."

"No, she's right." Helen looks directly at Sarah. The moment has come to show her hand, lay out the truth before them. "Please, you two, sit down."

Stephen is reluctant to surrender the floor. At last, he sits and looks up at Helen with a baffled expression, awaiting her next move.

"It's true," Helen explains. "I don't have the experience you do, experience I tried to pretend. Outside high school, I'd never performed in front of an audience." The liberation of confession is sudden, overwhelming. "Everything I've told you about performing was a lie designed to get me to the Aleutian Islands so I could find my husband, a writer who's not supposed to be here, but I hope to God he is."

They all look to her hand for a ring.

"I've kept all these things from you because I was afraid I'd get passed over or sent home. I didn't tell you because I'm embarrassed to have lost my husband. I can't imagine the future without him . . . And because telling you might make you feel sorry for me, which I can't abide. I have never lied to anyone the way I've lied to you. I'm sorry."

Gladys looks at Stephen, then Sarah. Jane can't take her eyes off Helen. The pause is brief, but excruciating. It is Gladys who brings it to an end. She gets up, throws her arms wide open, and embraces Helen. "God," she says. "That's romantic." Jane, and then even Sarah close in. Never before has Helen felt such a flood of feminine affection.

At last, Helen says, "Sarah should sing the song."

"This is all very touching," Stephen says. "But Helen is going to sing it. She's improved more, and faster, than the rest of you. She's a strong all-around soprano. And she has the kind of presence that song needs . . . As far as padding résumés is concerned, I think it's safe to say we're all guilty as charged."

Helen is at once humbled and overwhelmed.

"All we have out here is each other," Stephen says. "I need you to trust me. Let's meet back here at thirteen-hundred hours."

REHEARSAL SPACE ON ADAK is at a premium. Privacy, a quaint memory. Everywhere Helen turns men gawk as if she's some sort of circus attraction.

She borrows Judith's umbrella, grabs the sheet music, and marches out toward the hills wondering whether—despite Stephen's glowing review—she's about to let them down again onstage tomorrow night. Whether her father was able to wake up this morning and if the neighbors will be home if he's forced to stagger over for help. If she's wrong, and John's not on this island, how is she ever going to find him? In search of answers, she only piles on the questions. All her research, plans, schemes, and lies have brought her to this improbable place. She has no fallback plan. She must move swiftly, efficiently, make each hour count.

Helen trades the muddy road for the flat, sodden weeds until she's well away from everything, save the wind. She stops, keeping her back to the tents and unwanted observers.

She spreads the sheet music between her fists. Rain taps the paper with a dissonant beat. Regardless, she lifts her chin and sings.

FIFTEEN

ASLEY TOSSES THE SKIS AND POLES INTO THE gully and considers their effect on the overall composition. The face of Uben Kubota rests directly atop the gravel, his arms outstretched as if to embrace the land. The stream washes over the left boot and calf. Suspecting the skis might be too far away, Easley scrambles back down a third time and kicks one closer to the body. It gives him a twinge of regret to leave the man this way, but there is little choice in the matter. It is his faint hope that it will appear as if Kubota slipped and fell to his death.

Over the past few days, the Americans have been hammering the enemy harder than at any time since Easley arrived over a month ago. Yesterday afternoon, and again today, the skies broke open with P-36s and B-24s spilling untold tons of explosives on the Japanese encampment. The intensity of the attacks is likely the only thing that keeps a search party from setting out in pursuit of Kubota. But now, the skies fall silent. Soon they will be coming for him.

So rapidly does the snow lose ground to the rain, it is difficult to remember its completeness the day before. On this, his second attempt to dump the body, Easley has been careful to haul it to the base of a cliff a full quarter mile toward the camp and away from the cave. It has taken several hours and all of his strength. He is soaked to the skin and shivering.

Easley returned the pistol and fur hat, and resisted the urge to take the coat—which is warmer and in much better shape than his own or Karl's. He rifled through every pocket in search of a lighter and cigarettes. He found instead a flask of water, two wet and crumbling matches, a broken watch, a spare button, lint. He did take the scarf, gambling on the chance that its absence would go unnoticed.

On his return to the cave, Easley hooks his thumbs into the waist of his trousers and holds them away from his skin. His hip bones have become so sharp that sores have formed where they rub against the filthy material. He walks like this back toward the cave, reveling in the temporary relief, never looking round to see if he is being watched— never looking back toward the body.

Should anyone be watching, he'd provide quite a spectacle. Easley wonders what his kid brother would say if he could see him now. So many times during this ordeal he has wondered what Warren would have done. Where Easley always played by the rules, Warren instinc- tively did end runs around every rule or convention. He was usually too careful to find himself in compromising situations, reliably able to charm his way out of the few he could not avoid. When all else failed, he'd turn to his older brother.

Six years ago, Warren found himself in that rarest of predica- ments, facing a problem he could not outmaneuver. He got a girl preg- nant. A girl his parents were never to know about, a girl who wanted nothing more to do with him. This was well before Warren landed his job with the timber company. Easley loaned him money to support the girl while she waited for the day she would hand over their child for adoption and put this mistake behind her. Warren wept openly, and was sullen much of the time, but finally agreed not to call or visit her, to simply leave her be.

It now seems Easley will take the knowledge of this abandoned child with him, along with his and Helen's own regrets, along with his parents' belief that they are the end of their line.

WHEN EASLEY RETURNS to the cave, Tatiana is waiting for him in front of a roaring fire. He is not surprised to see her sitting there, to smell her skin, soap-fresh from the bath. He is aware that she has entered the cave through his imagination. He chooses not to hold this fact against her—then suddenly changes his mind.

Easley rushes back out into the ravine and stares into the smoke gray sky. He tracks a growing swarm of floaters in his vision until he is dizzy and forced to sit down. Easley can see and feel his body getting weaker, feel it lightening, preparing to float away. He can still tell the difference between the real and the imagined, but for how much longer? How many more hours spent waiting, wandering, hiding from what's certain to come? The cave contains his only consolations, however they came to be. Must he deny himself the last comfort this cold hell affords?

She sits in the same dark coat she wore in the photograph, weaving a basket from blades of rye. She looks up at him and smiles. Easley does not disturb her. He continues up to his nest and lies down on the silk parachute. She hums a tune he is convinced he has heard before. When he asks how her day has been, she smiles and looks up at him. He feels something come unstuck, then begin to flow.

He tells her how tired he is and how he's ready to sleep forever. He explains that he came to this island to show the world what is happening here but has failed so utterly. Landing feet first in the snow, the hunger and cold. Hunting with Karl, releasing him to the sea.

How he tries and fails to conjure Helen. A punishment, he has come to believe, for the way he took his leave. How the past now seems to have forsaken him. Perhaps everything that went before was preparation for this, for Tatiana.

She tucks and weaves the blades of rye. Fingers graceful and long. The basket takes shape in her hands. Despite the outward flow of affection, there is sadness as he watches her work, knowing she could vanish any minute. He wants to both gather her up in his arms and scatter her like a reflection in a pool. He stands paralyzed, gaping by the fire. Her song surfaces above the hum, she gives words to the tune.

> *"A-tisket a-tasket*
> *A green and yellow basket*
> *I sent a letter to my love*
> *And on the way I dropped it . . ."*

Planes growl overhead. The Americans are at it again. Tatiana lets the words fall away, but hums a little louder to drown out the noise. Antiaircraft fire answers in a crackling stream. The bombs tumble down all the same. *Thump, thump, thump.* She shakes her head and defiantly hums even louder. Eventually, she looks up—*Go out so they can see you.*

Easley bundles up the parachute and walks outside.

He bounds up the ravine. The drone of Navy bombers, unseen in the folds of cloud, is overcome by his own voice calling out for the pilots to look down and see. But they are focused elsewhere: on to the enemy encampment, antiaircraft guns, adjacent airspace. He works quickly, spreading the silk on flattened rye. He hobbles around, pulling the edges out to form a circle. He looks up and sees a plane briefly freed of the clouds. Before it disappears, it makes no sign of recognition, no bank or tip of the wings.

And then the bombing stops. Through a widening gap, a second plane curves out into the open. It comes in over the hills toward his beach. He cannot tell if the pilot sees him. It continues toward open sea.

Easley jumps up and down around the parachute, waving desperately. The pilot still offers no response. Then, as an afterthought, or to lighten the load for the journey home, a single, whistling bomb escapes as the plane pulls up and climbs. The bomb traces an elegant line down over Easley's head. It sails over the cave, and Tatiana. It enters the water just offshore, sending up a geyser of rock and spray. The concussion sends him to his knees. He palms his ears, but this only keeps the pain ringing close to his brain. By the time he looks up, the plane is just a dot, lost in the gauze of another cloud.

The end is now in view. No—he chides himself, yet again—he only needs a good meal or three, prepared and served by Helen's hands. But this lie no longer has effect. For too long now, Easley has been consuming himself. If Helen were here she would see a different species altogether. A wretch with another man's blood on his clothes. Someone who cannot discern between shadow and light. Someone whose heart has been untrue. If only they had succeeded in starting a family. *That* would have been a form of continuation, a life beyond this one now set to end.

Easley gathers up the parachute, then walks back toward the ravine. No sound can be heard inside. He glances back at where the bomb shattered the sea. The waves have closed over and healed the breach swiftly, as if it had never been. He spies white specks floating in the surf, sees a couple of fish up on the beach. Easley drops the silk and runs.

He manages to snatch eight fish before the tide pulls the rest away. He removes the lace from his right boot, threads it through gills and gaping mouths. He dips them back into the water, rinsing sand from glistening skin.

At the cave, all signs of light and life have vanished. There is no hum or song. Tatiana is back in her frame—only the ringing in his ears remains.

SIXTEEN

THE STAGE IS SET AGAINST THE BACK WALL OF THE hangar. Aircraft have been rolled outside to make room for an audience of two thousand, their biggest show yet. A broad, three-foot riser has been custom built, with a little dressing room off stage right. Inside is a bench, a mirror, a washbasin and pitcher. The only notable part of the construction, the truly creative touch, is a row of bombshells lined up along the front of the stage like a row of menacing, moss-colored teeth separating the entertainment from the entertained.

A man drives nails into fresh plywood. His khaki jumpsuit covers an athlete's frame. The toes of his boots are nearly worn through from working too often on his knees. Unruly brown hair sticks out from under his cap, considerably longer than regulation. Helen approaches with her arms folded tight against the cold. She watches as he pounds a nail, stands up, then jumps up and down to test its integrity.

"I hope you made a trapdoor," Helen says to his broad back. "I'll need it when the crowd gets ugly."

The man stops jumping but does not turn around. He's been aware of her presence from the start.

"It looks great," she adds. "Thanks for all your work."

"Lady, you don't need to thank me. You're doing us the favor."

He turns to reveal a thoughtful, intelligent face, jaw pronounced and set. He hasn't shaved in days. He avoids looking directly in her eyes.

"We put an electric heater in there for you to warm up before the show." He points with his hammer. "Or for when you take breaks between numbers."

"We saw it this morning. Thanks again."

He jumps up and down in a few more spots, paying her no further heed. When he discovers a board that squeaks, he pulls a nail out of his pocket and pounds it down in two smooth strokes.

"I'm Helen. I hope you enjoy the show."

"Perera. Airman Thomas Perera."

She extends her hand and waits. He seems unused to the custom, or civilian company. Finally he steps forward and shakes her hand, all the while avoiding her eyes. His are blue, set deep in the shadow of his brow. Italian, but from the north. He turns and shifts his weight to a new board, which gives no reply.

"We've been looking forward to your show forever."

"Well, I hope we don't disappoint." She observes a moment more, then catches herself. She turns to leave.

"The shells are empty," he says. "Nothing to worry about. I just thought they add a little something."

"They do. They do indeed . . . I was wondering. Ever meet any journalists out here? Writers coming out to file a report?" She's grown skilled at cultivating such entrées, turning most every conversation to her purpose.

"They say loose lips sink ships . . . I've heard of no reporters. But you can bet they'll be arriving by the boatload once we mop up the last of the mess."

"Of course. I just thought a friend of mine might have come through."

"But I've only been here nine months," he says, lightening his tone. "Long enough to forget my manners. If you're looking for someone in particular, you can try asking at the Supply Corps' office. There's a manifest for every ship and plane that's landed here. They might be able to check the records, if they're in the right frame of mind. You could try Ralph Rosetta. Tell him I sent you."

To him, it's a small thing. A common courtesy. He has no idea how his generosity could change everything.

"Well, I don't know how to thank you."

After what appears to be serious thought, he says, "Just make me laugh tonight."

STEPHEN SITS FORWARD, pipe in hand, elbows on knees. He's lit it twice, but the bowl's gone cold from lack of attention. Judith hides behind her wool curtain, feigning sleep. Gladys sets the mirror down with a sigh, unhappy with her hair, the way her nerves have mottled her skin, telling herself she's ready to take the lead. Sarah purses her lips and shifts her eyes about in a kind of aimless searching. Jane adjusts her earrings, apparently relaxed and content. Helen finds it best to focus on quiet, uncomplicated Jane because she projects confidence. She has proven herself to be their most accomplished actress. Stephen glances at his watch again, stands up, and nods. It's time.

Outside, the weather seems determined to drive the audience underground. The troupe, now reduced to a quartet, cinch their coats to the neck, cover their heads with scarves, and hustle to the hangar through the back door, which is veiled in parachutes. The silk leads in an unbroken curtain to the stage and dressing room. The unseen audience asserts itself on the other side, laughing, singing in anticipation.

The tiny dressing room offers barely enough space to contain them. Gladys, Sarah, and Jane sit on the bench, Stephen stands along with Helen. The heater glows orange in between. The air, saunalike, sets Helen's cheeks tingling. The multitudes beyond begin calling out for action. Helen reaches into her purse for a jar of Vaseline. She rubs a small pearl's worth on her teeth to lubricate her smile. She looks at her shoes and mutters a chain of Hail Marys just under her breath. They all freeze when they hear an electric *click* followed by two dull thuds.

"Ladies, please take your seats . . . God, what an ugly crowd we have here tonight!" The voice reminds Helen of her father. "Church services will now begin. Please open your hymnals to page two hundred twelve."

Laughter.

"They say no one cares about the heroics of Aleutian flyboys." This is met with catcalls and jeers. "They say no one gives a damn about the men who provide top cover for America." More displeasure. "What I want to know is, who the hell are *they?*" Cheers. "*They've* never flown through a williwaw, or put a B-24 down on a soggy Marsden Mat." Louder cheers. "Let me tell you a little something about the show you're about to see tonight, about the girls from the USO. They know where to find the hardest working men in the Pacific. And that's why they've come to Adak—to show their appreciation on behalf of a grateful nation. Now, at ease! Take a load off, enjoy yourselves tonight. And please give a warm, warm Aleutian welcome to the USO Swingettes!"

The lights go down and the little dressing room is hit with a sustained volley of applause.

Stephen grabs Gladys's hand, leads her out the door and across the darkened stage. Sarah, Jane, and Helen follow close behind. En route, they pass the resident twelve-piece band that's been rehearsing this set for weeks. Each girl takes her place onstage. Stephen mounts the piano stool and taps out the first notes in the dark—then pauses. He starts again, gets a little further, then pauses a longer beat. He's teasing it out. The tune's so familiar, it's the stripped-down piano rendition that throws the audience off. Then, from deep in the crowd, someone lets out a howl. Stephen attacks the keyboard and the horns join in. The lights go up on the girls. They have their backs to the audience, hands on hips, whistling the first phrase of "In the Mood."

The response from the crowd is unlike anything Helen has experienced. It hits her at the base of the spine, nearly shoving her off balance. As the applause rolls on, she steals a sideways glance at Sarah, sees the smile stretch wide across her face. One by one the girls turn round, approach the microphone, take up a line of song.

"Who's the lovin' daddy with the beautiful eyes
What a pair o' lips, I'd like to try 'em for size.
I'll just tell him, 'Baby, won't you swing it with me'
Hope he tells me maybe, what a wing it will be . . ."

Helen stares into the light, over the heads of the men. When she allows herself to look into their faces, she feels both powerful and disarmed. When it's her turn to lead, she holds back half her volume. She has to trust it first before pushing it out beyond the front of the stage. The result is that each verse gains weight at the end. She glances over at Stephen for reassurance.

Four songs in, the lights narrow down to a spot. Sarah steps forward with "T'ain't What You Do (It's the Way That You Do It)." Helen slips offstage and back into the dressing room. She opens the door and steps through a wall of heat. It takes a moment, but when her eyes adjust she finds Judith sitting in the corner, blanket around her shoulders, looking up with a colorless smile. She reaches for Helen's hand and gives it a squeeze. Together, they listen as Sarah works the crowd.

About halfway in, Sarah's classically trained voice pulls back and the trumpets clamber over top one another. Helen and Judith pause in anticipation of the shim-sham routine Sarah has honed to perfection. They stare into the shadows, then Helen catches Judith's eye just as the crowd roars for the pirouette Sarah always breaks out before picking up the verse again. When it's all over, the applause seems to last as long as the song. Sarah sings two more.

Helen's stomach tightens when the time comes to slip back onstage. She's sung well so far, but now she must carry a song. She leans against the piano and concentrates on Stephen's shiny black hair, hair too beautiful to waste on a man. Her pulse quickens when she hears men whistle and shout. Time to slow things down. Stephen looks up and nods. He waits for the slightest sign, then leans forward and presses into the keys. A few notes in, Helen sings.

"It's not the pale moon that excites me
That thrills and delights me, oh no,
It's just the nearness of you."

Helen turns and takes the next verse downstage. Just beyond the bombshells, a man stands, reaches up, and claps above his head.

The verse wasn't perfect, but it'll do. No sour notes, no fumbled lines. She knows Judith's songs as well as her own, as well as every other song in their repertoire. A little deeper in, she has a high-wire moment, unsure of the next phrase. But she trusts, stays present with the music, and when she reaches for it, it's there. She finds the current, lets it pull her through. What would John think if he could see her now?

Helen plays it soft, vulnerable. She turns her back on Stephen, glances over her shoulder at him, teasing, making eyes. But the love she must win is from the crowd in front of her. These men want the song sung to them. They want to believe, for a moment, that if they are not in love, then at least they're someplace else, someplace warm and easy. To help keep her equilibrium, she scans over the heads of the audience, avoids making eye contact with individuals, tries to think of them as one.

But by her final verse, she can no longer help herself. Through the glare and haze she picks out tall ones and short ones, men swaying, leaning, standing transfixed. She has made herself the object of unblinking attention for two thousand men. She takes an unsure step, then looks to Stephen. His smile pulls her up, brings her back into the moment.

> *"I need no soft lights to enchant me*
> *If you'll only grant me the right*
> *To hold you ever so tight*
> *And to feel in the night the nearness of you."*

Stephen rises with the cheers. He takes Helen's hand and strides to the middle of the stage. They bow deeply as the men jump to their feet. Sarah, Gladys, and Jane emerge from the shadows to join Stephen and Helen at center stage with the trumpet player from the band. They cap the set with "Tuxedo Junction." By the first *Way down south in Birmingham,* some of the men have opened up a hole in the crowd at the foot of the stage, taking turns at the Lindy Hop, lead and follow, a few attempting lifts and tricks. At last, the girls wave and bow into the wings as the crowd calls out for more. And this is only the intermission.

In the shadows, they nearly collide with three men each made up as Carmen Miranda. They wear bright flower print dresses, turbans of fruit, hoop earrings. They won a talent contest and with it the honor of performing during the girls' break. As the Mirandas make their way past and onto the stage, they shake false breasts and purse red lips. One of them is flat-out gorgeous.

Stephen discusses the set list with the show's MC and the girls make a beeline for the dressing room. As the band cranks up a samba, Helen strays down behind the parachutes. She lifts back a fold of silk and sees the audience in profile. She scans for John. The men well back from the stage sit on folding chairs, tires, and tarps. Reactions to the drag routine are mixed. Some men grin and shake their head, others glare disapprovingly. Most cheer or shout lewd and encouraging things.

Helen spots Airman Perera, reclined on a folding chair. She pulls the silk a little farther aside. He turns in her direction but looks instead at the man seated beside him, doubled over with laughter. Perera slaps him on the back, then jumps to his feet and whistles piercingly.

AFTER THE SHOW, a bottle makes the rounds of the dressing room, lipstick wiped following each pull. The heat and postperformance euphoria mix with the drink and soon they're losing their heads. There's talk of meeting the boys from the band. Gladys and Sarah undress in front of Stephen, tease him with it, kiss him all over his face. Like a boy caught in his sisters' room, he blushes, takes it good-naturedly—for a while—then slips out at the first opportunity. Helen isn't far behind.

The hangar still resonates with energy, although only a scattering of men remain. Up near the giant doors, two men roll electrical cord on a drum, shoving each other like a couple of kids. When they see

Helen, they turn to each other to sing a few lines of "The Nearness of You," which makes her blush.

Now is the moment, the afterglow of shared experience. The men will want to help with any and all of her questions, compete with each other to find answers. She will put this to use for John. Helen pulls her coat around her shoulders and heads in their direction.

Airman Perera appears out of nowhere, unlit cigarette dangling from his lips. His face is freshly shaved, his hair neatly combed. Unlike their first meeting, he can't take his eyes off her.

"Well," she says. "Say something."

"Good show." He lights the cigarette and stares hard into her eyes, then at her mouth.

"But did you laugh? That was your only request." She looks past his shoulder and returns the wave of men heading out the door.

He steps forward and puts his hand on her cheek. It's warm and smells of tobacco. Caught unaware, she stumbles back a step.

They both turn at the sound of a metal chair toppling over onstage. Helen can hear the girls inside the dressing room, Gladys's hysterical laugh. She glances around at the mostly vacant hangar. Then the door near the stage bangs open. Billowing parachutes whip and twist in the sudden onrush of wind.

"I have to be getting back . . ." Helen turns and walks away.

Perera quickly covers the space between them and grabs her hand. She yanks it away. Unperturbed, he stares directly into her eyes. "Where to?"

"I don't know what makes you think . . ."

His shameless gaze contains ownership, a claim to inevitability. Again, he says, "Where to?"

She slaps his face, frightened at what she's unleashed. "My *husband* . . ."

He fingers his jaw and stares at her mouth again, then down at her chest. He bends over and retrieves his cigarette. He takes one last drag before flicking it away.

Smoke trickles from his lips. "I don't see no ring."

She turns and marches to the dressing room.

Helen rushes inside and discovers that the girls have already left. She slams the door and sits down on the bench, trembling. What now? The air close and muggy. She switches off the heater and the grate clicks as it fades from purple to gray.

Helen waits for her pulse to settle, her breathing to return to her control. As she shoves her brush and scarf into her bag, her father's words come back to her. Her anger spikes at the memory of having brushed off his warning. Stephen had told them more than once not to give the men too much individual attention. And still she's shocked by the sudden, physical liberty. Like that man in the chapel at Fairbanks. And now Airman Perera. Did she somehow lead him on? What is she projecting? She tells herself it was simply gratitude. She refuses to treat these men as if they are in prison. But what entitles anyone . . . She'll march directly out of here, then catch up with the girls. Someone must have noticed what was happening. He won't risk approaching again.

How has she arrived at this moment? She was raised to believe that to look astray is to commit adultery in your heart. A mortal sin. Better to tear out your eye and throw it away than have your whole body cast into hell. From catechism up, we've been warned. So far, this logic has gone untested. There is no question of her love for John. But now she calls into question all she's been taught. Is there really no difference between a careless thought and taking action? *One* stray thought? What rational adult could believe such a thing?

Perera pushes his way in and closes the door behind him.

"Get out!" she cries. "Who do you think you are?"

He stands directly in front of her. Where are the girls? Will anyone hear if she screams? She scrambles to get up, but he presses down on her shoulders, pinning her against the wall. He quickly shrugs off his jacket, pulls his undershirt over his head as she fights to get past. He grabs her by the back of the hair and pulls her in, pressing her face against his belly. Helen braces herself, then springs forward using all the power in her legs, back, and shoulders, shoving with upward momentum. He stumbles and falls back over the heater and against the opposite wall as she scrambles out of the room.

When she opens the outer door, the storm pushes in. All her strength is required to pull the door closed behind her. A sharp sheet of tin metal flies past, spinning into the night. She has never encountered such a storm. Will the planes snap their moorings? The tents and buildings roll into the sea? Helen clutches her coat to her neck and leans into the wind. *Our Father, who art in heaven . . .*

The water lashing her face and eyes is neither rain nor sleet—it stings with the salt of the sea. She has no idea where she is. Darkness presses in with only a few distant pinpricks of light. She attempts to unfold the map in her mind. The hospital, the mess hall, tents, and Quonset huts all the same. She stumbles on. *Thy will be done on earth as it is in heaven . . .*

The roar is disorienting. Why was there no hurricane warning? Fifty yards beyond the building and it's now impossible to see where she's going. Mud sucks at her shoes. Puddles up to her shins. A seam of flat earth feels as if it might be a road. She will follow it toward the cluster of light she hopes is the mess hall. *Lead us not into temptation, but deliver us from evil . . .*

A new magnitude of gust rises up. All progress comes to a halt. She swings her arm up to protect against what sounds like more cart-

wheeling sheets of metal, a gesture that costs her balance and sends
her to the ground. Helen pushes herself up. She must find her feet.
Carry on.

From behind, a flashlight beam cuts into the darkness. A voice
calls out, but it is impossible to distinguish words. There is no cover,
no place to hide. The voice—urgent, persistent—struggles through
the wind once again.

The flashlight bounces and swivels in pursuit, grows brighter on
approach. She catches sight of her shadow against the ground, stretching out from her feet to infinity. The syllables, repeated, "Hel-len!"
He is bearing down on her. She stops and turns to face the light straight
on, buckling her knees, crouching to stay upright in the wind.

The figure is less than a dozen feet away before she sees that it
is Stephen, wet hair pressed down over his forehead, soaked clothes
clinging to his limbs. The shocking whiteness of his hand as he reaches
for her shoulder. He shouts, "What in the world are you doing?"

She shakes her head.

"You'll get yourself killed! You're headed in the wrong direction."

He draws her in under his shoulder, she wraps her arm around his
back. Together, they carry on. The flashlight beam refracts off the
larger puddles, illuminating countless streaks of spray. A man trudging past, a fleeing sheet of canvas, a terrified dog scampering under a
truck. Eventually the light strikes the back of a covered jeep. Stephen
flings open the passenger door. Helen scrambles in as he races round to
the driver's side. Once inside, he switches off the flashlight. The wind
shakes the jeep like a toy.

"Where the hell were you? Everyone's worried sick!"

"Lost," she says, catching her breath. "Beyond lost."

"What happened back there? You bolted outside like the place
was on fire."

She is unsure how to give it shape, definition. Where the story should begin. She is sure only of this: "He came at me, but I got away in time."

In the moment it takes Stephen to sort this formation, Helen can feel him seething beside her.

"Believe me. I'll find that piece of shit . . . Helen, are you okay?"

She nods her head, shivering with the wet and cold.

"That prick will rot in jail."

They listen to the wind have its way.

"I should have been there to protect you. I can't let you girls out of my sight for a single, goddamn minute . . ."

"Stephen, please. I said I'm all right."

"Helen, listen . . . I'm sorry to bring this up right now, but I can't hold it any longer. I came to tell you that I just met a guy who might have seen your husband."

Her heart stumbles. Her mouth falls open. She turns to Stephen but can't discern his face in the dark.

"The guy's a mechanic. Part of the hangar crew. He knows what goes up and what comes back. He said a man rode along on a bombing run a couple of months ago. An advance man for the Royal Canadian Air Force. No mention of a reporter, but when I heard 'Canadian' I thought it might lead to something. He said the guy's name was Warren Easley."

Helen leans forward, covers her face with her hands.

"His brother."

How could she have missed it? All along, she was looking in the right place, but for the wrong man.

"Must have faked the paperwork. Stole a uniform?"

Helen lifts her head and takes a deep breath. She fixes her gaze on the few, distant clusters of light. Between here and there, all is black.

She can see John rummaging through his brother's papers and personal effects back at his parents' house. He took the chance that the wheels of bureaucracy wouldn't catch up to him in time. How would the U.S. Navy, on Adak Island, know about the death of a Canadian airman over the English Channel? Written orders from the RCAF requesting access? She smiles at the thought of John taking pleasure in choosing the precise military jargon. All along, she had been looking for signs of a journalist, a writer. Months of research, two thousand miles. Although she knew Adak held the key, it took Stephen to find it.

"Where's John?" Her voice, flat, barely audible over the storm.

"Helen . . ."

"Damn it! Where is he?"

The wind mocks his hesitation. "The plane went down somewhere between here and Attu. He was with a crew of six. Helen, they never made it back."

"They could have made an emergency landing someplace." As the words leave her lips, she realizes the idea felt much more powerful held close and unspoken.

"They say life expectancy is five minutes in the open water. Give or take."

"He could have been captured. On Kiska, or Attu."

Stephen finds her hand in the dark. "Helen . . . I need you to listen to me. I'm told there's no chance they survived."

She hears the finality of the words but scrambles to find cracks in the logic, the missing details. There's been some kind of mistake. John was not on that plane, Stephen's source is confusing his facts. Again she finds herself outrunning pursuit. She's scaling fences, kicking open doors that have been shut in her face. John is too smart to die.

Stephen leans over, kisses her hand, then cradles it in both of his.

"It takes time, months, years even. But eventually you find comfort in knowing that you're not alone in having lost somebody," he says. "Pearl Harbor. It's like the *Mayflower*, the way everyone claims a connection. The truth is, I did lose someone at Pearl."

Helen blinks, draws herself back to the here and now. Replays the words she's just heard.

"Stephen. My God, I'm so sorry. You never said anything. Tell me—"

"Another time."

And then she forces herself to imagine it, John's plane falling from the sky—to feel it happening. The cry of wind through dead propellers. The impact of metal on concrete sea. Cold water folding in, pulling him down beyond the reach of light. Just like his brother. She cries out loud, surprising herself with the sound. Stephen puts his arm around her shoulder and gathers her in.

Here she would reach for the comfort of heaven, the knowledge that they will be together again, but is stopped by John himself. Because admission into heaven calls for faith in its existence. All along, he made it clear he won't be going. This life is all they have together.

Unless, on occasion, forgiveness is granted to those who do not ask. Unless the faith of some is strong enough to carry others through.

Eventually Helen sits up and wipes her nose. "How many islands between here and there?"

"I don't know. Half dozen?"

"Help me find a map."

SEVENTEEN

THE INCREASED ACTIVITY AT THE JAPANESE CAMP has made it impossible to steal coal. The lack of coal makes it impossible to coax a flame from the last sodden sticks of driftwood. And now there is no way to light either coal or wood. While Easley knew the absence of fire would gnaw away at his nerves, he was wholly unprepared for the damage it would inflict on his feet.

He sits in the damp cave comparing the boots he has just removed with the boots he keeps in the nest. The first set is wet and warm, the second damp and cold. He's long since removed the laces to allow his ballooning flesh room to escape. All the socks are wet, and there is no way to make them dry. The ones he wears are sticky with pus. He carefully peels them away.

The left foot has increased in size by half. The right is slightly smaller, but topped with a half dozen blisters, several as wide as Coke bottle caps. So far, only two have ruptured. The color of both feet is mottled burgundy and blue. The contrast with the dirty white skin of his shins makes them look as if they belong to another body altogether. He thinks of the stories of the Great War and the trenches.

Of all the ways he imagined death overtaking him—starvation, cold, poisoning, a fall—he never dreamed it would crawl up from his toes.

Easley spends the day inside listening to the wind and planes. Yesterday's steady drizzle has been replaced by fog and the pilots cannot see their targets below. He listens to them circle the island, looking for a hole through which to rain down their rage. Finding none, the planes eventually turn away from the island with their bellies full, leaving no fresh wounds behind.

HE AWAKENS in the middle of the night, surrounded by darkness and cold. His exposed feet are numb. He pulls them in and wraps them in silk. The surf sounds unusually distant, even accounting for the tide. The drip near the front of the cave calls his attention because it keeps time for a tune. He hears faint whistling and wonders if Karl has come back for a visit.

He suspects his imagination is taking advantage of his weakened condition. He has always been able to see these things for what they are—hallucinations—but now he runs toward the phantoms, chasing down what has become more important than his hold on reality. Easley finds himself humming along, then he calls out into the darkness.

The whistling grows louder and he can see a yellow light coming up the ravine from the sea. When the light reaches the mouth of the cave, Easley sits up to greet his brother. Warren wears a clean undershirt and underpants, black socks with garters. The light shows his handsome face, his hair disheveled from sleep. The lantern he carries paints the cave with a warm and comforting glow. Warren whistles the notes, but Easley remembers the words.

So long, it's been good to know you
So long, it's been good to know you
There's a mighty big war that's got to be won
And we'll get back together again.

The lantern is set atop the flat rock Easley uses as a table. Next to the lamp is what his brother has come to collect: his RCAF uniform, starched clean and folded to regulation. Atop the uniform are his hat and leather gloves. As he gets dressed, Warren whistles the tune in a continuous loop. First the shirt, then the trousers, jacket, and boots. He pulls the hat snug on his head. Easley becomes anxious when he sees his brother getting ready to leave.

"I only borrowed it," Easley says, "because I figured you wouldn't need it anymore."

Not wanting to miss the chance, he tells his brother how much he's missed him. That he always admired Warren's way with family and friends, teachers and coaches, strangers on the street. His inborn confidence and ease. His faith in others, as well as his belief that everything will somehow turn out for the best. He never realized—or allowed himself to believe—that his older brother wanted all these things for himself. Wanted to shoulder him aside, out of the flow of attention and praise, out of the way altogether. Warren never seemed to suspect that the natural roles had reversed, the firstborn idolizing the second.

Warren whistles contentedly.

"Forgive me," Easley says. "For not being a better brother and friend. For keeping everything wrapped up inside. I have lived my life as a professional stranger. What's the use in that? Now I see it for the waste it is . . . I always knew I would never equal the man I saw in you."

Warren has no reply. He straightens his tie and tugs his cuffs, then looks up and nods. He touches the brim of his hat, the lantern sparkling in his eyes. He walks out the way he came, swinging the lantern out into the ravine until the light grows fainter and the night fills back in.

Easley sits up and feels the blood surge to his head. He stands on blistered feet and gropes his way outside.

The wind has abated. Sleet falls on upturned cheeks. The sea is asleep and the world so remarkably still he can hear the slush as it strikes the land. Easley suspects he's about to die, or die again—whichever the case may be. He unbuttons his trousers, drains his bladder, then stumbles back into the cave.

AT DAWN, the distant clang of metal echoes across the waves. Easley puts on wet socks and Karl's cold boots because they are slightly bigger and because he's afraid that if he doesn't do it now, they might never fit again. The pain he knows he should feel from his feet never reaches his brain. He peeks outside and scans the water. After staring long and hard into the fog, he thinks he can hear the sound of engines in the chop.

A new kind of bombardment begins. One after another, a distant bang then heavy thud in the direction of the village and camp. The attack goes on for the better part of an hour, then silence reigns again.

Easley spends the balance of the morning cocooned inside the cave, leaving only once to drink from the stream. When he's had his fill, he stands and catches a whiff of bunker fuel on the wind.

He studies Tatiana's photo and opens her precious tin. He stares at the bright white linen, the icon, the harpoon tip, the roll of bills. He touches nothing. Inside, everything is clean and bright and made by human hands. He will not risk contaminating it with his filth. He replaces the lid and slides the tin into his pack. Next, he collects the spent lighter, the knife, the Japanese book where he's written his tribute to Karl. He places it all neatly inside the canvas, then cinches the pack closed. He slides the photo into his pocket.

He lies down and gazes out through clouded light.

THE NIGHT IS WELL ADVANCED when he opens his eyes again. The tingling in his feet is gone and when he reaches down to squeeze his boot he feels nothing at all. The last decision left to him is the choice of place and time. He stands and steadies himself, slips the pack over his shoulders. He removes the boy's dog tags from around his neck and places them upon the nest, then leaves the cave for good.

A quarter moon darts in and out of the clouds making it possible, with imagination, to see the land before him. Easley marches along the beach. He makes his way above the high tide line surprised at how easily he travels. His feet no longer give him any trouble. He feels neither the ground beneath him, nor the frigid current as he fords the shallow river. It's as if he walks on air. He holds this as further proof that he has become a ghost—until he trips and cuts the heel of his hand.

It is still dark when Easley passes the spot where he left the body, but he sees neither skis nor poles. He sees no sign. He carries on.

He envisions two scenarios. A bullet, fired from a great distance, will pass through his chest and he will fall back into the grass. His blood will flow into the ground, enriching this forsaken land. On that small patch, the flowers will grow fat this summer. The other possibility is capture, then torture and imprisonment in some hole in the ground. It doesn't seem all that different from his current situation. At least there will be some kind of regular food. Easley feels no real attachment to either of these outcomes, only a measure of contentment that soon it will be over and he will never be alone again.

By daybreak, he is within a mile of the village. His clumsy feet have slowed his progress. He will arrive in time for breakfast. What do Japanese soldiers eat for breakfast? When he reaches the rise with its view of the village, there is an unexpected sense of calm. The village and encampment are both silent and still, caught in the deepest sleep. If he walks another hundred yards in the same direction, someone will surely see him. He smiles—so close to the finish line.

Easley sits down and inspects his feet. They are expanding to new, grotesque proportions. There is no pain, but now a tingling deep inside. He pulls down the sock and pokes the taut skin with his index finger. Although his eyes register the contact, there is no felt response.

He could walk into their camp with his hands in the air and they might take him alive. Remembering Tatiana's embroidery, Easley pulls the tin from his pack and holds it in his lap. He pops the top and removes the linen with fingertips, then shakes it open. He grabs his pack and stumbles to his feet.

He is disappointed to see no smoke rising from the buildings or tents. Without a hot fire, it will take them forever to warm his bath. Easley raises the white flag above his head and lets it flutter in the clammy breeze.

The clouds shift behind him and the sun paints the mountains a flattering pink. He remembers the omen: red sky in morning, sailor's warning.

His arm gets tired before he reaches the ruins of the first building. He has given up singing for calling "hello"—soft enough to be heard but not so loud as to cause alarm. Easley rests his arm by letting it fall across the top of his head, the white cloth dangling by his ear. His heartbeat quickens.

The bombs have scattered the place. Easley stops and surveys abandoned vehicles, tire tracks still fresh in the mud. Houses with open doors, walls torn away, roofs opened to the sky. Walking past the home where he hid those weeks ago, he sees no signs of life. No hint of Tatiana or her people, no troops or their laundry. Only splinters and shattered glass. Where has everyone gone? He continues up the road to the oil drums and bunkers. There is no smell of coal or smoke of any kind. He stops at the first tent.

"Hello," he says. "I give up."

Easley squints and hunches his shoulders like he's about to receive a blow. Nothing. He reaches out for the canvas, slowly pulls it back, and sees a mess of papers inside. A smashed box and a blanket tossed on the gravel floor. Sticking out from under the blanket is a broken fishing pole and a tangle of line.

He walks from one tent to the next, politely offering his surrender, but finds no one to accept. Instead he finds foxholes and gaping tunnels, all dark and mute. Every shelter is strewn with paper, empty crates, heavy tools discarded on the run. Outside, he finds a shoe—even wetter than his own—and a spoon, dry and clean.

Easley picks up a damp, official-looking paper with Japanese characters printed at the top of the page in blue. Below dangle columns of runny black ink and a seal in the bottom right corner. He folds it and puts it into his pocket. Then, changing his mind, he pulls it out and tosses it away. Better not surrender with stolen documents.

He walks to the edge of the tents and looks down the abandoned paths to the desolate beach, then back to the mountains above. The lifting clouds reveal patches of snow and the gray-black shale beneath. The only sound is wind, waves, and the ongoing complaint of gulls. Easley holds the linen up over his head and shouts, "I . . . fucking . . . WIN!"

No hail of gunfire or lobbing of grenades, no enemy faces rushing from the shadows—just a new loneliness that's somehow even larger than before. Easley walks back to the tent where he saw the blanket. He lies down on a mildewed tarp and removes his boots and socks. He wraps his feet in Japanese wool and falls fast asleep.

A herring gull is busy giving him the eye when he finally comes to. It stands at the entrance of the tent, gawking in. When Easley sits up to grab it, the pain in his head is such that he is forced to lie back down again. The bird hops back a few feet, then waddles away.

Judging by the light in the sky, the better part of a day has come and gone. He will black out again if he doesn't eat and drink something soon. Easley sits up, but falls back over with the throbbing in his head. The pain is slow to subside.

His feet are now too big for boots. He pulls out his knife, cuts a hole in the blanket, tears off a strip. It takes all his effort to accomplish this task and he waits awhile before attempting it again. When he does, he has two long strips of wool to wrap around his feet. He pulls the bootlaces out of his pack, wraps them around the wool, then struggles to stand up.

He finds a photograph of a young Japanese boy smiling in front of a dark mountain, plus the tail and bones of a fish. He picks up the skeleton and holds it to his nose. It is foul, gray with decay, reminding him of his feet. He finds a soiled undershirt and mountains of spent shells. Between drifts of debris are the craters of recent bombs. He finds nothing to eat, but plenty of abandoned tires, glass, wire, artillery. Then treasure: a half-full bucket of coal.

Where are the Japanese? Are they truly gone, or is their disappearance merely proof that he has passed to the other side? No, he decides. The gull has confirmed his existence.

The cloud lifts and the peaks loom over the village—the ruins of which Tatiana would scarcely recognize. Something moves at the edge of the snowpack. A thin river of white spills out along the black rock and travels uphill toward the pass. It is alive. The white line grows thinner and then separates itself from the larger pack of snow, traveling slowly along the rock until a cloud drifts across, obscuring it from view. This is no product of his imagination, no trick of shadows in his eyes. The Japanese are on the move.

Then the veil drops away and he can see this for what it is: the abandoned camp and village, the enemy taking to higher elevation . . . The smell of fuel, the clang of metal across the water, the lack of planes in the air.

Karl explained weeks ago that the Navy would not risk a landing on the well-defended village shore. To avoid the heavy guns, the infantry would probably land beyond the rise, a half dozen miles south of the village, perhaps at Massacre Bay—a place-name that stuck from Easley's own research. Two hundred years ago, fifteen Aleuts were executed by Russian fur traders there, perhaps daring to resist the invaders, or their subsequent state of slavery. The other choice would be to approach from the west of the village. They could land on the wide beach not far from his cave. He had so often imagined this day but gave up hope long ago. And now, as the moment arrives, has he walked in the wrong direction?

Easley slings his pack over his shoulder and limps along the beach—away from shelter, blankets, shiny lumps of coal. He goes back the way he came.

The rain is light but quickly finds its way down his neck. He exhales in raspy clouds.

A FEW HOURS ON, not far from where Tatiana buried her tin, Easley falls for a third time. He lands face-first in old brown rye. The numbness has migrated up from his feet to his knees. Above that, his thighs are buzzing warm. He turns over on his back, closes his eyes, shakes with the wet and cold.

His hand does not reach for the small picture in his pocket. It is Helen's face that appears to him now, hair hanging down, warm sun full behind. But he blinks and she is gone.

Which birds will be the first to arrive and take their revenge? Stand on his chest, pull at his lips and eyes. When his body is found, no one will know who he was or what happened here. All this will be lost. Perhaps they will think he is Karl.

These are the thoughts of a coward. Get up! Time's wasting.

"Helen?" He calls her name aloud.

She has a head start down the beach, barefoot through hot sand. He must jump up now, run after her just as fast as his legs will go.

But the body won't obey. A short rest is all he needs.

Get up! Open your eyes!

Then the warm rush comes, followed by a sense of sinking. The cable cut, the elevator in free fall. The flailing, inescapable plunge.

EIGHTEEN

SHE LIES BURIED IN BLANKETS, PILED THREE DEEP, the wool rough against her neck and cheeks. They smell of dust and mildew, and the sweat of men who've lain here before. She stares up at the ceiling, listening for signs of Gladys's breathing. She can detect none. There's no human sound to comfort her, no laughter or murmur of conversation. No whine of a passing jeep. Only wind. She peers into the darkness and marvels at how the view barely changes whether her eyes are open or shut.

Following the Navy's abrupt cancellation of their final show, Judith, Sarah, and Jane were flown out yesterday afternoon on the only three seats available. Stephen made such a scene, puffing his chest, declaring he'll be damned if he'll let any of his charges out of his sight ever again. They will neither travel, nor remain behind without him. Look around, they said. The accelerated pace of bombing runs, the sudden arrival of ships in the harbor, the relentless pace of the ground crews. Something has changed, there is no hiding the fact. The war is closing in. Because of this, and Stephen's outburst, the remaining members of the troupe have been confined to quarters pending evacuation. Helen insisted she be allowed to remain with Gladys and Stephen. Weather and space permitting, they will be flown out tomorrow.

Gladys turns over in her cot, unseen in the dark.

Before their house arrest, Helen learned from the clarinet player that a plane out of Adak was forced to make a successful crash landing on an uninhabited island. This was three months before John's plane took to the sky. The crew was promptly rescued with no lives lost. Helen took this news as evidence, a shield of reason to help protect her faith.

All day she wondered, is John on some similar island, surviving off the land with members of the crew? Each plane that leaves this island is stocked with survival equipment and supplies. She was told his plane was a flying boat. Perhaps they were able to make a water landing close to shore. She let the thought germinate and bloom. And now, at three o'clock in the morning, it withers in hungry shadows, the unrelenting cold, and the thought of John coming to the conclusion that no one is looking for him. She sits up, pushes the blankets aside.

Is this it? Is this all she has to show for her lies and schemes, for leaving her father behind?

John would want her on that plane tomorrow, heading home and safely removed from whatever danger is headed this way. Of this, she has no doubt. Just as surely she knows that if it were *she* who had gone missing . . .

Helen lies back, draws the covers close, takes refuge in a memory suddenly close at hand. A hot August day. A small canvas tent pitched on the British Columbia coast. The sky textured with a cloud filigree, the sea a placid blue.

She followed his lead through the understory, past sheltering cedar and fir, until they emerged into bright sunlight. Spread a picnic on a dry hillside and uncorked a bottle of wine. Before he had a chance to pour, a pair of eagles tumbled from the sky. They landed less than fifty feet away. One tried to dominate the other—wings outstretched, flapping, posturing as if preparing for battle. The second bird finally relented, and its mate swiftly mounted. It was over in a matter of seconds. The eagles separated, but flew off in the same direction. John filled their glasses. They toasted the amorous display, the birds that mate for life. On the way back to camp, he tugged at her pants, then pinned her against a tree.

TWO HOURS LATER, Helen shakes herself awake. The aircrews can be heard warming engines and loading bombs earlier each day. She wipes the sleep from her eyes, then swings her legs over the edge of the cot.

The wind is on furlough. Beyond the windowpane, wisps of smoke can be seen floating up from the tents, passing fat flakes of snow coming down. Helen bundles up by the stove, stokes the coals, waits for the heat to rise. From her bag she retrieves a file and grinds her nails down to the quick.

Gladys lies on her back in the dim light with the covers up to her chin. Her face is pale, clean of all makeup, and Helen thinks it makes her look a good five years younger than twenty-eight. To fight the chill, in want of a cap, she wears a white sweater over her head and ears, tied in a big bow under her chin. She looks ridiculous and sweet. Helen carries over two of the blankets from her own cot, lays them over Gladys, then returns to the stove.

She must find a way to stay. If John can be found, these are the men who will find him. This is where they will bring him. But she will not stand idly by—she will make herself of use.

HELEN SITS ALONE, dressed, and waiting. The morning is already slipping away. Gladys is out at the airfield, posing for snapshots and signing autographs, covering for Helen's absence.

Stephen appears in the doorway nibbling the inside of his lower lip. Helen has developed the ability to read the thoughts written on his face before he has a chance to cloak them. In this, he is not so different from her father or brothers, from John or most any man closely observed. Stephen spends nearly half an hour pointing out the unlikeliness of her new plan, the certainty of her husband's fate, the peace she must make with the facts. The trouble *he* will face if she's not on that plane. He is determined to change her mind.

Helen looks up at Stephen, backlit in rare sunlight, realizing how much she'll miss him.

"So that's it," he says at last. "You don't even want to come out to the plane."

"I can't."

"Well. I don't know what more to say."

She gets up and throws her arms around him, feels it at the back of her throat. His friendship was unexpected. Given instinctively, without reservation. If she were to utter a single word, she would unravel at his feet. Instead she kisses his cheek, runs her fingers through his hair. She is pleased to see him smile.

"If I don't go now," he says, "I'll get sentimental, and then everyone will know I'm soft." He turns and steps down into the mud. "I'll write, and I expect a reply."

Helen watches him walk down the road toward the airfield, aware that she's letting go of something precious and rare. She keeps him in her sights until his path bends round a tent, then suddenly—he's gone.

WHEN HELEN ARRIVES, she is offered a seat across from the number two man on Adak. She shakes his hand, settles in, and tries to compose her opening argument. The room's low ceiling results in a kind of forced perspective, making Rear Admiral Styles and his tin desk appear disproportionately large. Maps the size of bed sheets cover the walls. Roosevelt beams down from his frame with that earnest look of optimism most everyone finds reassuring, saintly even. Helen tries to take courage in the president's gaze as the rear admiral flips back and forth through a ledger.

"I am sorry we had to cut your schedule short. The men are so grateful—*I* am so grateful—for what you've all done up here. But as you can see, the ground is shifting beneath us. We should have gotten you girls out days ago. Now, what is it I can do for you?"

"I am here to volunteer my services," Helen declares. "I want to stay on, help out in the hospital. Please, hear me out. I've seen the load your medical staff is under. I've spoken with your head nurse, Lieutenant Mayfield, and she says she'd make room for me. I know I can—"

He raises his hand, with a look of wide-eyed disbelief. "Pardon me, Miss—"

"I am not a trained nurse, but I can assist. I can clean, make beds. I can help feed and change dressings." She can hear her own desperation but is unable to stop. "Tell me your doctors can't use an extra set of hands."

The rear admiral caps his fountain pen and sets it aside, ceremoniously. He presses his fingertips together and rests his elbows on the desk. Helen can see a twitch under his left eye.

"I appreciate your eagerness to serve. But this is the front, and as you can plainly see, we're not set up for civilians. They'll welcome you with open arms back in Anchorage or Fairbanks."

Helen feels the blush rising in her cheeks, sees her anxiety register in his expression.

"Wait a minute," he glares at his watch. "Weren't you scheduled to fly out, half an hour ago?"

He reaches for the phone. She interrupts him with a fresh tactic: the better part of the truth.

"You lost a plane on April first, en route back from Attu."

He puts the receiver down.

"A PBY Catalina flying boat went missing that day with seven men aboard. My husband was on that plane."

He leans back in his chair, reconsidering the problem sitting across from him.

"You have him listed as Lieutenant Warren Easley, RCAF."

"Mrs. Easley." His tone is respectful, patient.

"Like me, you're not wearing a wedding ring, so I can't tell whether you have someone back home waiting for you . . . Someone you love enough to make you do foolish, or improbable things."

"I did not know your husband," he explains. "I am truly sorry for your loss. I can understand your desire to stay, but it's simply not possible. I must—"

"There was another crash landing back in January. Those men survived. And I know—"

"Not *another* crash landing, Mrs. Easley. That was on Great Sitkin, the island you can see outside that window, twenty-five miles away. Not four hundred and fifty miles down the chain and under the flag of Japan. Your husband's plane was seen falling into the sea some ten miles east of Attu. If those men somehow survived, you can bet we would have heard about it. The enemy likes to brag about this sort of thing. One of their radio operators speaks perfect English, with a Harvard accent. He taunts our pilots every time they approach Attu."

The room is no colder than any other on this island, and yet she is forced to grasp the arms of the chair to keep from shivering.

The phone rings and he snatches up the receiver, leans forward on the desk.

"I see," he says. "No. That will be all."

He hangs up, then stands and straightens his jacket. He lifts his coat off the rack and pulls it around his shoulders. He extends his hand to her.

"Please, let me stay."

"Mrs. Easley."

"Please."

"I would be greatly honored if you'd take my arm. Walk with me."

Helen is unable to move.

He reaches for Helen's coat, opens it wide to receive her. This act of grace allows her to find her legs, turn, slowly thread her arms through.

He lifts his elbow and she places her hand in the crook of his arm. Together, they step outside the room. Past the clerk who looks up from behind his desk, out the door, and down the muddy track outside. Alongside bouncing and careening jeeps, and men roused with a newfound sense of purpose. He walks Helen past the barracks and the hangar where they performed, to the edge of the airfield, where returning bombers circle overhead. They approach the plane where Stephen stands smoking his pipe, chatting with members of the crew. Two men climb up inside the aircraft while another pair pull blocks from beneath the wheels. Rear Admiral Styles nods and shakes Stephen's hand. He shouts something over the general roar. Helen cannot make out the words. She feels a hand placed gently on her back as he turns and walks away.

NINETEEN

IS FIRST POINT OF FOCUS IS THE MUZZLE OF A
rifle. The rifle is trained down at Easley's chest by what
appears to be a giant. Thick neck, the bulk and build
of a linebacker, eyes of Nordic blue. The soldier nudges Easley with
the toe of his boot. He looks frightened, unsure of what to do. Easley
rubs his eyes, blinks at the light, trying to get a read on how long he
has been unconscious. An hour, perhaps two? His attention is drawn
past the giant's knees to the unbelievable sight beyond: men running
across the grass, hauling boxes and guns. They yell and point and
look in every direction. A shot echoes somewhere in the mountains.

"Speak English?" The soldier holds the rifle straight, elbows out,
in a state of readiness.

Easley nods.

"Where'd they go?"

"The Japs?"

The soldier looks over his shoulder. "I got a prisoner here!" he
yells to the men behind. Then, reconsidering, asks, "You a prisoner?"

Easley doesn't know.

The number of men who come running now is too large to count.

The pairs of green legs surrounding him soon block out the land. Easley sits up and slowly raises his hands. The soldier lowers his rifle a notch and says, to no one in particular, "What the hell am I supposed to do with this?"

Gunfire crackles down the beach. Men crouch and hold their helmets in place. When the firing stops, some of them jog away. Finally, someone says, "Search him."

"You hurt?" the soldier asks. "You look like shit."

Easley considers his own appearance: filthy beard, mangy hair, the thinness of his arms and legs. "My feet," he says. "They're pretty well shot."

The soldier looks at the mud-soaked and bandaged feet, then glances over his shoulder again like he should probably be someplace else. Finally, he says, "This is what we're gonna do."

A soft-looking medic pushes past the linebacker. Soaked to the armpits, he must have just waded ashore. He appears as frightened and confused as the rest. Late teens, face plump with baby fat, cheeks of ruddy pink. He tells the others to carry on, which they do, then he pulls out his medical bag. He opens a fresh pack of gauze without giving much thought to the injuries. When he realizes that he's getting ahead of himself, he looks at Easley's feet—then sits back on his haunches.

"What are you doing here? What happened to you?"

"Better start with my feet."

The medic unravels the wool, then promptly leans over to retch. He heaves a few times, but nothing much comes up. Likely, he left his lunch back on the deck of his ship. He wipes his mouth, then looks round to make sure no one else has seen. "Sorry. I think I'm going into shock."

"Why don't you sit down for a minute or two," Easley says.

The medic ignores this and quickly packs his bag. "Can you walk?"

"Think so."

"Does it hurt?"

"Can't feel a thing."

"You shouldn't walk. I'll carry you."

The medic slings his bag over his shoulder and stands beside Easley. He doesn't look strong enough to manage it.

"Put your arms round my neck."

Easley does as he's told and the medic scoops him up. It smells as if he's bathed in fuel. The ease with which he's being whisked away makes Easley wonder how much of himself he has left behind.

Everywhere soldiers run and crouch, set up equipment in spongy rye. A gang tries to push a tractor out of the mud. It traveled up from the beach, then promptly sank under its own weight in the bog. Some men scan the hills with binoculars and rifles, others run between hills with pistols drawn, like clueless cops in a gangster film. Most wear thin jackets and leather boots—they haven't dressed for the weather. Hundreds whisk past shouting, pointing, stumbling as the fog lowers down over the harbor. The medic stops, then yells to another man who comes rushing over directly. They each get under one of Easley's shoulders and hook their free hands together to form a seat. Easley rides like royalty across the land.

They travel along the beach near Easley's cave. Ungainly boats beach themselves, then lower landing bridges down onto the sand. Men gush forth like blood from a new wound. Once ashore, they crouch with their hands out like wrestlers, ready for action. Easley fights to stay awake.

The pudgy medic and his mate lay Easley down in a cluster of litters and crates that form the beginnings of a field hospital, then they're promptly sent away. A jolt passes through Easley's body as he remembers the tea tin and the treasures it contains. Somehow, it got left behind where he fell.

"My pack." Easley nearly rolls over, struggling to get up. "I've gotta go back and get it."

"Lie down, buddy." This senior medic looks to be either Spanish or Turkish, some class of Mediterranean. His beard can't be much further along than a couple of days but is already coming in solid and blue. He seems to be in charge.

"I need my pack."

"You're gonna lie down." The medic leans over a litter where another man winces in pain. Easley decides he's Greek.

"It's all I've got."

The Greek calls another man over to help, then wipes his hands on his thighs. He gets up and walks over to Easley.

"Who the hell are you?"

"John Easley."

"Rank?"

He will no longer play his brother's part. "None."

"POW?"

"No."

"They do this to you?"

He kneels down and grasps Easley's thin arm, pulls up his shirt, runs fingers across the ribs inspecting his emaciated frame. "Sweet mother of Christ! How are you still alive?" he says. "When was the last time you ate?"

"My pack. It's got all my things. Things that don't belong to me. Please. It's not far."

"Lie down."

The Greek makes a pillow of an empty duffle bag and shoves it behind Easley's head. He inspects Easley's feet and recoils in disgust.

Next, he reaches into a carton and pulls out a syringe and vial. He draws fluid through the needle then gives it a tap. He unbuckles Easley's trousers and pushes him over on his side. A cold trickle of alcohol washes over his hip and where his ass used to be. The Greek rubs the site with cotton, throws it aside, then repeats the procedure again and again. Finally, he plunges the needle in. He hikes Easley's trousers back up and says, "Get some sleep. We'll have food here by tonight. We'll get to those legs soon enough."

Gunfire in the foothills draws everyone's attention, momentarily.

"There's nothing wrong with my legs," Easley says. "My feet are a little numb."

"Sure."

"Promise you'll get my pack."

"Go to sleep."

"There's cash. You can keep all the money. Please. Just . . . *please*."

The Greek tosses a blanket over Easley and walks away. Everyone scrambles and shouts. There seems to be no direction or plan. On the adjacent litter, a man mumbles the rosary. The rain starts up and yet Easley feels incredibly warm.

WHEN HE COMES TO AGAIN, there's a tent overhead and an Army major staring down into his face. The major looks impatient and exhausted. The Greek has hold of Easley's wrist, reading his pulse. Easley's eyelids droop again but the major shakes his shoulder.

"Where are they?"

The man means the Japanese. Easley strains to see through the billowing fog inside his brain. They were here, now they're not. He recalls the figures traveling in a line up into the mountains.

"I don't know."

"Did you see them leave?"

"No. But they must have known . . . you were coming. Saw some of them heading up into the snow . . . They were all . . . dressed in white."

"How long you been out here?"

"Since . . . the first."

"Of May?"

"April. April Fool's."

The major trades glances with the Greek. "What did you tell them?"

"Never talked to them. I was hiding in a cave . . ." Easley looks down but can sense nothing below his knees. It is as if his feet belong to another man. "I killed one," he declares, glad of the chance to finally speak the truth. "Then I came to turn myself in, but they were already gone."

Easley can see out the front of the tent. It's dusk now and the color has gone out of the light. The gunfire is steady and seems to be coming from the mountains, but he can't be sure. The major appears suspicious, eager for much more information. Easley would start at the beginning, tell him every last thing, if he could only find the words.

The major's lips move, but Easley can't make out what he's being told. It's as if he's listening underwater. The major takes off his helmet, scratches his scalp, then covers his head again. As he speaks to the Greek, Easley watches their chins bob up and down until he can watch no more.

* * *

WHEN EASLEY AWAKES AGAIN, a sudden movement catches his eye. A man picks up an empty wooden crate and hoists it high overhead, scraping the ceiling of the tent in the process. He carries the crate between rows of litters, then lands it in the mud next to Easley. In place of gloves, he appears to wear socks on his hands. Next, he makes a trip to the stove, returns with a steaming bowl, then sits down on the crate. With front teeth, he pulls the sock from his right hand then drapes it over his knee. The newly freed hand spoons up a mound of mush.

At least one night has passed, of this Easley can be certain. The pain is now centered deep between his eyes. The light hurts, as does turning his head. The man scoops, then holds the spoon near Easley's mouth and waits.

"It's my feet," Easley says. "There's nothing wrong with the rest of me."

Easley's own hand emerges from underneath the blankets and reaches for the spoon. It is a struggle to sit up. The man sees Easley's trouble and sticks the spoon in his own mouth. He quickly takes a second bite, sets the bowl on the ground, then wads a blanket behind Easley's shoulders. Unsatisfied with the result, the man finds another blanket and props Easley even higher. He helps himself to yet another bite of porridge before Easley reaches up and grabs the bowl away.

"You're one lucky bastard." Chapped lips, stubbled brown hair. Gray shadows below his eyes make him look like an addict. "Wounded get special rations. You're classed as wounded." He pulls the sock back over his hand.

Easley takes a bite of porridge. Warm oats, sugar, salt, salvation.

Although the headache does not abate with the introduction of food, Easley knows it is important that he finish. It is all he can do to remain upright.

A grenade goes off in the distance. It is the first sign of war Easley has heard all morning—if indeed this is still morning. He turns in the direction of the blast, but the wall of canvas limits vision to a matter of feet.

Easley's new companion does not flinch, doesn't seem to hear a thing. "How long you been here?" He retrieves the empty bowl, then pours a cup of water from a canteen. He hands it to Easley.

"Month and a half, I'm told."

"And you weren't captured."

Easley shakes his head.

"You're not military . . ."

"Journalist, of a sort." Overcome, Easley lies back down again.

"That so. Well, have I got a story for you." The man moves the crate closer to Easley's head. "Tell them the Seventh Infantry Division trained in desert combat for North Africa, then got shipped to the opposite end of the world. Tell 'em they gave us shitty clothes that don't keep you warm or dry. Tell 'em they didn't bring enough food and that no one seems to know what the hell they're doing. But I guess nobody wants to read about that."

The Greek looks up from four litters away, bandaging another man's head. "No one promised you a vacation. Spare us your complaints."

The man jumps to his feet. He snatches up the canteen and marches past a dozen other litters, out the tent and into the light.

It is then Easley notices the corner of his pack peaking out from under his litter. There is a surge of elation, followed by a sudden drop as it occurs to him that he had forgotten Tatiana. Surrounded again by other people, he can no longer sense her presence.

Easley closes his eyes to the rise and fall of adjacent conversations, the rhythm of boots passing by outside, the percussion of artillery fire in the mountains beyond. He falls into a deep and dreamless sleep.

* * *

THE VERY GROUND betrays him. He remains stretched out, and yet levitates away from the earth. It is a struggle to open his eyes. When he does, he focuses on the inverted jowl of the same pudgy medic who first picked him up and carried him to safety. The back and shoulders of the Greek are visible down at his feet. In between, Easley sways on his litter. He is back outside again.

The fog falls on his face in atomized mist. They are moving him someplace else, but where he cannot say. His stomach seems full, but the memory of porridge feels several days old. Another trick of the mind? Since his deliverance, Easley has felt himself continue to sink as his body grows weaker. The medic gestures with his chin and they set Easley's litter on the ground, then quickly walk away.

He is caught in a stampede of mud-caked leather boots. Men are busy putting up tents nearby. To his right is a man with a bandaged neck and blood dried black about the ears. He opens and closes his mouth, as if trying to speak. Easley sits up, but the rush of blood nearly puts him under. He steadies himself on the rails of the litter. All around, the hills teem with helmeted men.

The Greek returns with a doctor, a balding man with a squint that says he can bear no more discouraging words. The Greek speaks in hushed tones as the doctor nods his assent.

A pair of soldiers rushes up with yet another litter. They land it in the mud and beckon the Greek. Now three men crouch over the litter as the doctor stands, staring in the opposite direction, over ryegrass, beach, the sea beyond.

"I told you not to bring me corpses." The Greek stands up. "I've told you before. Check them out."

Easley closes his eyes. When he opens them, the doctor and the Greek loom above.

"This is the guy." The Greek pulls back the blankets and reveals Easley's bandaged feet. He pulls a pair of scissors out of his pocket and cuts the bandage away from the right foot. "It's been three days.

Someone better do something soon. He's been passed over every time."

The doctor looks up toward Easley's chest, careful not to meet his eyes. He grabs the scissors from the Greek and pokes the putrid flesh. "Feel that?"

"Around the shin. Feels itchy."

Easley watches the doctor poke the purple flesh again. It is as if it is someone else's body.

"Clean him up. I'll take him third, after the enlisted men," the doctor says over his shoulder, en route to the next decision.

The man who fed Easley porridge passes with a new litter, which is placed alongside the rest. He pulls off a sock and briefly holds the wounded man's wrist.

The Greek leans toward Easley's face. "It can't wait . . . You don't have any tags or papers, do you? We'll need a next of kin."

Easley shakes his head. "John Easley. Civilian. Writer."

"That's right. It's all coming back to me."

"My wife's in Seattle," he says, imagining her there, picking up the phone and taking the call.

The Greek pats his pockets but comes up empty-handed. "Easley, John. Seattle. I'll try and remember that. Turner will be by to prep you." Then, as an afterthought, "You'll be home before you know it."

And then the Greek is gone.

TURNER MOVES THE CIGARETTE to and from his lips in smooth, unhurried arcs, not the sharp strokes typical of the other soldiers. He looks clean-shaven and fresh. Rested, even. Perhaps he's just arrived. And yet when he bends over Easley the reek of nervous sweat is stifling. Before Turner has a chance to put him under, Easley asks for news of progress against the Japanese.

"Progress?" Turner seems surprised Easley can speak. "They've got the high ground, but we're still here. The Navy says they can keep their ships out, but who knows? And they've got thousands more soldiers over on Kiska . . . Our guys have been standing in mud for over a week. They're coming down with trench foot and exposure. There's not enough food to go around. Ask me again in a week."

He rests the cigarette between his lips then cuts Easley's trousers away, pulls them out from under his body, tosses them to the mud.

"One of the guys threw a grenade in the lagoon," he says. "You wouldn't believe how many fish they got. They're cooking 'em up now. I'd say that's the best thing that's happened so far."

Easley can feel himself smile.

Turner takes a clean white cloth and wipes Easley's feet. The cloth comes back brown with gore.

Easley lies back and looks up at the seamless cloud. A new set of hands comes from out of nowhere and places a damp cloth over his mouth and nose. Easley grabs the wrist, then releases. Floaters move across his field of vision like plankton in a jar. Soon, all is lost in the light.

EASLEY AWAKENS with bile charging up from his stomach. There is nothing to expel, so he leans over the side of the litter and wretches down at the mud. It is then that he realizes he is back inside. A larger tent this time. At first it seems as if no one notices him, until he spies the Greek, hands on his hips, standing beside another litter. He stares directly at Easley. But then Easley's stomach settles and he lies back down again.

Suddenly, he's buoyed by a wave of relief. Everything is new— blankets and clean shirt. He reaches below and discovers that he wears no other clothes. Even the fetid underpants are gone.

The man on the next litter observes Easley's assessment, the inventory, and waits until he is through. "You'll get the Purple Heart," he says.

Easley looks over at a kid still in his teens. A bloom of acne colors his chin and where his nose meets his cheek. Beneath the blanket, he wears his jacket and helmet and still he shivers with the cold.

"I'm not a soldier," Easley says.

The kid introduces himself as Garret, Pfc. "They're taking my foot off tomorrow."

Easley raises his head and looks down his own legs. Where twin peaks should rise at the end of the litter, only one remains. His left knee ends in a flat, undisturbed expanse of gray wool. His mind rejects this view.

This new tent has been pitched in a different location altogether, the slope of land seems more severe. Easley builds the mental map of where the field hospital had been, where the Japanese are holed up in the mountains, where the front might be. He pictures the waves of men still coming ashore without any hope of cover. However many they are, they'll still need boatloads more.

"They've got good false legs these days," Garret continues. "You can walk around just as pretty as you please. Of course, shorts are out. I'm bowlegged, anyhow."

A sustained volley of gunfire erupts from up in the hills. The inability to see the mountains or beach is disorienting. Easley wishes he could get a look outside.

"I shot one in the mouth. He was hollering in English. Fucker was yippin' at us for an hour. 'Damn American dogs, we massacre you!' He must have said it a hundred times. Sounded like the only English he knew. I waited. Buddy chucked a grenade and they all jumped out like rats. Came right over the top. And still he was shouting this shit.

I plugged him. I wasn't aiming for his mouth, but now, when I think on it, it makes me laugh. Didn't kill him. He grabbed his mouth and tried to run. Someone else nailed him in the chest. I guess you could say I scored the assist."

Easley is famished. Do they bring food around at set times, or do you have to ask for it? Everyone seems too busy to bother.

"Had my boots on for eight days straight. Never once took 'em off. By the time they were handing out socks and saying 'dry your feet' I was already in trouble. I hope I don't lose 'em both."

Easley looks over and considers the thin blond beard poking through the pimples. "You say you've been here eight days?"

"Nine."

Someone starts to cry. Opposite side of the tent, three litters down. Easley sees the man's hand go up to cover his face in shame. The sobs are unrestrained, rendering unnecessary anything anyone else has to say.

* * *

NO ONE BOTHERS TO explain what's happening. And it isn't because Easley's a civilian. No one explains anything to anyone, so far as he can determine. He concludes that no one really has a view of the big picture or the small.

The crates and medical equipment are carried out first. Easley props himself up on his elbows as men strip the tent amid machine-gun bursts and sporadic sniper fire. Empty-handed soldiers bump into those loaded down as they rush to get everything out. There are too many men for the job. Why can't they organize a chain and shift the loads from one man to the next?

A soldier marches in wearing proper rubber boots, a thick, knee-length greatcoat, and fur cap—all of it Japanese. Easley does not need to ask why he is wearing the enemy's clothes. He only wants to know when and where he got them.

"They had a little foxhole up the pass. They shot four of us before we got them. Pulled a rice ball out of this pocket two days back . . ." The soldier reaches inside, like there may be food he missed the first time around. "Sticky. Some kind of fish taste in it. Only thing I had to eat all day." He picks up a jerry can and marches outside.

It isn't long before Easley is carried out into the open and parked with the other litters.

Pfc Garret is only now emerging from the fog of ether, beginning to mourn that part of himself left behind.

Easley averts his gaze from the south end of his own litter, where the surgeon popped the kneecap, sliced between the femur and tibia, then tossed the ruined leg and foot away. The Greek explained that they *hope* they have cut off all the gangrenous flesh that would have soon claimed the rest of him. In the space left behind, his mind plays tricks, tells him he can still feel a burning itch in the arch of his foot and the tips of his toes. And yet the foot and lower leg are dead and gone. Surely this isn't what happens when the body dies entirely, the memory of pain lingering on.

Easley is grateful he no longer has to suffer such thoughts alone.

Garret draws a heavy sigh and rubs his face. Then opens up, full of talk.

A few guys are saying we've been had, he declares. The attack on Dutch Harbor? The occupation of Attu and Kiska? No more than a diversion for Midway. The enemy's plan to spread U.S. forces thin around the Pacific didn't work. The Japanese got clobbered at Midway, but that was eleven months ago. The only reason they're still here is for the propaganda mileage it gets them back home. They include it in their maps of Greater Japan. Others, himself included, won't stand such talk and are convinced the Allied invasion of Japan will be launched through the Aleutian Islands—if they don't try and use them to invade us first. Now that he's seen the place for himself, and the enemy's determination to stay, he can feel it in his bones. We're in striking distance, he says. A short hop to Japan. This is no diversion. This place, this fight, is where the war will be won or lost. The key to the whole damn thing.

He pulls a pitcher out from under his blanket and pours the contents into the mud. He taps it twice on the rail of his litter, then tosses the bottle to Easley. The kid has a point. This might be the last chance they will get for the foreseeable future. Easley turns on his side, positions the pitcher, and relieves himself awkwardly.

INFORMATION, AT LAST. The Greek announces that they are on the move again. The whys and wherefores, however, he leaves aside. There must be some strategy in having the wounded near the beach, perhaps for their long-awaited evacuation. Whatever the reason, two dozen litters have to be humped down the slope then lowered over a cliff.

Easley's breath makes little clouds in the drizzle as two soldiers carry him away. The sniper fire seems more frequent, machine-gun blasts closer than before. His heart pounds at the recognition of their complete exposure, and Easley's own helplessness. Each heartbeat sets off a wave of pain in his brain.

The man at the head of his litter neither speaks nor looks down at Easley. His face is grim with fear. Older than most—thirty perhaps—the man has a runny nose. Easley sees him struggle with the mucus dripping down his upper lip, wishing he could drop the litter and blow. Short of that, he attempts to wipe it on his shoulder while keeping the load in motion. This results in all manner of contortions. Then three sharp cracks have everyone crouching lower, moving quicker. Easley tugs the cuff of his own right sleeve so it hangs like a rag, then pushes it up toward the soldier's nose. At first the man seems startled, as if Easley has lost his mind.

"It's all right," Easley says. "Blow."

The litter bearer leans forward into Easley's cuff and blows like a tentative child. On second attempt, Easley grips his nose, and the man blows with satisfaction. A few steps on, amid the numerous pops and booms, the man lets out a groan, stumbles and falls. Easley's head and shoulders go down with him. The wooden rails plow up the mud until the man left hauling the litter drops his load and likewise hits the deck.

Sniper fire goes on for what seems an eternity and Easley is left with nothing to do but gawk up at the dripping sky and wait for it all to come crashing down. Some of the men, sprawled on their bellies, shoulder weapons and return fire. When the attack settles down and men are back on their feet again, the litter bearer with the runny nose fails to rise. Easley struggles to look around, but sees only the back of another man, checking for signs of life. "Jesus," the man declares. Three more arrive and Easley's litter is under way again, rushing toward the cliff.

A soldier kneels down and winds a rope tight around Easley's body and litter, securing him in place, pinning all of him save his arms. Easley lies there, bound and waiting, while the other litters disappear over and down.

When Easley is carried to the edge, another rope is hastily secured to the head of his litter. There is a quick gray sweep of sky, then the dangling view of the rocky beach below. Easley is lowered in short, jerking increments, a controlled, four-story slide. All he can do is brace himself and hang on. Below, two sets of hands reach up and then guide the foot of his litter down toward the beach. When Easley is flat on the ground again, he gasps for breath, despite the fact that he had no hand in this journey.

The litters are lined up side by side. The wounded lie in wait, listening to the rise and fall of battle and the waves scrambling ashore. Easley allows himself to imagine the sweltering furnace of a ship that will carry him home, the view of this island disappearing forever in the fog, the outstretched arms of Helen. Then the order comes down to haul everyone back up the way they came.

The return trip takes twice the time and effort. The only consolation is that sniper fire seems to be on the wane. When Easley is a little over halfway up, a gust of wind twists his litter, turning his palms and cheeks against the jagged cliff.

By the time all men and materiel are back atop the ridge, the howitzers are thundering through the mountains. The Japanese withdraw farther into the clouds as the Americans below scramble to decipher what it all means.

The decision is made to bring the wounded back to the original site and set up shop once again. To Easley's surprise, no one complains about this wasted effort, and by the time the tent has risen on the exact same spot, and the litters are safe inside under the red cross, the Greek is back in business calmly dispensing orders and morphine as if they had never left.

TWENTY

O
N HER DESCENT THROUGH THE CEILING OF CLOUD, it is not the huddled rows of fishing boats, tidy homes, orderly streets, or other signs of civilization that hold Helen's attention in the emerging world below—it's the profusion of trees. Marching down mountainsides to the waterline, they are living proof that she's found her way back to the edge of that safe and familiar world, the one that does not include John.

Helen is now the only woman on board. She had flown out of Adak with Gladys and Stephen, but because Seattle is her final destination, she was transferred to another flight out of Dutch Harbor. Stephen threw his hands up at his own powerlessness to keep the last of his troupe intact. In the end, he removed his hat and gave a theatrical bow as her plane sped forward and curved up into the clouds.

The plane circles twice above the airfield and town of Sitka. When the onion-domed cupolas of an Orthodox church come into view, Helen is reminded of having read somewhere that this was once the capital of Russian America, before the colony was sold to the United States and renamed Alaska. She recalls the Russian cross on the windowsill of Ilya and Jesse's hospital room in Seattle. They had mentioned their people were brought here from Atka to wait out the war in a camp nearby.

At last the plane touches down, almost seventeen hundred miles east of Adak. Here, the crew will rest overnight while the plane is serviced and refueled. As Helen steps down, an earnest young seaman steps up and offers his hand. Jug-handled ears, cockeyed smile—he doesn't seem old enough to be in uniform. He gently separates her from the crew and explains that her quarters are ready and waiting.

"But it's still early," he says. "I could drive you into town to have a look around, if you'd like. You know, go for a spin."

Helen is hollowed out, beyond words, unsure of the hour or day. She pauses for a moment to consider his question, then says this sounds like a wonderful idea. His smile retreats, however, when she asks to be taken directly to church.

INSIDE THE CATHEDRAL of St. Michael the Archangel, Helen finds neither kneelers nor pews. She has seen the interior of only one Protestant church, never a Russian Orthodox cathedral. Unsure of how to proceed, she stands at the back of the nave and bows her head. She is not alone. There is no service under way, no priest in evidence, but a half dozen people are praying separately. Middle-aged women with scarves covering their heads glance up now and then from tightly knit fingers to the panels of sacred paintings and through the gates to the altar beyond.

Helen takes the opportunity to thank the Lord for His protection on her journey and for the deliverance of John—from whatever trial he finds himself in. She prays for her father and brothers. She prays for the end of the war. She finds herself considering adding new prayers to the roster, one for the repose of the soul of her husband, and one for forgiveness of his disbelief. But she cannot form the words. She prays instead for the strength to accept His will, come what may.

A pair of women and one young girl each make the sign of the cross, turn, then pass Helen on their way out the door. She glances up and into native faces—Indian? Aleut?

No matter how ridiculous the impulse seems, she asks herself, What if they've met John? Maybe answered questions about their village, history, or way of life, saw him out snapping pictures of birds on his *National Geographic* assignment. He would have been wide-eyed then, taking it all in, the culture of the people, studying the landscape, flora and fauna, pulling out that notebook he keeps in his hip pocket, jotting down impressions, expressions, telling details that would somehow find their way into the weave of his story, the story that would have gone some way toward helping the rest of us understand something about that place. Tell us why those islands are worthy of our attention and give us a glimpse of their frightening beauty. Have they seen him, talked to him, shook his hand? She follows them out into the light.

The women are gathered on the steps in ill-fitting clothes, conferring quietly. On Helen's approach, they step aside.

"Hello," Helen says. "I'm sorry to bother you, but I'm on my way home from the Aleutians, and thought I'd take the chance . . ."

One of the women turns and guides the girl away, as if Helen might be contagious, or the bearer of bad news. The woman left behind, perhaps fifty years old, avoids eye contact but nods respectfully. "Which part?"

"I made it as far as Adak."

Her expression brightens a shade. "We're from Atka, the island to the east."

By now this upwelling sense of connection—proximity—is so familiar she reflexively tamps it down. "I stopped in to pray for my husband," Helen says. "His plane was lost near Attu."

The woman looks up and into Helen's eyes. "The Japs got every-one on Attu. What they did with them, nobody knows."

"And hardly anyone knows they're missing . . ."

"I pray for them every day."

Helen leads with her strongest card. "Ilya Hopikoff, and his boy, Jesse. Do you know them? We met in Seattle. Are they back at the camp?"

"Ilya's wife was my cousin," she says, taken aback, considering Helen anew. "They're still stateside, far as I know."

"I hope they come back to you soon."

"They're better off where they are." The woman states a matter of indisputable fact. "We're up at the old cannery. Eighty-three of us. Everyone from Atka. They dumped us out there for the duration. We just come in for the doctor and the priest."

"My husband has been to your island. Did you happen to meet a reporter last spring? Tall man"—Helen marks his height with her hand—"lean, brown hair, thirty-eight . . . handsome."

The woman shakes her head. "We had quite a few outsiders in the community," she explains. "They kept asking if we'd seen any strange ships or submarines. We were all on the lookout for the Japanese."

Helen nods.

"I'm sorry about your husband. God rest his soul."

Helen finds herself unable to respond.

The woman says good-bye, then makes her way to the others, waiting a safe distance down the street.

HELEN TRUDGES BACK through town. Shops, gardens, a primary school—bright and cheerful sights that fail to shift her focus. But when the airbase comes into view again, she wonders which plane was hers, and what its make and model might be. Her father will want a report about each and every plane she's flown on, as well as the kinds of bombs they carry. He'll shake his head when she admits she forgot to take any note of the latest radio equipment.

She tells herself that the sound of rapidly approaching footsteps is no cause for concern, and yet the memory of Airman Perera's face comes back to her. She stiffens her spine, resists the urge to glance over her shoulder.

A young man rushes up from behind then stops beside her, bent over panting, hands on knees. Thick black hair and warm complexion. He stands and reveals high cheekbones and dark, almond eyes. No more than nineteen or twenty. He wipes his mouth, then introduces himself as the son of the woman Helen spoke to back at the church.

He's got to hear what she knows of Attu, whether she's seen anyone, whether anyone's managed to escape. Has the military got a plan to finally go out there and save them?

"You heard what the Japs did to civilians in China? Place called Nanking?" His throat tightens on the words. "What they did to old people and women?"

She sees and feels it, physically. Their shared anxieties. Someone else set adrift on the questions surrounding Attu, someone else left spinning endless hypotheses.

"They're still dug in," Helen says. "Over on Kiska, too. They're getting bombed almost every day. But our guys are building up to something. One way or another, the war is set to break wide open— and soon."

He has none of his mother's reticence. He tells Helen that his father was the lay priest serving both Atka and Attu. For as long as he can remember, he accompanied him on trips between the islands, helping with the boat and church duties. On Attu, he met a girl and fell in love. She said she'd marry him.

"Then Attu's radio went quiet. That was June seventh of last year. A few days later, we all got shipped out here. There's been no news of Attu 'til you showed up asking questions."

But Helen has arrived empty-handed. If only she could offer him what she seeks for herself, some fresh reason for hope, some new path for him to pace.

"I wish I had some answers for you."

"Her father was building us a boat of our own. But he's getting old. And she's got no brothers. I should have been there to protect her. *I* should have been . . ." he says, jabbing his finger at the middle of his chest.

He does not look away, or cover his agony. He cries so hard he looses the power of speech. Helen reaches out to hold him but his body is a rigid knot. He neither responds nor pushes her away.

At last he steps aside and wipes his face. He reaches into his pocket, withdraws two dollar bills, and gestures back up the road. "Can you go into that shop up there and buy me a fifth of brandy? They won't sell to me."

Helen does not hesitate. She takes his money and marches back toward the store.

Around the back of the building, away from prying eyes, she uncorks the bottle and takes a swig before handing it over. He tilts the bottle to his lips and closes his eyes.

* * *

THE YOUNG SEAMAN who drove Helen to church pulls up outside the window of her otherwise vacant quarters. It's just shy of eight o'clock in the morning. He jumps out of the jeep and jogs around to her door with a kind of boundless energy. He wishes her good morning, asks if she found breakfast in time. Grabs her bag and lobs it into the back of the vehicle before holding open the door for her. Helen steps in, feeling as if she's aged ten years in the past few months without having gained the wisdom she's due. He hustles back around and slides behind the wheel.

"This is for you," he says, pulling a folded sheet of paper from a clip on the dashboard. "Came in late last night."

She unfolds a handwritten note that is the product of several authors. The message first made its way from California with a pilot heading north to Kodiak Island. From there, it was dictated to the radioman here at Sitka.

> *Dear Helen,*
> *This telegram arrived for you at the office almost two weeks ago. They tried to get it out to us, but somehow it got lost at Fairbanks. I'm sorry for this news and hope things turn out for the best. Let me know how you are when you get home.*
> *Yours,*
> *Stephen*

And then, in tight block capitals:

HELEN EASLEY, C/O USO PACIFIC

DAD'S IN ROUGH SHAPE. WHERE ARE YOU?
WE GOT THE CALL FROM ST. BRIGID'S.
GET HOME AS SOON AS YOU CAN.

FRANK CONNELLY

In her eldest brother's typical haste, he neglected to fill in any details. So Helen fills them in for herself.

ROUGH SHAPE . . . Did her father have another, more damaging stroke? Have things gotten worse since this note was written? Did his funeral come and go while she was asleep somewhere, or onstage singing one of her songs? She abandoned her father when he needed her most. Now, for all she knows, she is both widow and orphan.

They drive past the hangar to the very shadow of the plane's wing. As the crew approaches, Helen excuses herself, jumps out of the jeep, and runs past them and into the hangar where she finds a desk and a telephone. She asks the operator to place a collect call to her father's house. When no one answers, Helen asks instead to be connected to her brother Frank in Jersey City, where it is just after noon. She tries twice. When her second attempt goes unanswered, she tries the rectory of St. Brigid's parish—where it seems no one picks up the phone outside of office hours.

She is sentenced to a new state of limbo until her plane touches down in Seattle. Helen is left to reread and parse her brother's words, make plans and contingencies, try to comprehend all that has taken place and what it could possibly mean.

If John were here with her now, he would hold her hand and tell her not to fill the void with fear. Be realistic, he'd say, but do not jump straight to catastrophic conclusions. Remember how abrupt your brother can be and the fact that there were no further telegrams. There are enough hard facts to confront each day without letting our imaginations get the better of us—without letting worry drain our real lives away.

She sets the note aside and closes her eyes, savoring the memory of him.

TWENTY-ONE

THE MORNING IS STILL SO NEW IT CAN SCARCELY BE distinguished from night. An oil lamp hangs from the post, dimmed by a too short wick. Easley opens his eyes to a sensation he has long been dreaming of. The stovepipe in the middle of the tent radiates heat, and the air inside is summer. He lifts his head to see if the others are feeling it too, but most everyone else is caught in the deepest cycle of sleep. He is dry and warm and can feel the skin of his face flush with the joy of it.

It is the heat, he is certain, that results in another sensation from what seems like a lifetime ago: an erection so stiff and full it borders on the painful. Easley looks down the blanket and sees the form of it hovering over his belly. It aches in time with his pulse. He can't recall having had one so strong and sure since arriving in this barren place. He rolls over on his side to protect it.

The promised evacuation of wounded men has been delayed yet again. Easley no longer believes anything he hears from officers. He puts stock only in what the enlisted men are saying. They claim there are easily over two thousand Japanese concentrated in the mountains above the village. The Americans have landed more than twelve thousand men, several hundred are dead or missing, over two thousand injured or wounded. The invasion that was to have taken seventy-two hours is now stretching into its second week. Despite the determination of the Japanese, and their constant sniping from the heights above, half the American casualties result from exposure to the elements. Hundreds of men are losing their feet, others are coming down with hypothermia.

The positions are now well defined: the enemy holds the high ground, the Americans hold the lowlands and the beach. Are the Japanese waiting for some imminent rescue from the air or sea? If and when that force arrives, the Americans on the ground will be caught—exposed—in between.

Although the wounded are being fed regularly, there is never enough food for the troops. The gear they've brought is insufficient for the weather and terrain. It all seems patched together. Rumor is, the commanding officer of the whole operation is about to get pulled. The men wonder aloud if this change will come in time. When they discover that Easley is a journalist, they eagerly spill their guts, as if cooperation might somehow reduce their current sentence.

A familiar face enters the tent. He nods to the Greek, who looks up from counting vials by the stove. The man removes his helmet, followed by the socks from his hands. He scratches his scalp, then scans the row of litters on his left—until he meets Easley's gaze. He winks, flips the helmet back atop his head, then sets a pot of water on the stove to boil. A cough emanates from a litter near the flap. The man grabs a wool blanket, then walks over and unfurls it over the patient.

When the water boils, he pours some into his helmet then sits down on a crate. From his pocket, he produces a safety razor and a bar of soap. He lathers his neck and cheeks and begins to shave. He lifts the little mirror from his knee and considers the result. He catches Easley's eye in the reflection. "Pain?"

Easley nods his head.

The man drags the razor through the water, then starts in on the hollows of his cheeks. "You still have a fever. You got to keep an eye on that kind of infection. There could be complications down the road."

"Then what? Cut it off at the hip?"

He glances at Easley, then back to the job at hand. "At that stage, we shoot you and put you out of our misery."

Gusts shove and bully the walls of the tent.

With great effort, Easley manages to prop himself up on his elbows. His body seems to have grown weaker from lying constantly prone. "Any news?"

"More of the same. They're starving faster than we are. The blockade is holding—for now." Before shaving his upper lip, he pinches his nose like a diver. The man even holds his breath. On the exhale he says, "Either they can't face the fact they're trapped, or they know something we don't."

With both hands, he rubs his face. Satisfied, he opens his jacket and pulls up the front of his shirt to wipe his cheeks. "You should sleep while you can. It's bound to get busy around here, one way or another."

"I sleep too much."

He now retrieves a medical bag and walks over to Easley. He pulls back the blanket and inspects the bandages and stump, then the remaining foot, where skin peels away as the swelling recedes. He pulls up a crate, swabs Easley's weeping wound, then unrolls fresh white bandages. When finished, he sits back, frowning at Easley's face.

He rummages through his kit and pulls out a pair of scissors. "I'm getting tired of looking at you. Time to lose the disguise. You want me to do it or do you want to do it yourself?"

Easley takes up the scissors and pulls a lock of beard. He cuts weakly, then tosses the whiskers aside. He makes two more cuts, then his arms get tired and he lies back down again.

The soldier retrieves the scissors and starts in on Easley's beard. Once it is cut down to stubble, he gets fresh hot water, rubs the soap between his palms, and lathers Easley's face. Easley closes his eyes, drifting in the warmth and touch.

Warren insisted they go for "proper" shaves on his brother's wedding day. Easley felt like bolting as soon as he leaned back in that barber's chair. Bearing his throat to some sweaty old guy with bad breath and a blade. He swore to never repeat the experience. A few months later, Easley found himself in that big soaker tub, wrapped around Helen's fine form. Slick, soft, warm, and soapy. Lean back, she says. Relax and let me at those whiskers. And Easley says no. The mistakes we live to regret. This moves up near the top of the list of things left undone . . . And now she steps out of the tub and toward the bed. It's the right time of the month, she declares. Time's wasting. He manages to hoist himself up on his remaining leg, balancing, unable to move any further.

"Buddy!"

Easley awakes with a start.

"You're swearing in your sleep."

Easley closes his eyes again. "Can I ask something? It might seem like a small thing, given the state we're in."

"Don't tell me, you want a haircut too."

"How am I supposed to greet my wife if I ever get to see her again? I can't even stand when she enters the room. I want you to tell me that with a good false leg and a cane I can learn to get up and around again. Tell me practice will smooth the gait. Tell me one day I can toss the cane, hold her hand, walk down the street like an ordinary man."

"Sure. You're rich and handsome too."

Over at the flap, the cough starts up again.

"Since we're on such intimate terms," Easley says, "I think I should know your name."

"Cohen."

All at once, the world outside erupts with high-pitched, maniacal cries surrounding the tent, closing in. Cohen turns, looks up, then bolts outside. The disorienting charge descends from every direction. Over and over, they scream *banzai!* Easley's heart leaps past wakefulness, past the choice between fight or flight, to the realization that such physical response is no longer available to him. His one fixed point of reference is the Greek, now standing like a pillar at his side.

The screaming escalates, and before Easley can raise his head to look, the flap of the tent pulls back and the enemy rushes in. The first man's voice seems to frighten himself almost as much as his intended audience. His comrades barge in behind him. The Greek raises his arm to shield himself as a long blade flies toward his chest. Easley tips his own litter in a pathetic attempt to flee. The bayonet thrusts, then thrusts again. The Greek steps back, topples over the litter and falls, pinning Easley to the ground.

The enemy spreads throughout the tent, moving from bed to bed, slaughtering wounded men with bayonets and swords. Shielded by the body of the Greek, Easley can see at least three pairs of Japanese trousers moving through the tent. Blood flows warm from above, soaking Easley's shirt at the shoulder and down the back. The Greek's right hand dangles in front of Easley's face—life reduced to small, spasmodic tremors in thumb and index finger. The lamp goes down then all is black. English shouts and curses mix with *banzai!* cries until the tent is swamped with a chorus of murderous screams. Easley closes his eyes and assumes his place among the dead.

The attackers runs outside, then one suddenly stomps back in to ensure they finished the job, shouting and kicking everything in his path. A boot glances the Greek's head. Easley holds his breath as rifle fire fills his ears.

He remains pinned beneath his camouflage as the wild attack surges and retreats. Beyond the cluster of tents, the sounds of what seems like a concerted assault disintegrate into confusion. A few minutes later, a grenade goes off in the distance. Rifle and machine-gun fire reply. Then, the sounds of battle move away.

The stillness inside the tent is disrupted by a woeful sigh. In vain, Easley strains his ears for further proof he is not alone.

After what seems like the better part of an hour, unseen men approach, panting, whispering in frantic Japanese. A new surge of panic wells up, along with the understanding that this must be the end. But then the enemy fades away.

The boom of a 37 mm gun is followed by popping grenades and the distant hail of rifle fire. A muffled cough just inside the entrance to the tent is followed by the growl of Easley's own stomach.

Hushed English voices a few yards out mix in the wind with distant and unintelligible shouts. Inside, that cough can be heard again, louder and more defined. Easley slowly cranes his neck to see. Finally, a bandaged and bare-chested soldier flings back blankets, staggers to his feet, and wanders out into the weak morning light.

EASLEY MARVELS at the range of response to this horrific scene. Deep, uncontrollable sobbing. Cold rejection. Anger silent and smoldering. From where he lies near the back of the tent, Easley can see numerous men peer inside. One makes the sign of the cross, the next spews a torrent of obscenities.

When they begin pulling bodies out into the fog, one man shouts, "Praise the Lord!" A survivor has been found near the entrance of the tent. He is lifted up and carried away. Easley now calls out for help—timidly at first, then with determination. A pair of boots approach as Easley struggles to push the Greek away.

"I'm alive." It's all he can think to say.

A teenage soldier inspects the Greek's body, gasps, draws back his own blood-covered hand. He crouches down and gazes into Easley's face with stunned disbelief.

Easley's bloodied shirt is pulled up over his head. He is hastily searched for wounds. Finding nothing new, the soldier lifts him up and carries him past upturned litters, twisted blankets, arms, and legs. Outside, Easley blinks against the light. His beardless face tingles in the chill as men look up and gawk, as if he has risen from the dead.

Easley is set down upon an empty litter beside his fellow survivors. He learns that not one but two medical tents were attacked, tents clearly marked with the Red Cross. The slaughter was part of a suicide charge to capture the big howitzers and turn them on the Americans. It very nearly worked. Caught in the dark and fog, the disorienting rampage and screams, some men ran, others resisted, desperate hand to hand combat ensued. The Japanese regrouped, but grenades blew holes in their advancing line. The attack was finally put down a stone's throw from their objective. But farther up the valley, the battle is heard moving on.

Above Easley's litter, men huddle with arms crossed, murmuring in low, reverential tones. One of them turns and looks down with glassy eyes, then yanks a sock from his hand as his pale face breaks out in a grin. Cohen bends over and palms Easley's cheek, inspecting the quality of his work. He pulls a smooth line across the jaw that ends with a snap of his fingers.

Cohen stands, glances over his shoulder, past the gutted tent, toward the rifle fire just a few hundred yards deeper into the fog. His expression falls as the shock creeps back in.

"WHERE'S THE REPORTER? I want that goddamn reporter." A staff sergeant strides with his rifle cradled across his chest, at the ready, as if the enemy might be lurking among the wounded. Smoke-blackened face, twisted with the urge to avenge. Someone points down at Easley. "Get him up there. I want you to see this. See what kind of enemy we're fighting."

Two men are ordered to lift Easley's litter and follow the staff sergeant and a half dozen soldiers over the sodden and pockmarked fields. They travel so far the men are forced to take turns with the litter. All the while Easley fights the pain pounding in his head and stump. He shivers against the cold. He forces himself to take in every detail of the scene surrounding him.

At the top of a rise, the men set down their burden and help Easley up into a sitting position. Together they stare out over heaps of bodies strewn across fields of last year's rye. A pair of disembodied legs still joined at the hip. An arm, severed at the shoulder, with the hand still balled in a fist. Dead men splayed, tangled, split in two by hand grenades clutched tight against their chests. Dead men in the hundreds. All of them Japanese.

"*This* is how they fight." The staff sergeant points at the gruesome sight. "First, they kill their own wounded before coming after ours. Kill the helpless men, then blow themselves to smithereens. This is the value they place on human life. Even their own. Where's the honor in that?"

Easley has no answer.

"Take a good, long look. Write about how crazy these fuckers are. And this is American soil. Just wait and see how crazy they get once we invade Japan."

It seems so long ago that Easley returned to these islands to bear witness and report. The writer's vainglorious belief that he can somehow make sense of the world by capturing events, rendering them down to words on a page. Easley never really accounted for the possibility that this place, these events, would rewrite his own life so utterly.

The soldiers spread out among the dead, testing intact corpses for signs of life with the toes of their boots.

"Count 'em," the staff sergeant shouts. "Lay 'em out in some kind of order."

He and Easley watch as the men set about the hateful task.

"Mark my words," he says. "This war will never end."

TWENTY-TWO

SHE GENTLY PULLS THE FRONT DOOR CLOSED AND
finds her way back to the kitchen. Helen braces herself
against the sink, gathering her wits, staring past the soaking pots and pans and through the open window to the apple tree
beyond. The fruit is barely the size of crabapples. Despite this week's
welcomed sun, it will be a couple more months before they swell,
sweeten, and blush in the heat.

"Who was that?" Helen's father is in the living room, shouting
over the radio.

"Just a minute."

She stands up straight again, sticks her hands into the water, and
resumes soothing task. She needs a moment to collect herself, to think.
The sight of Ilya Hopikoff at the door, hat in hand, still has her weak
at the knees.

It's been thirteen days since the Battle of Attu. Helen read the
reports of the amphibious assault and the resulting death of 549
Americans and 2,351 Japanese. A handful of accredited war corre-
spondents were brought in to cover the battle. She chased down the

bylines of the few published articles she'd seen, enquiring whether the authors had encountered any prisoners held by the Japanese, or survivors of a missing plane, whether they had made the acquaintance of an RCAF lieutenant, Warren Easley. None of them had even the slightest lead. To stay focused, she keeps lists of people to contact, leads to follow up, things to do. It makes her feel as if progress is being made, as if progress is still possible. She heard that there might still be casualties at Fort Lewis near Tacoma, and has been working up the courage to go down and search. Thousands of soldiers who fought on Attu have already been reassigned to fight elsewhere—Italy, the South Pacific. They've been forced to move on with their war. Since Helen returned from the Aleutians, she has told herself that she too must learn to live in the present, move beyond her failure, even as she continues her search. She had learned to ration hope, along with life's other necessities. And then came the knock at the door.

Ilya Hopikoff was on his own today, his son Jesse still has a few more days of school. Compared to his ashen appearance over two months ago, today he looked rested, revitalized. He stood several yards away from the door, declined her invitation to step inside. While Jesse recovered quickly from pneumonia, his own symptoms were more persistent. The doctors discovered that he did have tuberculosis, but he is no longer contagious and is well on the mend. He sent Jesse to live with a family from the Orthodox church and had him enrolled in the third grade. That way, all this time won't have gone to waste. Jesse thrives in the society of other young boys. Ilya finally joined his son almost two weeks ago.

When Helen explained that she had met his late wife's cousin in Sitka, he looked down, fiddled with the hat in his hands. He said, as long as the people from Atka remain interned at the cannery, he and Jesse won't be joining them. Better for both of them to stay safe and well cared for here, then return to the Aleutians after the war is over and all the outsiders have gone home.

And then he found himself arriving at the business that brought him here.

Last week he met a soldier in the hospital who'd fought in the Battle of Attu. The man had never heard of the missing Aleuts but had vivid tales of what it took to rid the place of Japanese. He also mentioned hearing of an airman who had been marooned on the island before the invasion, hiding from the enemy, surviving off shellfish and birds. April in the Aleutians? Alone on the land? He initially dismissed this rumor but then recalled Helen's visit, found her card, and simply couldn't let it go. "I don't want to raise hopes unnecessarily," he said, "but wondered if you had heard the story. Wondered if this might be your man."

Joe calls from the living room. "I said, Who was at the door?"

"*I* said, I'll be there in a minute."

Joe has been impatient of late. His initial excitement about his upcoming journey is now tempered with reluctance and apprehension—at leaving the home in which he raised his children and nursed his wife, at leaving his daughter behind. His train departs on Saturday.

Four weeks after Helen left for Alaska, a pair of swallows built a nest among the pipes above the organ at St. Brigid's. Joe wanted to remove the nest before the birds had a chance to lay eggs, patch the breach that allowed them to come and go as they please. But the birds came back to claim their space and startled him on the ladder. Joe fell, sprained his one good wrist, and suffered a concussion. The priest couldn't track Helen down, so an urgent telegram was sent east to his sons. To her surprise, Joe allowed himself to fall again—this time for Frank's urgent plea for help with the booming family business. He and Patrick could use their old man on any number of building sites,

he said. Remarkably, Joe has consented to living under the same roof
as his eldest son. But he refused to leave until Helen was safe at home
again.

Helen knows he will pay careful attention as she recounts the
details of her conversation with Ilya Hopikoff, searching for signs
she's indulging in impossible dreams again. She can already hear his
objections: This could be another man from the same lost plane, a man
from any number of lost planes, a light-skinned Aleut who escaped
the Japanese. All these cautions seem so reasonable, mature. So why
can't she stop smiling?

TWENTY-THREE

HE FINDS HIMSELF ALONE AGAIN, ALTHOUGH OTH-
ers are close at hand. As when he lived like a shadow
in a cave, Easley is free to move about and yet remains
trapped—now by his physical limitations and the law. After several
rounds of shifting between hospital bed and prison cell, he passed
the last two nights in a surplus office in the hospital at Fort Richardson, a few miles outside of Anchorage. He assumes he remains under
arrest until otherwise informed.

They said they no longer know what to do with him, and yet
this room appears to have been designed to mock him. A ribbon-less
typewriter sits alone on a sturdy desk not ten feet from his cot. He has
not felt compelled to touch it. He remains forbidden from contacting
anyone outside this building: not editors, wire services, lawyers, or
relations. He is under strict orders not to write about Attu, or the
Aleutian campaign, until his case is "settled." When he first arrived,
he was unable to do much more than raise his head from the pillow.
And yet they remain worried he might try and file a story, somehow
compromise the official account of the Battle of Attu.

Easley gazes out the window at blue sky over birch and black spruce, vibrant and alive in the northern sun that beams so earnestly. He reaches for his shirt and trousers, then sets about getting dressed. These civilian clothes were given to him by a junior officer from Bellingham, a town midway between Vancouver and Seattle, between his childhood home and the life he built with Helen. He swings his leg over the side of the cot, pulls the wheelchair into position. He readies himself for departure.

Easley pleaded with the officers, doctors, nurses, and guards to let him get word to her, to let her know that at least he is alive. Helen would then let his mother know that she still had a son. The knowledge that he could not relieve their worry plagued him, especially at night, when the lingering northern twilight pushed sleep well beyond reach. All in due course, they said. But due course stretched into twelve days before he learned of his imminent release. Now they say he will be home by tomorrow afternoon. At last he might be able to beg the use of a telephone, hear her voice echo and fray across the miles, but he holds himself in check. In just one more day—less than twenty-four hours—he will be able to deliver his message in person. He will see his joy reflected in her eyes, he will return her embrace.

When Easley was first evacuated to the mainland, he was debriefed extensively. He freely admitted to having impersonated an officer, trespassed U.S. military installations, defied the terms of his previous expulsion from the territory, proved himself a nuisance. The book Karl stole from the Japanese camp—the book with Easley's tribute to him scrawled between the lines—was seized and scrutinized. It turned out to be classical poetry. Easley took his time, told them everything. They shook their heads in disbelief. What little intelligence he was able to provide on the Japanese occupation was welcome, and earned him some grace. But he doubts he was able to provide anything of use for their inevitable assault on Kiska, where the larger enemy force awaits.

He has not seen his interrogators for over a week. Perhaps they have been reassigned. This morning the armed guard outside his door was downgraded to an orderly, who chain-smokes cigarettes and strikes up conversations with whoever happens by. In the case of displaced person John Easley, the U.S. military seems to have lost interest.

The doctors, however, are paying increased attention. It is now clear that what remains of his left leg is not healing properly. The infection has returned, the heel of the femur seems intent on breaching the surface of the skin. This will require more surgery, a procedure and convalescence best undertaken stateside and in civilian care. The doctor has arranged for this transfer, but no one seems to know what this means for his status, or the charges that were to be laid against him. Easley has not been told if he will ever hear of the matter again. He concludes it is best not to raise his hand.

It is a surprise to learn how much can be accomplished with three points of contact. Remaining foot on the floor, two hands on the rail of the cot, then push up and away. Pivot, grab the arms of the wheelchair, reverse pattern, knead thigh until the throbbing subsides. Easley reaches into his shirt pocket for the pills the doctor said to save for the flight to come. He tosses them back and swallows them down.

Over the past few days, he has begun to stand at the urinal, lean against the sink to shave, even shower in an upright position. He forces himself to stand before the mirror and face the hollow eyes, sunken cheeks, and butchered limb confronting him. The doctor won't hear mention of getting fitted for a prosthesis until the infection is under control, until after the next operation, when the stump has fully healed. Still, these simple victories have his thoughts shifting from regret to possibility.

True to his word, Easley has not written about the events that brought him here. It has not been a difficult promise to keep. He has neither the strength, desire, nor clarity of mind to summarize events, to face writing about solitude or war. Such an undertaking demands a measure of time. Time to weigh all he has seen and endured against the new life yet to come. Time to let it settle and cure, reveal its shape, see if he discovers any kind of meaning at all. Easley dwells on none of these things. Mostly, he thinks of Helen.

Easley set himself the goal of reclaiming some of this stolen time by writing to her each day, describing his progress, his purgatory, his dreams for their future. These letters he keeps in a growing stack. He put down all the things he felt but seemed unable to say in his waking life, his life before the war. He began by asking for forgiveness for leaving her alone and bringing back so little in return. Then he found himself not describing the degrees of diminishment their separation has caused, but compiling a list of the small, the innumerable, the previously overlooked pleasures of their shared life that now seem to tower over all.

But given what he encountered on remote Attu—the all-consuming urge to self-preservation, an enemy willing to self-destruct—it is difficult to shake the feeling that this war might yet prove a curse passed on to the generation to come. A new Hundred Years War. If, somehow, he lives long enough to see it end, he will do things differently. Together they will buy and learn to tend a modest piece of land, plant and grow their own vegetables. If not children, then they will raise dogs and rabbits, keep chickens and bees. Perhaps he will start a small, local newspaper, or try his hand at teaching. Neither of them will ever sleep alone again.

There is a knock at the door. The orderly has come to escort the amputee to the airfield, make sure he gets settled and safely strapped into position. The decision as to whether the patient should be lying down or seated for this journey—a topic of some debate between hospital and hangar—has yet to be revealed. Should he be allowed to sit, Easley will spend the time composing one more letter to Helen, a letter describing this long-sought emancipation. The letter to complete the stack.

He calls the man in, hands over his bag, but declines the offer of help with the chair. He will roll through the door and return to his life with whatever strength remains.

TWENTY-FOUR

IF ONE RELIED ON APPEARANCES ALONE, TOM SORENSON might be suspected of having spent the war playing tennis. Only two weeks into June and he's deeply tanned and toned. In fact, Easley's former colleague has just returned from Sicily, where he saw his fair share of violence while filing dozens of stories. But he has also played by the rules. Easley does not hold this against him. Sorenson pumps the clutch and presses the gas, crosses one big, burnished forearm atop the other to turn the steering wheel. Easley has never owned a car himself, never considered himself a driver, but now realizes that the option has been taken from him entirely. This latest, newfound loss must find its place in line.

Easley's plane landed just after noon and he was taken directly to the hospital for an assessment. They weren't quite able to mask their response at seeing what was once his knee. Although far from any front line, Easley expected the staff would have developed a more practiced bedside manner this deep into the war. The doctor has given him three days—seventy-two hours—to rest up before surgery. Time enough, they hope, for the antibiotics to take effect and the recent swelling to subside. Sorenson tossed his newspaper

aside and grabbed Easley's hand as soon as he rolled into the waiting room. He went to the trouble of purchasing Easley a new suit of
clothes. A spare set of Sorenson's own would have been too short
in the legs and sleeves, too baggy everywhere else. For Easley, this
generosity called to mind when the two of them first tried to sneak
back into the Aleutians. Sorenson did not hesitate to share his food,
booze, or leads when all were becoming scarce. Stood firm beside
him on Kodiak when four merchant seamen were spoiling for a fight.
What Sorenson sees in him, Easley does not know. But the sight
of him, and the new pills the doctor supplied, have Easley feeling
revived. Good enough to see him through a shower and shave without undue pain. Easley imagines himself looking about as present-
able as one could hope.

Sorenson called ahead to let Helen know that Christmas has
come early. He said she cried out for joy when he promised they
would be by her house directly. Easley has a clear picture of how this
reunion ought to be. He has composed the scene in his mind, worked
it through time and again. He will reenter her life as complete a man
as possible. He will stand before her again—see, hear, and touch
her again—in her childhood home, not some emasculating hospital
room.

"There are a few things you need to know," Sorenson explains.
"She followed every lead, hounded every writer and editor in town.
When that didn't work, she made her way up north. Followed you
right out to the Aleutians . . . I'm telling you, she doesn't take no
for an answer. She'd make a better reporter than the two of us com-
bined."

Easley is told how Helen remade herself in order to pursue her
goal. How she chose to leave her ailing father behind. How she worked
her way out to Adak with a troupe from the USO, learned he had
assumed his brother's identity. How his plane was seen shot down

near Attu and yet still she believed. How, in the end, a source she discovered here at home gave her a tip about a man found alone on Attu. How that tip led her to call a high-ranking officer she met on Adak, how Adak led to Anchorage—

"The hospital at Fort Richardson?"

Sorenson turns to face him. "She called there pretending to be a reporter from the *Post-Intelligencer*."

Easley sits with the thought for a moment or two, then slowly shakes his head.

"Said she wanted to confirm the rumors of a man who survived being shot down over Japanese-occupied Attu." Sorenson clearly delights recounting the tale. "A man who 'outlasted the invaders.' But by the time she had connected the dots, your plane was in the air."

Easley stares out the window, tries to imagine it, but comes up only with the image of Helen's mouth set in determination, her small fists clenched at her sides. During his ordeal, he had tried so often to conjure soothing images of her waiting for him, safe at home. Tried to draw comfort from such wishful thinking. Faced with the account Sorenson now provides, it is clear he has almost everything to learn about the woman who shares his name.

A few blocks more and they will take a right at her family's parish church, travel west, under the shade of those old maple trees, pull up to the curb with the passenger's side facing the house. Easley will open the door, hoist himself up with as much grace as he can manage. Helen will see him achieve his natural height, stand on his one good leg without help from anyone. Then he will take up the crutches. He will hide nothing from her, but he is intent on showing her all that he can still accomplish.

When Easley pictures her now, and reflects on what he will say, he feels both a profound fragility and an abiding sense of peace. The reasons he had for leaving her side seem far away, smaller somehow, betraying their relative worth. He thinks only of her touch and companionship, and how—starved of these—he became a man he does not know.

Sorenson now affords him time to prepare in silence. Bright sunlight through the side window sets Easley's pale arm aglow. He folds his hands in his lap, watches buildings float past, notices how the shop fronts jostle for position. And everywhere he looks people are walking, daydreaming, greeting one another—more or less at ease.

Helen, he knows, would offer up a prayer in this moment. Once upon a time, he too would have been so inclined. And he feels a rush of gratitude unlike anything he has felt before. He is grateful for the continued safety and security of this city and the entire Pacific coast. For the silent and sturdy friend beside him. For the knowledge that Helen awaits his arrival in that big, empty house. And yet he feels no urge to thank what he once imagined was God. To do so would mean holding this same being responsible for allowing his brother to die—for Karl, the Greek, the litter bearer, Sergeant Major Uben Kubota, everyone else who lost their lives on Attu. For the disappeared Aleuts. But there is nowhere else to lay the blame, no one else to thank. No need to look beyond ourselves to find the responsible party. And yet his gratitude continues to expand. It is unfocused, sweeping, reaching out to everyone, every thing.

Sorenson turns the steering wheel and guides the car to the curb. He shuts off the engine. Easley turns to him and sees that his eyes are shy and brimming. Easley offers his hand, the two men shake, then he opens the door. But the house is shut, there are no signs of life.

Sorenson plants a cigarette between his lips. "She's probably shaving her legs." He pats his pockets for a lighter, glances up—then quickly removes his hat.

Easley sees the front door draw in and the screen push out all in a single gesture.

As Helen clears the shade of the porch, the sunlight illuminates the auburn curls about her neck and shoulders.

Easley braces himself, shifts forward in his seat, left hand on dashboard, right hand on doorframe. He plants his right foot on the pavement just before the curb. He shifts his hips, pushes up and away, but she is on him before he has found his balance. Her arms reach out for him, her eyes never leave his face. Her forward motion meets his ascent and suddenly he's tipping back. Seeing the trouble, Sorenson lunges across the seat like a goalie. He gives a steady shove to Easley's rump to keep them from falling in. Helen is forced to bend her knees and splay her legs in a most unladylike fashion. And then she has him in her arms.

John feels thin and frail. Sunken chest, withered arms, sharp shoulder blades. Tom assured her that he had gained back some of the fifty pounds he lost on the island. But it's not nearly enough. It is as if she holds an older version of her husband, one who has lived twice his chronological years. And yet his arms, hands, his body respond as before. The sent of wool and tobacco, the slight tang of sweat—he even smells the same. As she reconciles the past and present, he kisses her lips, her cheeks, her forehead. He kisses the palms of each hand. They begin to totter again, hang on to each other like a pair of drunks. They laugh with awkward relief.

Tom offers up the crutches, then reaches back for a tattered knapsack. John sets the pace across the path and through the yard then, remarkably, up four stairs to the porch. Helen holds open the screen as he bounds inside.

Tom rests the bag on the porch. In want of some closing observance, he offers Helen a hug.

"Iced tea?"

He shakes his head, then retreats down the stairs with the promise to return Friday morning to drive them to the hospital. He jogs back to the car.

John sits poised on the couch, crutches laid discreetly aside. He won't take his eyes off her. She stands before him, unsure what comes next, awaiting some kind of lead or cue.

"You went looking for me."

She nods, feels her face tighten with remembered grief. He reaches out a hand. She steps forward to take it.

"You love me."

Again, she nods helplessly.

"As I love you," he says.

He pulls her close, caresses her hips, searching, as if to confirm that they are both really here. Next, he extends his hand down and around the back of her right leg, pulling in at the knee. He draws his hands down, strokes her calf, then tugs the shoe away. He gestures for her left leg then removes the other shoe. She stands barefoot before him.

She opens her blouse, gathers him in.

He falls into her with the realization that this is the center, the place to rebuild his life, the only real beginning or end. This is a truth he does not believe, but embodies. This is the faith he will keep. And so here he gives thanks.

She holds his head between her hands and feels electric life within. She cannot contain her gratitude to the Lord, his Blessed Mother, the Holy Spirit for bringing him home to her. He is her living proof. Her faith, her hope, her questions satisfied. Is it right to pray at a moment like this? This is the finest, most heartfelt prayer of thanksgiving she will ever give.

TWENTY-FIVE

ELEN HAS BEEN HUMMING IN THE KITCHEN SINCE early afternoon. The weather's so inviting she decides they'll eat outside. With warm temperatures and abundant light, the days seem almost endless now, easily able to contain both their indolence and ambition. Her first instinct is to ask John to fetch the card table and take it out back, but she manages to catch herself in time.

He sits with her in the kitchen, watching her go about final preparations. After this meal, he will be forced to fast before tomorrow's surgery. From the icebox she pulls deviled eggs. She peeks inside the oven to check the onions browning atop the roast. He swirls the ice cubes in his whiskey as she moves between cupboard and pantry, gathering plates and bowls. He takes as much pleasure and nourishment observing her as he will from the resulting meal. He downs the last of his drink, then picks up his crutches.

Helen unfurls a tablecloth beneath the lone apple tree, the tree her father planted the day after she was born. As she unfolds the chairs, he makes his way out to her, past the clothesline and across the open lawn. He takes his seat and watches as she brings him a bowl of bright red cherries, a plate of salad greens. He hasn't the heart to tell her that the sight and smell of such a feast is mostly lost on him. His appetite seems to have gone AWOL these past few days and he scrambles for ways to explain. She's even made a cake. She wipes her hands on aproned hips, saunters back across the yard. She returns with two glasses of lemonade. It is all so beautiful.

Go easy, he says as she starts to fill his plate. It must be the long journey, he explains. The pills, the unaccustomed heat. He makes no mention of what's been tying him up inside.

At last Helen sits beside him. A breeze has begun to stir. The old Douglas fir in the neighbor's yard gently sweeps the sky. She glances up at the young green fruit overhead and imagines the many fine pies and crisps to come. John leans forward and takes up his knife and fork.

Since his return two days ago, he has avoided discussing plans for the future. Helen can only guess how hard it must be for him to think past the operation, convalescence, learning to live without his leg. Is he anxious about how they will make ends meet? To ease his mind and encourage him, she offers up a few of her own designs.

"The house is ours for as long as we want. Dad has no plans for coming home." She looks to the window above. "We'll set up an office in Frank and Patrick's old room. There's plenty of light up there. We'll get you a proper desk, facing the window. You can look out at the trees while you write. Of course, I've thought about the stairs, but I've seen how you can get around. Unless you're thinking of going full-time at one of the papers. A columnist, or editor. Something here in town . . . And in a couple of weeks, I'll get a job. Things are so different now. There's much more women can do. That is, unless I become too pregnant to work."

Easley smiles at this unfolding panorama, wipes his mouth, drinks her in. But he cannot take up her dreams and help color them in. Not until she is made aware of the kind of man who now sits before her, the man who shares her bed.

To prepare himself for the road ahead, he starts down a gentler path. He recounts the telephone conversation he had with his mother, and his request that she wait a few days before coming down. "She insists we take Warren's savings," he explains. "Money he'd been setting aside for a piece of land. You know how she can be. Given the state we're in, I couldn't think of a reasonable objection." Saying it out loud like this, he is struck by the fact that his brother still retains the power to reach into their lives.

From his lap, Easley produces a packet and hands it to Helen. She lifts her napkin to her lips, then takes a look inside. There are dozens of letters, envelopes unsealed, dates and times inscribed where the return address should be, her name written on the front of each one.

"Save them for later. After the operation. After you've gotten used to me and I start getting on your nerves again."

He now reveals what's been weighing him down ever since he believed he would survive. He tells her of Karl, and their time in the cave, hiding out from the enemy. How he left the boy alone in the dark and failed to find a splint in time. Waiting with a boulder above the entrance of the cave, lining it up with the skull of a Japanese officer. To his surprise, he finds these heavy words flow easily, as if he were describing episodes from someone else's life. He pauses for a moment, sees her hands clenched around the packet of letters. He now tells her of the treasures he found buried in an old tea tin. How he would have lost what was left of his mind but for the picture of a young Aleut woman, her brief note, and the hope she afforded him.

"I have a hard time explaining it, even to myself," he says, "and I don't expect you to understand. But you need to know that she was as real to me as my own life, or you sitting here with me."

Helen sees it written in the tightness of his jaw, the weary slope of his shoulders. The guilt of having let down a friend, of having killed an enemy. But then she loses her way. These two deaths seem like a prelude to the note and the photograph. She is unsure whether this will lead to some larger revelation, or is some kind of test. She is at a loss for how to proceed.

"John. You're talking about a picture. Like some pinup girl."

"That's just what I'm trying to say. It wasn't like that at all."

Helen takes a sip of lemonade, brushes the hair from her eyes.

"She came to me in my darkest time. It was as though she *chose* to reveal herself to me. Helen . . . I loved that girl. And I felt her love for me. I would have given my life for her, but she saved me instead. I know this might sound like shell shock to you, but she is the reason I am back here today. Sitting beside the woman I have always loved."

"John—"

"Her name is Tatiana. We've never met in person. The Japanese took her away before I arrived. She could be dead for all I know . . . As I hear myself saying these things, I can only imagine what you must think. But I need you to know, and I need you to forgive me."

Helen sets the napkin and letters aside, leans back in her chair. So much food for two people with so little appetite. She recalls the hangar on Adak, the unfinished stage, airman Perera driving nails into the floor. For her momentary lapse, she has already paid in full. It's an event she sees no reason to relive or confess, to let confuse or spoil this day.

In the end, what remains is the trust he must have in her. The faith she will accept, without understanding, that what they have between them cannot be diminished. He does not know the relief of confessing to a priest. Hers is the only absolution he seeks. She sees the weight of his burden and is instinctively moved to relieve him.

"John, if I was left alone on an island, with a single picture? Who knows? I might have fallen for Herbert Hoover."

He takes this in, nods, looks down and away.

Whether real, or imagined, whatever he did up there, and with whom, is of no concern to her now. She has him here with her again. He is both changed and the same. On balance, she believes he is more than the man she knew before. She takes his hand and kisses it. He has been heard. It is time to forget. There is nothing to forgive.

His stomach seems to have settled, his appetite has begun to stir. They eat in silence for a time. With the back of her hand, Helen gently diverts a pair of wasps from the remains of the roast. He asks about this spring's salmon run and whether Joe had a chance to cast a line before he left the coast. She fills in the details of her father's stroke, his fall from the ladder, his remarkable resilience. Easley rolls his eyes at the sudden concern of the prodigal sons. He takes comfort in these latest episodes, featuring familiar characters and themes. But mostly he loses himself in the rise and fall of her voice.

* * *

BEFORE THEY LEFT for the hospital this morning, Helen was struck by the urge to bring one of her father's puzzles. The box at hand features a windmill at the end of a multicolored tulip field somewhere in Holland. Once settled in John's room, she scattered the pieces on the table. She sits beside him on the bed. He establishes the borders first, she arranges flower fragments by color. They work together in contented silence—until he reaches over and cups her breast.

The surgery is still two hours off. When the time comes, someone will be by to wheel him down. The doctor's best guess is that, during the amputation, a bone fragment was missed and is now lodged inside the muscle. Under the circumstances, the field surgeons did the best they could. The doctor will seek out and remove the problem, then ensure the end of the femur is made round and smooth again. Following this, a fresh stretch of muscle and skin will be pulled down over the bone and stitched in place. Once the scar tissue forms and the muscle heals, it should be able to bear his weight again. Next up, a custom-fitted false leg. If all goes well, the patient could be walking by the end of summer.

Few hours pass in which Easley is not visited by a glimpse of Karl's hungry eyes, or the weight of the Greek pinning him down. Some memories do not wait to be called up from the past, they reside in the here and now. Could it be that the future reveals itself in a similar fashion?

Strangely, Tatiana leaves him be.

As the rows of tulips take shape, Easley turns his mind to the image that's been occupying him ever since Attu.

"I've got it," he says, looking up from the table.

"What?"

"Yesterday, you asked if I had any plans. Well, I do. Not a plan really, just a picture."

Helen sits back and folds her arms.

"You, dressed in overalls, standing in a field, a couple of kids running wild in the distance."

In Easley's vision, the war is long since decided. Perhaps by then enough time will have passed and he will finally be able to excise his fragment of the story. It too seems like a shard of himself, misplaced, a danger to the healthy tissue that surrounds.

"Do you have the money I gave you?"

She smiles.

"While I'm in there, I want you to go out like we said."

"Yes, sir."

They manage to assemble a few more rows of tulips before the orderlies arrive. Two men enter the room and roll a gurney alongside the bed. When they move to help Easley aboard, he waves them off and swiftly accomplishes it on his own. Helen carefully sets the puzzle aside for completion later tonight, tomorrow, or the following day while she waits for him to awaken from the haze. They push him toward the door. Helen touches the shoulder of one of the orderlies, then reaches for her husband's hand.

"Something bright," he says. "See you this afternoon."

She kisses his cheek, stands anchored to the floor as the men roll her husband away.

Helen scans the empty room, recalls her father's vigil for her dying mother. She feels the sudden urge to run. But she calms herself, gathers her bag and shawl. Then she steps out into the hall and walks in the opposite direction.

Stark midday sun reflects off freshly waxed floors. She passes a series of windows, through succeeding columns of light, composing a new prayer. She is careful not to ask the Lord for further favors, but to thank him again for all that he has already done. She has been the recipient of so much grace she asks only for the wisdom to remain aware of her blessings. Out front, she boards a bus bound for the shops downtown where, despite rationing and shortages, despite the war, she will discover the perfect summer dress.

Easley lies in wait, picturing how Helen will look when she returns. Covered in a thin sheet, he is thankful for the warmth of the operating room, the sound of someone whistling just beyond the door. He becomes lost amid the voices now surrounding him, discussing the number and angle of lights, the height and availability of tables and trays. Then the lights begin to fade as the wind whips up against the canvas of the medical tent. There is the hard sag of his litter, the dank moisture in the air. Someone hums a few bars of a tune. Jazz? He tries to imagine one of Helen's musical routines. He will have to request a private performance. Snow falls past the mouth of the cave, the laden apple tree. How will she look when she returns? Then all these things seem to loosen their grip and float away until he is wholly unencumbered. He has never felt so clean.

TWENTY-SIX

NOVEMBER 9, 1945

T HE BACKYARD FENCE IS LOST TO HER, ALONG WITH the trees and telephone poles beyond. This is one of those rare, autumnal fogs that settle in a hush over the city, drowning both sound and light. The radio advises anyone expecting to cross town today to think twice. In addition to the fog, an unscheduled parade is reportedly moving through the streets. Traffic is at a standstill. Helen realizes that if she has any hope of arriving at her destination on time, she must grab her coat and walk. She slips the parcel into her bag, makes her way through the silent living room, then out into the cloud.

Beyond the reach of the stove, the house has been cool for weeks. It's not nearly cold enough for the pipes to freeze, so it makes little sense lavishing heat on empty rooms. Soon enough, the place will fill with life again. Helen recently signed a lease with the parents of four young children to rent it for a year. With both Joe and Helen gone for the foreseeable future, the house would have moldered in neglect. This way, someone will be here to look after things, keep the old place alive and breathing.

After fourteen months of serving with the local Red Cross, Helen has set her sights on Europe, where millions of people are still displaced in the aftermath of war. She has signed on with the relief effort in France. She leaves in eleven days. There, she will distribute clothing and food, fill out untold scores of immigration applications, teach English in refugee camps. She will help those seeking the lost. She will find her own mother's sisters and brother, if they have survived. Introduce herself, and offer whatever help she can give. She will remind them that they have family on the far, safe side of the world. Helen will do these things to keep herself in motion, to be of use, to try and fill the hole left behind.

The doctors gently reminded her that there are never any guarantees with surgery. Despite advances, the science is far from exact. What we don't know easily tips the scales. Clotting blood and embolisms, circulatory and respiratory systems weakened by malnutrition, the risks of anesthesia. When she thinks of it now, it is clear that John met his end in the Aleutian Islands, but somehow made it home to finally take his rest. His return, his brief visitation, was enough to confirm and then sorely test her faith.

John was restored to her for three days only to be lost again. Now two years, four months, and twenty-seven days have passed. His absence made her question whether there is a life beyond this one. It robbed her certainty. In that time, she has pulled down much of what she previously held to be true. She has only recently begun to rebuild, to pray once again. The one thing never in question was the necessity of hope—not some airy wish for better times, but a belief that calls for action, demands she make her own way there. Hope: not for its own sake, but for all that it reveals.

The city has seen its share of celebrations for the men who fought overseas, homecomings both spontaneous and planned. And then this morning, after the simultaneous arrival of two troopships at the Port of Seattle, soldiers poured off gangways, along sidewalks, then onto the streets as passersby cheer them on. Nearly three months past V-J Day and the appetite for jubilation seems undiminished. But Helen stands on the corner in the disbanding fog as thousands of uniformed soldiers stream through the disembodied cheers, hugging herself, wishing the men would hurry past. Only when they are close enough to touch can their deep tans and sun-bleached hair be seen. Family sedans, taxis, and military jeeps sail past with men hanging out the windows, honking horns and singing. Those on foot swagger in casual formation, eight or ten abreast, waving at the crowd. A band on a flat-deck truck plays "When the Saints Come Marching In." Civilians grab their chance to mix with some of the last men home from the newly liberated islands and atolls of the South Pacific. Helen wonders if there are any veterans of Attu among them. She skirts the crowd, unable to cross, forced to take the long way round. But the sky is brightening, the mist is in retreat—the heroes have the fog on the run.

WHEN AT LAST HELEN ARRIVES in the tattered lobby of the Cascade Hotel, she immediately sees him seated in a soft, high-back chair. He wears an old trench coat over white undershirt, suspenders tugging at the waist of faded dungarees. All of it second or third hand. His eyes are black and almond shaped, his skin the color of walnut shells. He appears to be native but could just as easily be mistaken as Asian, or even Japanese. It is difficult to tell, but Helen guesses he's partway through his sixties. She does not wonder whether this is her man.

Helen introduces herself as the woman he spoke to on the telephone yesterday. Alexander Seminoff shifts forward in his seat, pulls wire-framed glasses around his ears. He wants to rise and greet her, but she can see the effort this will cost and quickly grabs an adjacent chair. She sets her bag on the floor and asks how he's getting on.

"We've been in good shape ever since we got to Frisco. And everyone here is treating us very, very nicely."

She wants to sail through the small talk, the how-do-you-dos, and ask how they managed to survive. From the Bureau of Indian Affairs, she has gleaned this much: forty-five people went missing from Attu, only twenty-five survive. Listed among the living is a woman with the name Tatiana.

Helen now learns that after the Japanese invasion, the people of Attu were held captive on their island for three months, then shipped to the island of Hokkaido. There they endured three years of forced labor. Seventeen died of starvation and disease. They have been wending their way home ever since the Instrument of Surrender was signed.

"It's been a long journey," he says. "Before we left Japan, we had our first airplane ride. Some of us were scared, but to me it was kind of a thrill. Then, all of a sudden, the pilot tells us to look out the windows. 'Take a good, long look,' he says. 'You may be the first U.S. civilians to see the ruins of Nagasaki.'"

Helen nods. She can guess, but cannot know, what this point of view brings.

"On Hokkaido, we were left to wonder how bad things were back home. Over here, at least, it hardly looks like there's been a war at all."

"Mr. Seminoff, I'm sorry to say that few people know what happened in the Aleutian Islands." She considers her timing, holds back her opening lines. "If you don't mind my asking—"

"What happened to me is all upstairs in my room. I've got three boxes up there. The ashes of my wife, my brother, and his son. Now I'm bringing 'em home."

Part of her wonders what's left to say. The other part, the part she shared with John, wants it all out in the open, in the full light of day. She could put him in touch with Sorenson, any number of reporters and editors who could help make his story known.

"Don't you think people should know?"

The resulting pause makes it appear as if he's been put on the spot, asked to speak on behalf of others, speak with authority about things she cannot possibly comprehend. His gaze drifts to the steady flow of departures and arrivals.

"Ma'am? I thank you for your interest, but all we want is to get back home. We thought we had it pretty tough until we saw what we saw, and heard what happened most everywhere else. What's the use in dragging all that out now? Maybe one day I'll tell the grandkids, if they ask. When it seems they're ready to know."

Helen wonders whether he's been told that his village was destroyed, but she cannot bring herself to ask. She has not come to lay this new loss beside the others.

"You say you've got something for my daughter?"

Something Helen did not touch for almost a year. Something believed to be hidden safe.

"I do," she says, quietly.

"She's supposed to be here by now. Guess she got held up like everybody else. We can wait a spell, if you'd like."

"I'd be happy to."

He seems content to wait in silence. He is polite but seems incurious about who she is, or how she tracked him down. He does not ask how she came to be in possession of something belonging to a member of his family, or what that something could be. He does not ask about her war. Perhaps he has the wisdom to suspect she too has paid a price.

Together, they watch patrons come and go. So many men, recently discharged, ill at ease in jackets and ties.

Finally he asks if there's anything left in the way of waterfowl in and around these parts, what kind they might be and whether, like so much else, they were all used up in the war. She explains what little she knows of mallards and Canada geese, then smiles at the thought of John hearing this, jumping at the chance to fill in the details of at least a dozen other species beside.

A young woman enters the lobby. Shadows encircling tired eyes. Sunken cheeks. Hair black as ravens' wings. The woman who was once the girl in the photograph tucked inside the parcel at Helen's feet. She has been and will be beautiful again.

At the sight of her, Alexander Seminoff brightens. He leans forward in his chair. "That's her there with her husband. And those are her cousins."

By her side is a native man with a suitcase in his hand. He rests it on the floor, reaches his arm over the woman's shoulders, draws her in. Helen catches her breath. It has been over two years and eight hundred miles since she saw him on the road from Sitka's Orthodox cathedral, since their shared fifth of brandy out behind the store. He has grown in both weight and stature. He is transformed. Only now does she realize how terribly close she had come.

The couple greet the cousins, then launch into what appears to be a reunion long overdue. On the young man's face, Helen recognizes what she has come to know as resurrected joy—the rarefied happiness that was rumored to have died, but has sprung to life again.

Helen has lived in doubt this day would ever come. She has thought of it often over the course of the war, rejecting it as improbable in the extreme. John would have never expected her to do this, and yet she has wanted it ever since she learned of Tatiana's survival. She recognizes this as the moment to finally deliver her well-considered speech, the story of how these things came to be in her possession. What they meant to John Easley. How Helen has Tatiana to thank for bringing him—briefly—home.

Seeing them now, Helen considers the effect such knowledge might have on this young woman both now and in the future. The way this story might take root in the mind of the young man at her side. She imagines how she herself will feel trying to convey the unlikely devotion of her deceased husband. In an instant she weighs all these things, then hands over the parcel.

"I'm sorry," Helen says, "But I'm already late."

Late for what, she can't imagine. She has only just arrived where she felt destined to go. And yet the burden she thought she carried is suddenly gone. In its place is the urge to protect.

Helen rises to her feet. "Could you please make sure she gets this?"

"Don't you want to say hello?"

"Mr. Seminoff . . ."

He looks up, searches her eyes.

"God bless you," she says, finally. "Good luck to you and your family."

"And to you."

He shifts the parcel and offers his right hand. Helen reaches out to shake it, but he kisses her hand instead. In that moment, she closes her eyes, and opens them again on a world both changed and the same. Then she turns and walks through the lobby, out into the crowd and light.

ACKNOWLEDGMENTS

I am deeply grateful to my first reader and beloved wife, Lily Harned. She always believed.

With this book, I am supremely fortunate to have had the kind of editor who reads and rereads between the lines. Thank you, Lee Boudreaux. I am grateful to Daniel Halpern, for giving this book such an enthusiastic reception and supportive home at Ecco. Patrick Crean at HarperCollins Canada was first on the scene. He provided invaluable advice and staunch support. Iris Tupholme stood firmly behind this book from the start. Sophie Orme at Mantle/Pan Macmillan offered sensitive and welcome insight. Rachel Meyers delivered the copyedited manuscript before the baby arrived, and Allison Saltzman designed the gorgeous cover. Ryan Willard and Karen Maine kept everything on track. Thank you to Michael McKenzie, Ashley Garland, and everyone at Ecco/HarperCollins, HarperCollins Canada, and Mantle.

I am grateful to my extraordinary agent, Victoria Sanders, and her team: Bernadette Baker-Baughman, Chris Kepner, and Chandler Crawford. Their overwhelming support helped ensure this book would find its way into your hands. Special thanks are due to Mary Anne Thompson, whose early and passionate endorsement opened so many doors.

Over the course of this book's long gestation, I have been the recipient of tremendous generosity, encouragement, and support for which I'm deeply grateful. Early readers—including Edna Alford, Georges Borchardt, Joan Clark, and Michael Winter—offered sound critique. The MacDowell Colony, Banff Centre for the Arts, and Our Town Café offered welcoming places to write. Grants from the Canada Council for the Arts, British Columbia Arts Council, and Access Copyright Foundation allowed me to travel to the Aleutian Islands and afforded me the time in which to create.

I am indebted to the writers who came to the subject of the Aleutian Islands before me. Numerous books, journals, natural histories, government reports, articles, and essays were instrumental in my research. Foremost among those are Brian Garfield's excellent military history, *The Thousand-Mile War: World War II in Alaska and the Aleutians;* Dean Kohlhoff's heartbreaking account of the internment of the Aleut people, *When the Wind Was a River: Aleut Evacuation in World War II;* Corey Ford's extraordinary account of early exploration of the Aleutian Islands, *Where the Sea Breaks Its Back: The Epic Story of Early Naturalist Georg Steller and the Russian Exploration of Alaska;* and Ray Hudson's sensitive and insightful *Moments Rightly Placed: An Aleutian Memoir.*

Thank you, one and all.

AUTHOR'S NOTE

On June 3, 1942, war arrived in the North Pacific. The Japanese Imperial Navy bombed Dutch Harbor in Alaska's Aleutian Islands. Four days later, an invasion force of nearly 2,500 Japanese combat troops seized and held the islands of Attu and Kiska.

The inhabitants of Attu—44 Aleuts and 2 nonnative U.S. citizens—were taken prisoner. One man was killed; the rest were sent to Japan. The remaining 881 Aleut people scattered throughout the Aleutian and Pribilof islands were evacuated by the U.S. military and interned in southeast Alaska for the duration of the war.

For the next eleven months, U.S. forces sustained an aerial campaign against the Japanese-held positions. From May 11–29, 1943, one of the toughest battles of the war took place to recapture Attu. In proportion to the number of men engaged, it was surpassed only by Iwo Jima as the most costly American battle in the Pacific Theater. It was the only battle fought on American soil.

The war in the Aleutians was relatively small in the context of the global conflict, and yet some five hundred thousand people took part. Dozens of ships, hundreds of planes, and an estimated ten thousand lives were lost. Journalists were ordered out of the region, military censorship was tight, and most of the campaign was fought beyond view of the civilian press.

These events are forgotten footnotes in the history of the Second World War.